one True Pairing

A Fandom Hearts Novel

Cathy Yardley

contents

1. CHAPTER 1   1

2. CHAPTER 2   30

3. CHAPTER 3   61

4. CHAPTER 4   92

5. CHAPTER 5   127

6. CHAPTER 6   156

7. CHAPTER 7   188

8. CHAPTER 8   218

9. CHAPTER 9   238

10. CHAPTER 10   255

11. CHAPTER 11   275

12. CHAPTER 12   289

13. EPILOGUE   304

A Note from Cathy   309

About the Author   311

Let's Get Social!   313

Also By   314

CHAPTER 1

Just hang in there, Jake. You can do this.

Jake Reese sat in a crowded restaurant in Issaquah, Washington, surrounded by women. Many men would consider this ideal—hell, some would consider it a dream come true. For Jake, it was the job.

"These women have paid hundreds of dollars to have a sit-down meal with one of the stars of *Mystics*," his agent, Susie, had said when explaining the gig. "So you'll glad hand, you'll answer questions, you'll take selfies, you'll eat something. No big deal."

"Why don't they just see us—*me*—at the convention?" Jake argued.

"Because they want one-on-one time, and they're willing to pay for it," Susie replied, in that maddeningly patient way of hers. "Your original contract, the one for the first two seasons, stipulated you'd do outside promotional support, and this VIP stuff really does help. Still, we're renegotiating your new contract for the seasons moving forward, and they want to film season three soon. So, if you want that stricken . . ." She was using the tone of voice that screamed "this is a bad idea, but if you really want it, I'll push, even though I'm advising against it like any rational person would."

"I play ball."

Which was what he was doing now, sitting with fifteen or so "super fans" at a long table in a chic little bistro, trying to stay calm. Not that he minded hanging out with fans, generally speaking. He was actually looking forward to the *Mystics* convention where he'd be one of the star attractions, along with his two co-stars, Miles and Simon. And his secretly geeky heart was looking forward to it.

Once, a few years ago, Jake had gone in disguise to the San Diego Comic-Con, to see what the experience was like, and it'd been a blast: amazing costumes, throngs of people, video games, and the artist's alley and movie screenings, and he'd heard stories about *Supernatural's* own fan events, which was much more in line with what *Mystics* was aiming for: something more intimate, aimed at the true super fans. As a new show with only two seasons under its belt, their fandom was still young, so it was still developing its audience. These VIPs were the cornerstone of that audience.

Still, he'd been around his dad when there were fans, face-to-face interaction, and liquor. They tended to get rowdy in their adulation, an energy his father fed on. He shuddered, remembering. He couldn't help but notice that this time, the wine had been flowing pretty freely to a few of the VIPs.

He had a sense of foreboding, and forced himself not to look at his watch.

"Rick . . ." a woman sitting to his right said in a breathy voice.

"Jake," he corrected gently. "Rick's just, you know, my character."

She looked disappointed, but another woman, a redhead to her right, picked up the ball. The redhead had been one of the ones he'd noticed drinking steadily, ordering red wine after red wine as their meals were served. She was staring at him like he was dessert. He shifted uncomfortably in his chair.

"Jake," the redhead said, correctly, with just the slightest slur to her words. "You're even sexier than you are on TV, you know that?"

She was wearing a too-tight T-shirt that said All Knight Long on it—one of the memes from *Mystics*, referencing their Knights Templar heritage. The woman looked to be in her late forties, but well-maintained, passing easily for mid-thirties at least. She had an almost over-bright, predatory look in her eyes.

He'd admit it: it made him nervous.

"Mr. Reese," a serious girl, maybe in her late teens, interrupted. He wondered how she'd gotten the money to go to a VIP event, which wasn't cheap, then wondered if she was missing school for this. She had shoulder-length brown hair and was wearing a sweater, a nod to the brisk March weather. She studied him owlishly from behind smudged glasses. She had a binder of *Mystics* photos and paraphernalia.

Now here is my favorite kind of fan. He smiled kindly, relieved to shift focus.

"I was wondering," she asked, "what made you decide to go into acting?"

He stiffened, then went into his practiced spiel. "Some of you might know my father, Kurt Windlass."

There was an appreciative chuckle all around. Of course they knew his father, he thought. If you'd watched an action film sometime in the past twenty years, you knew his famous father.

"I'd always seen my father working from a young age. He always seemed to love what he was doing. I pursued acting when I was in my teens. He noticed, and encouraged me. I wound up following in his footsteps."

It was a glossy version—the P.R. version, he thought. Really, it was all they needed to hear.

"Are you planning on going into movies, as well?" Glasses Girl asked. She seemed earnest, intelligent, and kind. A nice kid. He could've probably talked to people like her all afternoon.

"I'm looking over scripts, but nothing's jumped out at me yet." He smiled gently. "My agent says I'm too picky."

She smiled back. "But you liked *Mystics*?"

"I loved it, right from the start. I'm a huge urban fantasy, epic fantasy, sci-fi fan. A total geek at heart."

"I find that hard to believe." The girl reddened.

"You were a model, too, right?" the redhead interrupted, licking her lips. Swear to God, *licking her lips*. She couldn't be more obvious if she'd written DO ME on her forehead in Sharpie. "I remember that underwear ad you did. So hot."

"Mom!" the teen said, burying her face in her palm. "Really?"

His eyes popped before he could stop them. The redhead was the teen's mother? Yikes.

"Yes, I did some modeling, but not so much anymore," Jake said, after clearing his throat. "I only did it because it helped pay the bills. The carpentry and construction jobs were a little light, and a friend of mine had gotten a campaign, so . . ."

"And that was your big break, right?" the teen asked. He got the feeling she knew more than she was saying. Probably she knew more than he was willing to say.

He nodded. "Modeling is what got me my first acting gigs, guest starring on some sitcoms and a few teen shows. Now that I'm on *Mystics*, I like to focus on that, instead."

"It's such a great show," the teen said. "I love the writing. And I love the interaction between you and the other brothers—Simon, Miles."

He grinned. "They really are like brothers," he agreed. "They were working together on that show, when they were teens . . ."

"*Double Negative*," the teen supplied, then blushed again.

"Right. So they've been best friends for a while. They even share a house in Vancouver."

"Is it hard, when they've known each other for a while, and you're kind of the odd man out?"

He paused, looking at her. This girl with her glasses was pretty perceptive.

"Yeah," he admitted. "Sometimes."

"They're so hot," the redhead purred, obviously bored with the line of questioning. For a change, Jake was okay with changing the topic back to hotness. "But you're totally the hottest. I'm so glad you're the one that got roped into this VIP!"

"I'm surprised it wasn't Simon," the teen noted. "I think he's from near here, originally, or something."

"So, you guys also going to the *Mystics* con, over at the hotel?" Jake asked, deciding to take the conversation into his own hands and start wrapping things up. "Looking forward to it?"

"Absolutely!" the mom said. "I wouldn't miss it."

There were quick cheers of assent from the women around him. He glanced at his watch, then looked for the handler, who seemed to be missing in action. He needed to get over to the hotel and decompress. He'd promised to do this extra pre-pre-VIP outing, but now he wanted nothing more than to get settled in to the hotel and get a good night's sleep. He wanted to be prepped for the first day of the *Mystics* convention.

"Well, it's been wonderful meeting all of you," he said, standing up. There was a chorus of disappointed "awwwwwwws," so he held up his hands. "I know, I know. But I do have to go. I hope to see most of you at *Mystics* con!"

His smile felt pasted on. The thought of being sur-rounded by all these people, a crush of bodies, and the subsequent feeling of being a beefcake on display made him feel like running as far as he could. But no—his job depended on him putting himself out there, objectified or not. He'd just suck it up.

"Can I get one more autograph?" the redhead said.

"Um, sure." He pulled out his pen. "What do you want me to sign?"

She got a mischievous smile, and he could see the teen's aghast expression just seconds before the woman yanked her shirt up, producing a pair of plastic-perfect boobs in a bloodred bra.

"Could you sign these?"

He blanched, as there were hoots and hollers. It felt like he was a stripper at a bachelorette party. He took a deep breath.

"Right or left?" he said, trying to stay game. *Just a few more minutes, you got this . . .*

"You pick," she said, winking. "Surprise me."

He quickly scrawled "Jake" over her right boob, a hasty, illegible autograph.

"Sign me, too!"

Crap. He had to escape before this got any worse. "I really have to go, ladies," he apologized quickly. "I'll be signing at the hotel, during the—"

"Can I have a hug?" the redhead said, and before he could respond, she'd thrown her arms around him.

"Gack!" he protested.

"Hey, I want a hug!" another woman said, and he felt another set of arms wrapping around him.

He felt panic start to set in. "Now, ladies. . . . Come on . . . I need to . . ."

He yelped as he felt hands cup his ass.

"Whoa! Excuse me!"

He glanced around. Where the hell was the handler? He saw a woman in the crowd, the one who had booked the restaurant for the VIP. The restaurant manager was yelling at her. Several waiters were trying to break up the now-frenzied women.

He felt a hand—Jesus, was the woman an octo-pus?—start to move around the front of his jeans, and he jolted away. Then there was yet *another* hand on his ass. He heard a rip.

"I got his pocket!" someone shouted.

He felt it—the back pocket of his jeans had just gotten torn the hell off.

What. The ever-loving. Fuck!

He felt cornered, angry—and unnerved, both by their audacity and what he might do to try to stop their advances. This was not okay, on so many levels. He hadn't felt this violated since his most persistent stalker had somehow sneaked onto his property and left him dozens of "love notes" in his bedroom.

He shoved a little, fear giving him energy. He moved his way to the door, ignoring the groping fingers that were tugging at him. Grabbing his leather jacket, he made a beeline for the door.

"Wait! Wait!" they protested. Several began following him.

He opened the door, taking a gulping lungful of air. Then, out of sheer self-preservation, he started running.

"Wait!" a woman shouted, and then he heard them tumbling out of the restaurant, calling his name.

He felt like a guy from *The Walking Dead*, being hunted by zombies. He had to get the hell out of here. He didn't have a car—his flight had been running late and he'd taken a taxi rather than wait for a rental—and he got the feeling waiting for an Uber or something was just going to make him a sitting duck for the eager, amorous, and vaguely buzzed women from the VIP lunch.

He needed to find a place to hide.

"There he is!" He heard a call, like a baying dog. "Over there!"

You can do this, Jake, he thought to himself, and started sprinting.

· ♥ · ♥ · ♥ · ♥ · ♥ ·

It had been an uneventful March day, but a long one. And for Hailey Frost, it wasn't even half over. "C'mon, Hailey! I just want to grab a Herfy burger. Please?"

Hailey looked at the ceiling, taking a deep breath. "I'm just about to go off shift here, Stan. You know that."

"Five minutes," Stan, her co-worker at the coffee shop, pleaded. "Six minutes, tops."

"Can't you just grab something here?"

He wrinkled his nose at the attractive offering of quiches, sandwiches, and pastries. "I eat here every day," he whined.

She huffed out a short sigh. She had almost an hour before she had to start her second job, but she hated feeling rushed. "Six minutes," she said. "The casino will have my ass if I'm late, so hustle, okay?"

"Thank you thank you thank you," he said, giving her a half hug and then bolting out the door. She smirked. Stan was a great guy, a good friend, especially in the last few months that she'd taken on the coffee shop as a second job. Helping him indulge in a burger seemed like the least she could do.

It was quiet, thankfully. There was a woman listening to an iPod and reading something, her head nodding gently. Two elderly women were having mochas and looking at pictures from a vacation on a tablet. And there was Mr. Temporary Office guy, who had set up his laptop and a mess of papers and was talking in an "aren't-I-important" tone of voice on his Bluetooth headset, even though she could tell he was middle management at best. She'd seen guys like him all the time when she lived down in L.A.: men who liked to act like they were more important than they were.

Their inflated sense of self-importance, and desperate need to be admired, tended to make them better marks than most, she remembered. The cocktail of insecurity and greed tended to make them ready suckers, just waiting for the right bait.

Not going to think about that, though. She was stressed enough. It was better if she stayed positive.

She liked living up here in the Northwest much better than Southern Cal, anyway, she thought as she cleaned off the counter and wiped down tables. More than that, she loved living with her sisters—the foster sister she'd bonded with through several years of hardship, and the half-sister she hadn't met until she was in her teens. Through the years, they'd become her reason for staying on the straight and narrow. Helping them, supporting them, gave her purpose. She'd jump in front of a bus for either of them.

Which is why I'm going to jet out of here and catch that double shift at the casino, she thought as she straightened out the food display case. Their landlord had given them the Christmas present of raising the rent on their house-slash-bookstore for the New Year. Now it was March, and they were making rent so far . . . barely. They would have to come up with some way to get the bookstore to be more successful, or they'd go under.

The door opened quickly, and she glanced up, ready to tease Stan for his burger habit. But it wasn't Stan. It was a gorgeous dark-haired guy, with a strong jaw and a leather jacket.

"Hide me," the guy said, in a breathless, raspy tone.

"Excuse me?"

Before she could say anything else, he glanced behind him, then—unbelievably—he dashed behind the counter, hiding on the floor.

"Hey!" she yelped.

He held a finger to his lips, then pointed at the door.

A minute later, the door swung open with force, pushed by an onslaught of about ten to fifteen women, all a variety of ages, body types, and wardrobes. The one common trait they shared was a sort of giddy bloodlust.

"Where is he?"

Hailey's protective instinct kicked in. She didn't know what the guy's story was, but she'd run enough cons to know when one went south. He was on the run, and these women were out for blood. It had all the earmarks of a guy hiding out from a gig gone wrong.

She also felt the familiar solidarity—honor, as it were, among thieves. God knows she'd had to dodge some marks when things had gone sideways, and she'd appreciated any help she could get—what little there was. At the very least, she'd figure out what was going on before ratting him out, if need be.

"Where is who?"

"Jake Reese!" a tall, red-haired woman said, holding her side as if she had a stitch in it and wincing. "You know—*Rick*, from Mystics!"

Hailey froze internally, and she mentally replayed the man's face in her mind. She refused to look down, knowing it would tip off the women.

Oh, my God. It *was* Jake Reese.

"*Mystics*? The TV show?" Hailey echoed. "The one with all those hot guys?"

"Yes!" the woman said eagerly.

"Have you seen him?" Another woman, sort of matronly looking with a sweater over a striped shirt, was searching the place like a bloodhound. "He'll have ripped

13

jeans." She held up a patch of denim and cackled. "I got his pocket!"

Oh, holy shit. These women were out for flesh, all right, and it had nothing to do with Jake running a con on them.

"Trust me, if I saw a guy that hot, I wouldn't be behind this counter," Hailey said, and her voice all but dripped with authenticity, just the right amount of longing and curiosity. She could tell the exact moment when they believed her. "What would a guy like Jake Reese be doing here, though?"

"He was doing a VIP thing, over at the Flat Iron Grill," a teenage girl said, pushing her glasses up the bridge of her nose, looking pained. "And before he was *swarmed* and *groped* . . ."

"Oh, don't be so stuffy, Amelia," the redhead said, rolling her eyes. "Guys love that sort of thing, believe me."

"He made a break for it. I wouldn't be surprised if he was running for the cops," Amelia shot back, scowling.

"Well, he *is* smokin' hot," Hailey commiserated, causing the redhead to grin triumphantly at the girl, Amelia. "And he's around here? Seriously? You're not kidding?"

The redhead nodded. "Not even kidding. Can you imagine?"

"Well, crap. I'm stuck here until the end of my shift. I thought I saw a guy running past the window, down the mall. Thought he was a thief, actually."

Don't oversell it, she chastised herself. She was out of practice.

"Which way did he go?" Pocket-Ripper said, gripping the edge of the counter.

"That way," Hailey said, pointing to the far end of the strip mall. "But he could probably . . ."

Before she could finish, Sweater-Woman was already moving. Redhead let out a hoot, like a baying hunting dog, and sprinted after the crowd. Only Amelia remained behind.

"Um, miss?"

Hailey bit her lip, hoping that the kid would move so she could hustle Jake out of here without incident. "Yes? Did you want some coffee?"

Amelia looked at her searchingly. "If you do happen to see Mr. Reese," she said, her tone serious, "please apologize to him. From me."

Hailey smiled. Amelia was no fool. "I'll do that," she said, nodding. Amelia nodded back, then strolled out.

Hailey waited a beat, then let out a breath, turning to the prone actor. "Well, that was a close one. You okay?"

"I am now," he said, smiling at her. He was wearing a pair of dark blue jeans, a black T-shirt, and a brown leather jacket. His eyes were shockingly blue—like, Paul Newman blue. He was sex in a pair of Levi's. "Damn. You're not a bad actress, you know that?"

"I'm a terrible actress," she corrected. "But I'm a hell of a liar."

He chuckled. "Thanks for covering for me."

"No worries," she said, feeling a little fluttery burst of sexual awareness hum through her stomach—and, just as immediately, felt a little irritated with herself for it.

So he's famous. So what?

"You'd better get out of here before the rampaging horde comes back, though."

"You said it," he agreed. "Can you tell me where this hotel is?"

He handed her a piece of paper, and she scanned the address. "Sure. It's not far. Maybe a five-minute drive."

"Can I call Uber or a cab from here?" he said, pulling out his phone.

"You could," she said, shaking her head. "Only problem there: this isn't that big of a shopping center. Those women are going to be back. Better make sure they know exactly where to pick you up, and wait until they're out front before you leave."

He glanced at her. "I don't suppose you could take me," he said with a hopeful smile.

She felt a jolt of awareness flash through her like an electric shock.

Dimples, she thought absently. They were her downfall.

Jake Reese gave great dimples.

She looked heavenward. "I have an afternoon shift, at my other job," she said, trying to fight the pull of attraction she felt. *This guy's not for you, kiddo.*

16

"You said it's only five minutes away, though," he wheedled.

"What is it with guys trying to get on my good side today?"

He deliberately turned, pointing at his ass. She saw the gaping hole where his pocket used to be. The guy was wearing striped boxers, she noticed. He also had an ass a woman could write odes to, she also couldn't help but notice.

"I don't think I'll survive another round with those women," he said, his eyes imploring.

Damn those dimples.

"Fine," she said, ignoring the flash of his blue eyes and her corresponding hormonal bump. "As soon as my replacement comes back, I'll . . ."

"Oh, thank you," Jake said quickly. Before she knew it, he was hugging her.

She was being hugged by Jake Reese, a.k.a. Rick from *Mystics*, the brooding bad-boy with muscles for miles and a kick-ass Shelby Mustang. His character had successfully taken on Illuminati alien assassins as part of a secret brotherhood of Templar knights. She knew this because she watched the show religiously, threatening to kill people over spoilers. If she had any spare money, she'd probably go to the *Mystics* con that was happening that week.

Now, she was in his arms. Her mind was temporarily blown.

He smelled like expensive cologne, just a splash of it, plus some pure rugged male. Her body tightened in response, her breasts crushed up against the rock-hard wall of his chest.

Oh, my.

Of course, it was at that point that Stan breezed back in, a paper bag of greasy goodness in hand. "Thanks, Hales, I . . ." He stopped, jaw dropping at the sight in front of him.

Jake pulled back away from Hailey, with a rueful half-smile.

"Well, I got a double burger and fries with a milkshake," Stan said, tongue in cheek. "What goodies did *you* grab for lunch, girl?"

She rolled her eyes. "Say good-bye, Stan," she said, grabbing her own leather jacket and throwing it on.

"Good-bye, Stan," Stan replied, chuckling. With that, she did a quick scan for the fangirls, then grabbed Jake's hand and tugged him toward the parking lot. She'd just take him to the hotel, drop him off, and head off to her shift. He'd get a ride, she'd get a story to tell her sisters and friends.

She glanced over her shoulder at him, then reddened, realizing she still held his hand. She didn't have to lead him like a two-year-old. She tried to let him go.

He didn't release her, though; instead, he squeezed. And she felt a resulting tension in her body as he winked at her before finally dropping her hand.

Her blush went a little deeper—she could feel the heat on her cheeks—and she looked straight ahead.

Drop him off and go to work, she chastised herself. The guy was hot as hell and twice as charming.

He was the last thing she needed. And she wasn't going to be his mark.

· ♥ · ♥ · ♥ · ♥ · ♥ ·

Jake followed his rescuer to the parking lot, staring at her as surreptitiously as he could. She looked like a forties pinup mixed with a goth. Her dark brown hair was done up in elaborate curls, tied at the nape of her neck with a navy-blue bow. She was wearing a maraschino cherry–red sweater and jeans that hugged every curve, of which there were plenty. She was also wearing Dr. Martens that looked like she could stomp a man into powder and a black leather jacket that looked worn, not from fashion but from hard use.

She was, in a word, awesome.

He was grateful that she'd both saved him and was now transporting him to the relative safety of his hotel. He also couldn't stop staring at her, which is why he didn't realize they'd come to her car until she stopped him.

"Hop in," she said. She gestured to a beat-up old station wagon, midnight blue except for the Bondo spots. It

looked like, charitably, a hoopty. Or, uncharitably, like a
piece of shit.

"This is your car?"

She lifted one perfectly sculpted eyebrow at the doubt
in his voice, and made a pursed pout with her full scarlet
lips. "Are you judging my ride?"

"No," he said quickly. It wouldn't do to have her strand
him here. He got in, ignoring the cold of the patched
vinyl seat. "It's . . . unusual. Vintage," he added, trying to
remedy the situation.

She patted the dashboard lovingly. "Don't listen to him,
Charlotte," she crooned.

"Your car's name is Charlotte?"

She slammed the door shut. "Of course," she said, as
if it were perfectly obvious. "And don't let how she looks
fool you. She's got it where it counts."

"I'll bet . . ." he started to say, and then the woman
revved the engine. It sounded like a lion roaring, or
maybe a mechanical T. rex. "Holy shit!"

Her smile was like the sun. "It's bored out, blueprinted
and balanced, with a radical cam and aluminum heads, a
four-speed transmission, and a three-point-seven-three
to one posi rear end. She does a twelve-second quarter
mile at Pacific Raceways. Like I said: don't let looks fool
you."

"I'm impressed," he said. Actually, he was dumbfound-
ed.

She shot him a curious glance. "No cracks about why a woman's driving a car like this?"

"Nope," he said, rubbing the crackled leather seat and feeling the thrum of the engine roar through him. "I'd ask about a price, but I get the feeling she'd never be for sale."

"Too right." The woman let out a throaty laugh that made his body tense in all the right places. It wasn't like he was hard up for female companionship, but this woman wasn't just any woman. Obviously, his body had noticed.

He cleared his throat. "So, you know my name. What's yours?"

"Oh! Right. I'm Hailey," she said. With ease, she pulled the large vehicle out of the parking lot, turning onto the main street.

"I owe you, Hailey," he said. "Did I hear you're a fan of the show?"

Her skin was olive-hued—maybe there was some Latina, or maybe Italian or Greek, in her background?—but it turned the greatest rose color when she blushed. "I do like *Mystics*," she admitted. "My sister Cressida's an even bigger fan."

"You going to the convention?"

"Gotta work," she said. "Even if I didn't, though, I don't really have the couple hundred bucks for admission to burn."

Guilt pricked him, and he shifted uncomfortably on the bench seat. She was obviously going from one job to

21

another, and he'd hijacked her into acting as a cabbie for him. "Can I give you some money for the ride?"

She shot him a quick, hard glance. "Wasn't fishing for cash, ace," she said with a tight grin. "Just pointing out the convention's a little pricey for a relatively new show, and the first time you've had a convention."

Now he felt his own cheeks heat. "Well, how about, like, a T-shirt or something? Some memorabilia? I can grab you some."

She smiled more gently this time. "Cressida would love that, actually," she said, then nodded, as if her sister was the deciding factor. "If it won't take too long . . . ?"

"It'll only take a minute," he assured her, feeling a little better. She was right, it took less than five minutes to get there—considerably less, the way she drove. She took one of the last spots in the hotel lot as someone pulled out.

He got out, then looked at her. "Come with me, I'll grab your stuff," he said. Sure, he could've simply run in and grabbed it, but that would mean he wouldn't get to spend those last few minutes with her—and then she'd just drive off into the sunset.

As they walked toward the building, he took her hand, grinning at her little jump of surprise. "Just wanted to show you where the lobby is," he said innocently.

Her eyes went wide, but she didn't pull away. He got the feeling that she wasn't stunned easily, and felt inordinately proud.

That is, until he reached the desk. The lobby was a cacophony of chaos. People were trying to sign in, wearing various costumes. He could see what looked like a convention organizer arguing with a hotel manager type. There were also a bunch of men and women in business-casual gear, gawking with irritation at the disorder swirling around. Everybody, it seemed, was trying to get either checked in or checked out, and were complaining about the same.

Hailey nudged him. "I have to get to work," she said.

He didn't know why, but he didn't want her leaving without anything. He didn't want to be some fast-talking Hollywood type, welshing on his offer. "This'll just take a second," he said, then went in front of the line, nudging past people who were getting gradually pissed about it. He stopped the manager. "Hi, there."

The manager, a thin man with a pronounced Adam's apple and receding hairline, glared at him. "You're going to have to go back in line with everybody else," he snapped.

Jake released Hailey's hand, crossing his arms in front of his chest and glaring back. "I'm Jake Reese."

The manager looked distinctly unimpressed.

"I'm with the show? The convention?" he said, feeling like a total schmuck to have to put it that way. "I'm supposed to have a room here."

"So does everyone in line," the manager said loudly. "You'll have to wait your turn."

CATHY YARDLEY

Jake felt humiliation burn at him. It wouldn't be so bad if it wasn't in front of Hailey, but he'd made a big deal about this, and now he was striking out. *Maybe if I used my dad's name, this guy'd snap to*, Jake thought bitterly. Which is why he wasn't going to use it. He felt like enough of a douchebag for saying he was with the show. He wasn't going to compound it by pulling the Hollywood royalty card, cementing the impression of "entitled asshole."

He glanced back at Hailey, ready to apologize, only to see her studying the manager shrewdly.

"Maybe you didn't hear properly. This is *Jake Reese*," she said sharply, her tone making the manager stand a bit straighter—as well as a woman at the nearby counter. "Don't you know who he is? He's one of the main attractions at the convention that's setting up—chaotically, I can't help but notice. He's the reason that all these women are shelling out three hundred dollars, not to mention the hotel fees. And you know a lot of them are going to be eating at your restaurants."

The manager blanched. She surreptitiously nudged Jake, and he took the hint, standing a little straighter, trying to look haughty. Maybe he should consider hiring Hailey to be his handler, he thought with a smirk. She seemed to have some skills in that area.

"Jake Reese?" the woman behind the counter said, stepping away from an irate customer. "I'm so sorry. I thought that someone had contacted you. There was a huge mix-up. The dental convention let out later than

24

we booked, and there's been a lot of miscommunication with the convention organizers. We have your bag here, behind the counter. Give me just a second to grab it."

She dashed off, and he stared after her, mystified. *What mix-up? And why is she giving me my bag? Why isn't it, I don't know, in my room?*

She handed it to him. "I've got a lead on a few rooms in other hotels," she said, "but it's kind of a busy season right now. There are conventions and business meetings all over the city, so, um, I've had a hard time finding anything available."

He stared at the bag for a second, blinking. "Are you telling me I *don't have a room*?"

"I'm so sorry," she said, and she looked near tears. He sighed.

"It's, um, okay," he answered, nonplussed. "Really. I'll figure something out."

"You can room with us, Jake!" a woman at the counter said, waving a key card.

"Oh, shit," he muttered.

"We are sorry for the inconvenience," the manager said stiffly. "You will absolutely have a room available tomorrow."

"I expect you'll ensure that it's more than adequate," Hailey said, and the manager guy cowered. Actually *cowered*. It was kind of glorious. "Come on, Jake. You can bet your ass that upper management will be hearing about this."

He took his bag and followed her out, ignoring some of the catcalls from fans who were starting to recognize him. "What are you doing?" he whispered.

"Just follow me," she hissed back. Pretty soon, they were back at her car.

"I'm sorry," he said, feeling like the hotel clerk. "Really, really sorry. If you give me your address, I'll make sure stuff is shipped to you." He rubbed the back of his neck. Saying good-bye to Hailey had just gotten a hell of a lot more awkward. "Now I guess I'd, um, better look for another . . ."

To his surprise, she burst out laughing. "Man. That is just one big clusterfuck in there, isn't it?"

Slowly, he grinned. "They're still figuring it out," he said. "They're a new convention company, so it'll take a while to work the kinks out, I think. Thanks for the rescue back there."

"Guys like that give me hives," she said, rolling her eyes. "Self-important, doesn't pay attention unless you're 'worth paying attention to' in his mind. And unable to handle stress. My sister Rachel does event planning up at the casino, and she'd have that place running like a Swiss watch without breaking a sweat."

He felt the warmth in her voice when she talked about her sister. "Yeah, he was kind of a dickhead," he agreed.

"Incompetence. *Such* a turnoff," Hailey said decisively.

Suggesting that a guy who knew what he was doing might be a turn-on for her. He filed that away mentally.

For . . . reasons.

"Anyway, they're right. Everything is booked around here," Hailey said apologetically as they made it back to her car. "I don't know if March is convention season or what, but I know that a lot of hotels are full."

"How do you know that?"

"I work at a casino that's also a large hotel," she said with a sigh. "It's sold out right now, too—there's a big tournament, and a lot of tourists—and Rachel told me they had to arrange for transportation to other hotels for some of the attendees."

He felt a pang of disappointment. It would've been cool to spend a bit more time with her—wander down to where she was dealing blackjack, maybe watch her work. Maybe see if she had a dinner break. He owed her that, at least.

And that's totally not why you want to stay in the hotel where she works, he admitted to himself.

Her smile was broad, and mischievous. "As luck would have it, though, I happen to have a room reserved there for tonight."

He felt a zing course through his body, like when he'd accidentally touched a live wire, back when he was doing construction. "You do?"

Was she asking him to stay with her?

Yes, please! His body clamored.

"And you can use it," she said. "I'm feeling generous."

27

"Really?" It sounded perfect. "That would be awesome," he said, with feeling. Then he cleared his throat. Just because she was sharing her room, it didn't mean she was giving him an open invitation to her bed—or other things. "I can, um, sleep on a cot. Or the couch."

She shook her head. "I live just down the hill," she said. "I don't need to use the room at all."

He frowned. "But . . . you got the hotel room for you, right?"

"I get a night every month," she said, shrugging. "Don't worry. I'll cancel my plans."

Now that he realized he was getting the room rather than her, and putting her out, he felt like a total jackass. "I don't want you to go through the trouble," he said. "Really, it's no big deal. I can figure this out."

"Do you want to go searching around for a no-tell motel for a while, or fight traffic and go into Seattle itself . . . or do you want to take me up on a nice room, in a casino with great restaurants, that's maybe fifteen minutes away?"

"When you put it that way," he conceded, but still felt a twinge of guilt. "Are they important plans, though?"

She shrugged. "Nah. It's not a big deal, really."

"Well then," he said, feeling overwhelmingly relieved, if disappointed, "I'll definitely take you up on it. Thanks."

She turned the car around and they started speeding toward the highway, like a large blue-gray shark. That roared.

"So, why do you rent a room once a month?" he asked, curious. "Just a little staycation? Spa day?"

She quirked her lips into a little smirk. "Something like that."

A mystery. Suddenly, he wanted to know *everything* about this girl. She worked two jobs. She looked like Rosie the Riveter in a street gang.

Who was this Hailey woman?

"What's 'something like that,' exactly?" he found himself asking instead.

She glanced at him, her violet eyes sparkling.

"If you must know," she said, sighing, "I was going to get laid."

CHAPTER 2

No good deed goes unpunished.

Hailey walked Jake to the hotel room. It wasn't anything fancy—not like the suites, or anything—but he got to be largely incognito. The people who crowded the noisy casino were more interested in pai gow and poker than sci-fi series actors.

As she walked Jake in and got her key from the front desk, she texted and canceled her plans for the evening with a tiny twinge of remorse. She enjoyed sex, the variety, the adrenaline rush. Most of all, the relaxation. She'd just worked from seven that morning to one in the afternoon at the coffee shop—now, she was closing in on her two o'clock start at the casino. At least it was a short shift, letting her out at eight or so, but still, it was going to be a long damned day. Especially since she no longer had a recreational "bounce" to look forward to.

Still, the grateful look on Jake's face had made it worth it. Besides, the whole "I rescued Jake Reese" tale would be a blast to tell Cressida, Rachel, and the book club.

She handed him the key card. "Okay. You're all set. It's room six-oh-four."

"I can't thank you enough," he said, dimples in full effect, and she squelched a soft sigh. Damn, the guy was gorgeous. He glanced at the card, and then at her. "If you've got a minute, maybe you could show me where the room is?" She raised an eyebrow at him, giggling when he gave her a look of exaggerated innocence. "What? I get lost easily."

She glanced at her watch—she had a few minutes to spare. "Sure. Why not?" She walked him to the bank of elevators, then down the hallway, noticing her pace slowed down a little. He was fun. Cute. She wished she could spend a little more time with him.

Hell, she wished she could do more than that.

They finally made it to the room. She cleared her throat. "Well, it's been great," she said. "But I've got to . . ."

"Please. Let me reimburse you for the room, at least," he said, turning a little red. "I mean, I've almost made you late for your shift, and you're, er, giving up a lot for me."

He looked so uncomfortable, she grinned. She'd stunned him to silence with her admission in the car. It was fun to watch.

The thing was, even though she was tight on money, she felt weird taking money from him. She'd felt genuinely good helping him out, and she didn't want to tarnish that by acting like she was using him to turn a profit.

Still, guilt wasn't going to pay the bills. "Sure," she said, shrugging. At that moment, her phone started ringing, blasting Drake's "Hotline Bling." She sighed. "Sorry, excuse me a sec."

She walked over to the door, holding it up. "Hey, Duke."

"Hey, Hellcat," he said, his voice a rough, only slightly affected growl. "What's with the text?"

"Lost the room tonight," she said. "Gotta raincheck."

"Damn. Seriously?" He sounded as disappointed as she felt. "After last time, I came back to town specifically to hit that, you know."

She rolled her eyes. This was Duke's way of being charming, unfortunately. *Perhaps I set the bar a bit low.*

"Yeah, well, the ride's closed, buddy," she said. Which was a pity. She'd only slept with Duke once before, and she'd probably want to shoot herself if she had to spend more than, say, forty-eight hours with him. But he was big where it counted, and had a few moves that she could work with. She knew he wasn't clingy. Even better, he had the stamina of a steam engine. Guy could go all night, which she appreciated.

"Well, shit." He sounded disgruntled. "We could get another room . . ."

"You paying?" she said.

"How about your place?" he quickly amended. That was another strike against the guy. He was a mooch.

"I never bring guys over to the house," she said sternly.

"Well, shit," he repeated, but she could hear the resignation in his tone. He'd accepted the situation, albeit not gracefully. "I, uh, guess I'll call back when I'm in town."

"Sure," she said, and hung up on him, deciding at that point that Duke wasn't going to make the playlist again. Tacky, she thought. She could do better, even for one-night stands.

She turned back to Jake, only to see him staring at her, wide eyed. Suddenly, she realized . . . he'd heard her say, "You paying?"

And he knew she was talking about sex.

Crap. She shouldn't care that he had the wrong idea. It wasn't like she was going to see him again. Still, she cleared her throat.

"The thing about paying—that was about another hotel room. Not paying for sex," she clarified. "Not that I have anything against that. I firmly believe that sex work is work. That said, I like men, I love sex, but I'm not a pro. Just a dedicated amateur."

She tilted her head up, with a little challenge, when he still stared at her. The guy had probably bedded starlets like it was an Olympic sport. Let him try to slut shame her.

"No judgment," he said quickly, hands up. "I just feel badly. I mean, you went through all this trouble, and now you can't, erm . . ."

"Get laid?" she said, just to watch his cheeks heat a little. "Nah. He wasn't all that great, anyway, honestly."

But Duke was good enough, and best of all, he wasn't usually around. Duke never got any ideas about "permanent." Duke barely did "temporary."

Jake handed over a few hundred dollar bills.

"Hey, this is too much!"

"You rescued me, you've driven me around, you stood up to a manager for me. This is the least I can do," Jake said, his eyes meeting hers. He looked so damned *sincere*. "Anything else I can do to make it up to you?"

The guy was a sweetheart, she realized. He'd probably be a beautiful mark—just enough naiveté, especially for Hollywood. Chivalry, nobility. The guy was a soft touch.

She couldn't help it. Her grinned curved wider, and she looked at him suggestively. "Have anything particular in mind?"

"What? Oh! No. That's not what I meant," he stammered. But she saw his pulse racing in the thick muscles of his neck, and the way his pupils dilated.

Might not be what he meant, but he was thinking about it.

And damn it, now so am I.

"Why not?" she teased, pitching her voice as if she were hurt that he wouldn't consider it, just to watch him squirm. And squirm he did.

"No. I mean, I'd love to, don't get me wrong. You are . . ." His gaze now swept over her, and she felt it like a chinchilla mitten, all soft and sensual and something you just wanted to rub up against. "Unbelievable. But I don't want you to think that I'm just taking advantage of the situation, or anything. I mean, I don't expect you to have sex with me."

"Relax, Boy Scout. I'm just messing with you," she said, laughing and patting his cheek. "Really, it's cool. Maybe score me a one-day pass to the Con? My sister's a big fan, she'd love to get some video of it." Since Cressida couldn't leave the house, video would be the next best thing to attending in person.

"Just because I don't expect anything," he said quietly, "doesn't mean I don't *want* anything, Hailey."

She blinked. Her heart started to rhumba in her chest. God. Sex with Jake Reese?

He was messing with her, she chastised herself. He had to be.

She started to take a step away from him. She had to get out of here, before she started getting ideas—reckless, ridiculous ideas.

Before she could pull away, he grasped her wrist—gently, but inexorably. He kept it against his cheek, then turned his face, letting her fingertips rub against the stubble before placing a hot kiss in the center of her palm.

Just like that, her body tingled in anticipation.

"Oh, my," she whispered.

"I'd like to take you to dinner," he said, his voice low, those blue, blue eyes mesmerizing. He'd lost his stammer, and he'd somehow switched from awkward suitor to hell-yeah, hot-fudge-sinful man. "Tonight. When do you get off work?"

Wow. Zero to turned on in three-point-two seconds. That had to be some sort of record.

She swallowed hard.

This is a bad idea.

"I guess I could have dinner." Her voice came out breathy, and she cleared her throat, getting more businesslike. "I mean, I'll be hungry. Gotta eat, right?"

From his grin, she knew she was suddenly rambling. She frowned. Men did not make her nervous. *She* made *men* nervous.

She had to get a grip.

"Sure," she said briskly. "I get off work at eight o'clock."

He released her, smiling a bit smugly. "Then I'll take you to dinner," he said, dimples in full effect. "And then I'll . . . thank you properly."

Ohhhh, he was good, she thought. She'd thrown him off balance. Now, he was trying to get some semblance of himself together, and do the same to her.

She stepped up to him, close, showing she wasn't intimidated.

He leaned down, getting even closer . . . waiting.

She waited, too. Her shift downstairs at the blackjack table be damned. This was her pride at stake.

He moved in, slowly, giving her plenty of time to pull away. She stood like a statue. She felt his lips brush hers . . . hot, firm lips, yet smooth as silk. Feathery strokes, gently exploring. Teasing.

She felt her knees buckle, just a little, when he moved in a little more seriously, his mouth caressing hers like an erotic whisper.

He finally pulled away.

"Till eight, then," he said. "And we'll see if maybe there isn't anything else I can do for you."

Sexy, she thought. And smug.

This man does not know who he is dealing with. And there was no better time than the present to educate him.

She let out a small sigh. Paused a long moment. Let him think he had the upper hand.

Then she gathered up his shirt in her right fist, and tugged him to her.

She knew she was a hell of a kisser. His sweet, sensual thing might work on the tender-hearted fangirls out there, but there was a world of difference between wooing and what she was capable of.

She ravished his lips with hers, working his mouth like a virtuoso. Her mouth parted his lips, her tongue tracing the soft inner rim of his smile, before he opened his mouth wider, pressing his own tongue forward, obviously trying to become the aggressor . . . trying to regain control. She took advantage, her tongue darting past, tangling with his. She felt him rub against her instinctively with the rest of his body, mimicking their meshed mouth play.

She tangled her fingers in his hair, pulling him closer, doing a full body press, molding herself to him. Feeling his hands on her hips, his fingers digging in, tugging her pelvis against his now rock-hard erection.

And it wasn't an inconsiderable hardness. *Nice.* She could definitely work with that.

She pulled away. His body was tense all over, firm as concrete, tense as iron cable. His breathing was ragged. His pupils were dilated. And his hands were still reaching for her, obviously itching to do more than one hot kiss.

"Sweetheart," she rasped, with some smugness of her own, "you couldn't handle me. But I'll let you buy me dinner."

With that, she turned and headed out, down the hall-way. Before she did something truly foolish, and missed her shift altogether.

· ❤ · ❤ · ❤ · ❤ · ❤ ·

Jake had spent the next six hours in a fog of lust and confusion, in roughly equal parts. He'd talked to Susie, who promised to chew out the handler, the convention staff, and the hotel. She also said she'd play it all up to the producers when she discussed contract negotiation, which they *still* hadn't finalized.

"Don't worry, I'll take care of everything," Susie had promised. "Just try to relax tonight, okay?"

He was ready to do a lot tonight, but he wasn't sure if "relaxing" was quite the right term.

Actually, what the hell are *you doing tonight, Jake*?

He wasn't sure. He wasn't the sort of guy who did one-night stands, and as an actor, he certainly wasn't the type to mix it up with groupies. Not that Hailey was a groupie, necessarily, even if she was a fan of *Mystics*.

So what *was* he doing?

I'm not going to sleep with her.

He was quite clear about that. He didn't do one-night stands anymore. There were too many crazies out there, which made the idea of getting intimate with no background check dangerous bordering on stupid. Still, he hadn't been out on a date with someone for months. He couldn't even remember the last time he'd asked a woman out to dinner that he'd had this kind of spark with, either. There was just something about Hailey that revved his engine. Not just sex, although, God, the woman was a walking, talking, breathing seduction. But she was funny, and challenging, and just . . .

He shook his head. At this rate, he'd start writing sonnets.

I'm just going out to dinner. Simple as that.

Still, his body was at least half aroused when she knocked on the hotel door. She looked tired, he thought, and felt a wave of concern.

39

"This still all right?"

She shot a smirk at him. "You weaseling out, Reese?"

"No, ma'am." He felt like putting an arm around her, but felt it was maybe too soon. "Want to eat in one of the restaurants here?"

"Nah. I work here, don't want the hassle," she said. "There's a place down the road a ways, though. They're open, and the food's good." She grinned, quicksilver and devilish. "I'll drive."

So he found himself in her small town, Snoqualmie, at a restaurant called the Black Dog. It was a funky place, more like a café from the looks of it. The walls were covered with artwork, obviously from a local artist, all swirls and designs that turned into recognizable items: crows, mushrooms. The tables didn't match the chairs or each other. There was a decent-sized crowd, but nobody was paying attention to him, which was a nice change. Instead, they all greeted Hailey warmly, with hugs and fist bumps and waves. She was like a local celebrity.

There was a trio playing jazzy blues up on the small stage in the back, forcing the two of them to sit side by side to hear each other. Feeling her thigh pressed lightly against his wasn't a hardship though, and having her lean close, feeling her breath against his neck, wasn't a hardship, either. Well, other than the fact that some parts of his anatomy were starting to get hard as a result.

"You live around here, then?" he asked, wanting to know more about her.

She shrugged. "Grew up here. . . . Well, since I was around fifteen or so."

"Where did you live before then?"

"L.A."

He waited for more explanation, but she didn't say anything. So he pressed a little. "Really? Where in L.A.? I grew up there, too."

She grinned at him. "I know."

"You do?"

"I'm a *Mystics* fan, remember?" Her dark blue eyes gleamed. "We know everything about you guys."

He winced.

"Don't worry. I'm not a stalker or overenthusiastic clothes-ripper-offer," she said, humor liberally lacing her voice. "I'm a fan, not a threat. I know where to draw the line."

"Having had someone write in lipstick on my hotel room mirror and my home broken into, I appreciate that," he said, but his laugh fell flat. He wasn't joking. The thought sobered him.

You're just *having dinner*. And there was a reason for that, he reminded himself.

"Which do you prefer: Los Angeles or New York?" she asked him, tactfully changing the subject as a waitress brought them their food: locally sourced burgers with pasilla peppers and homemade buns. "Seeing as you've lived on both coasts."

41

"There are good things about both," he hedged. "I could go hike upstate, when I was living in New York, even though it was kind of a pain in the ass. And in Los Angeles, I could go up to the mountains or go surfing."

"Nature boy, huh?"

"How about you?" he said, trying to get the conversation back on track. He wanted to find out about her, not the other way around. "What do you prefer: Snoqualmie or Los Angeles?"

"Snoqualmie. Absolutely no question," she said, with a touch of forcefulness. "I love it here."

"Why?" He took a bite of the burger. It was delicious, better than burgers he'd shelled out twenty-five bucks for in L.A. He was glad she'd made the recommendation.

Rather than answering his question, she toyed with a fry. "Why do you think?" she finally asked, taking a big bite of her own burger.

There it was again, that evasiveness. Answering questions with questions, turning things back to him. It wasn't about him, though, he could tell. She wasn't pumping him for information. She was just . . . hiding.

Curious. Especially considering she looked like a forties pinup girl meets Negan from *The Walking Dead*, with her leather jacket and boots. She didn't seem like the type that would hide from anything.

"Well, you don't look like a small-town girl," he said, and saw her bristle, just a little. "Is it the hiking?"

She leaned back, gesturing to herself: the hair, the clothes, the makeup. "Do I strike you as outdoorsy?"

"You seem like the sort of woman that would constantly surprise me," he said, and he saw her defensiveness melt away into a flash of confusion before her smartass smile snapped back in place.

"Well, I've hiked, but it's not my favorite thing. And I may not love all small towns, but I love this one," she said, and he heard the passion humming through her voice. "It's like the anti–L.A."

"How so?"

She smiled, and it was gentler this time—possibly the most authentic, revealing smile he'd seen from her yet.

"The police blotter."

He blinked. "The . . . police blotter?"

"There's a local newspaper that prints it up every week," she said, her violet-blue eyes glowing with amusement and affection. "In L.A., it'd read like a scroll of statistics: shootings, theft, rapes. Here? Someone's chickens got loose. A bear settled into somebody's backyard to raid their plum tree. A local bar had a suspicious guy who was freaking out the waitress, because he'd hung out for hours and she didn't know him. Police responded."

"Just because she didn't recognize him?"

"They take it seriously here," she said, with obvious pride. "Anyway, turns out he was homeless and couldn't get back to the bus station, didn't want to stay out in the cold."

"Nice of the cops to ask," he said.

"They took him to McDonald's," she said. "Then gave him bus fare."

He stared at her. "That's . . ."

"Total *Twilight Zone*, I know," she said. "Every week, there's something like that. You should see the Facebook page. If something happens, twenty minutes later everybody knows about it. It's like people gossiping to each other at their back fences, only online."

"No shit."

"People look out for each other. We take up collections for people who are sick or hurt. Sure, there's crime, don't get me wrong. But people just seem . . . better, here."

"You make it sound awesome," he said, suddenly envious. "I've never had anything like that."

She looked over at him. "I didn't, either. This place, these people, changed my life."

The quiet way she said it made him sense, deep down, that her life had been pretty bad before she'd somehow transplanted to this quaint little town. She looked at home.

He envied her. And more than that, he wanted to know more about her. He wanted that very, very badly.

Why are you so eager to get to know her better? his subconscious asked. After all, he was only here for a week, then it'd be back to Vancouver for filming. It seemed foolish to start up something with this woman that he probably wouldn't be able to follow through with. Besides, he barely knew her. It wasn't like he was going to be driving eight hours round trip to keep taking her out to dinner.

Yet he found himself compelled to dig deeper. To learn more.

It was his hormones. Had to be. Ever since his last girlfriend had dumped him for an up-and-coming action star (who had then fizzled when Mr. Up-and-Coming's much vaunted movie tanked), Jake had been gun-shy. He didn't want to get involved with the actress-and-model types that were the bulk of his acquaintance. He'd tried getting involved with people outside the industry, too, only to have a woman sell "his story," a bunch of made-up bullshit, to the tabloids. It'd been six months since he'd had sex. It was uncomfortable, sure, but it wasn't like it made him crazy. He wasn't the kind of guy who would bang just anybody because he hadn't gotten any action. If anything, he'd rather hold out, extend the dry spell, to avoid settling.

He liked to think of it as discernment. His father had other, less flattering terms for it. Like "get laid, for Christ's sake, and get out of your own head."

They finished their meals, lingered over ice cream for dessert. "It's getting late." Hailey's indigo eyes gleamed. "Guess I'd better be getting you back to your hotel. You'll have a big day at the convention tomorrow."

He cringed. "Guess I will."

She laughed at his expression. "Come on. Is it really that bad?"

"I don't know," he said. "This isn't like *Supernatural*, where they've been doing it for years. This is the first one we've done. But if the VIP event and that zoo at the hotel lobby was anything to go on . . ." He shuddered for comedic effect, and she laughed. "I'm not looking forward to it."

"Poor baby," she purred, then chuckled. It warmed his skin, made him almost shiver with anticipation.

Damn, this woman strummed every one of his strings.

He sighed, pushing aside the sensation. No matter what kind of string-strumming he was feeling, he'd have to handle his own instrument tonight. No one-night stands, no matter how cool she seemed. No matter how badly his body ached for her. No matter how funny, and smart, and awesome she appeared.

He paid the bill, and walked out with her to her car, reluctant to have the night end. The ride from the restaurant back to the casino/hotel was just too damned short, and he desperately wanted to stay in her company.

She pulled into the hotel's parking lot, then looked at him. "Well, thanks for dinner," she said brightly. Dismissively. "I'd say we're even."

He swallowed. "Say, do you want to grab a drink?" He gestured at one of the casino's bars.

She quirked a perfectly curved eyebrow at him, those pillowy lips pursing. "A drink?"

"It's not *that* late," he argued. It was weak, and he knew it, but he just wasn't quite ready to have her walk out of his life. Not yet.

So what are you going to do? He chided himself. *Ask for her number? Email her?*

"Why do you want to have a drink, Jake?"

He found himself warming at the way she said his name. What about this woman didn't turn him on?

"I don't want to end tonight just yet," he said, his voice almost growling. His body tightened. He couldn't remember the last time he wanted anyone as badly as he did this woman. *Just want to torture myself for a little while longer . . .*

Her smile was heated, her eyes low-lidded. "I get that," she said, and the warmth in her voice made his toes curl. "You're just here for a few days. It's flattering that you want to get to know me better, but why?"

"Can't a guy want to get to know a woman better?"

"Were you planning on becoming my pen pal?"

He barked out a laugh. She'd followed his thoughts exactly.

"I have to assume you're interested in me. And trust me, I'm interested in you," she said, and he went hard as iron. "But the thing is, you're just here for a few days, then you'll be about four hours away. I sincerely doubt you're interested in a relationship."

He started to protest, but she held up a hand, cutting him off.

47

"And even if you were, I'm not."

"Huh?" He spluttered. "Why not?"

"It's not you," she said quickly. "I just don't do relationships."

He stared at her. "Why . . ."

"I do hookups," she clarified. "I'd be lying if I said I wasn't curious about what you'd be like. You're hot, but more importantly, you're funny, and sweet, and . . . I don't know. There's something real about you."

It was, perhaps, the best compliment he'd ever received.

"But short term is all I've got to offer," she finished. "If you're not interested, that's fine. No harm, no foul." She leaned forward. "But if you *are* interested, let's skip the drink and just go to your room." His mouth went dry. She was sincere. And hot. Holy crow, she was hot.

He should say no.

"Come up to my room," he said instead.

· ❤ · ❤ · ❤ · ❤ · ❤ ·

Hailey's heart was racing as she parked the car and they made their way into the hotel, to his room—which originally would've been her room. Which would, for one night only, be *their* room.

Dear Penthouse, she thought with a grin. *I never thought it would happen to me . . .*

This was crazy. The guy was a celebrity, for God's sake. He probably had all the women he wanted, and a boatload he didn't, and yet here she was.

She wanted this. Every nerve ending felt on fire, and she was drawn to him like a damned electromagnet. Not only because Jake made her libido red line, although that was a great perk. And even though she loved his stoic, physically badass character on Mystics, she was under no illusions about who she was going to have sex with tonight. She wasn't pretending to get with "Rick," wasn't pretending that she was going to be having sex with anybody other than Jake Reese. And she was certainly not looking forward to getting with Jake because he was famous.

It was because he was *unexpected*. Everything she'd learned about this man, through her interactions with him all day, and over dinner, made her more and more eager to get to know him on the most basic of levels.

He had a fun sense of humor. He seemed at ease with himself. And he wanted to know about her. Not that she wanted to share, granted, but it was nice . . . a guy who seemed to be genuinely interested in who she was, instead of downloading a bunch of stuff about what *his* life was like, *his* interests. Why she should be impressed with *him*.

They walked next to each other, but not too close. Since they'd gotten out of the car, he hadn't touched her, and she hadn't touched him. Probably for the same reasons—once they did, there was probably going to be a high probability of outright combustion.

She noticed his hand was shaking a little as he struggled with the key card to get the door open. She felt herself smile with a purely feminine sense of satisfaction. He wanted her badly.

She knew exactly how that felt.

She placed her hand over his, steadying it. "Allow me," she murmured, then pulled the key card out, watching the doorknob's unlock light go green. She opened the door.

He gestured for her to enter, following her in. The door shut behind him, and he locked and latched it. For a long moment, he simply stared at her, like a starving man at a buffet, unsure of where to start first.

She took a deep breath, then moved forward, body-pressing him against the door and locking her lips to his. She felt his body tense, both with attraction and with surprise. She fucking *loved* kissing, the tactile quality, the taste and the feel and the way it made her body thrum. Too many men she'd been with saw it as an unnecessary appetizer, something that distracted from the "main meal." Jake had a great mouth—firm lips, but velvety—and he knew how to use it. His tongue darted forward, tracing the soft inner flesh of hers, and she growled in appreciation. She shrugged out of her leather jacket, letting it fall to the floor, not pulling away. Her breasts were straining, making her bra straps tight.

Damn. This was going to be *good*.

He tore away, breathing hard. "There's something I need to tell you," he said, his voice breaking slightly.

"Oh?" She nipped his neck, and he gripped her hips, moaning softly. "Right now?"

"Um, yeah. Sorta important."

She froze. "Oh, Jesus. You're not secretly married, are you?"

"What? No!"

"Seeing someone?" She grimaced, backing up. "I may play, but I don't poach."

"No. In fact, the opposite." He took a deep breath. "I, um, haven't had sex in a while."

Of all the confessions she was expecting, this wasn't it. "Define a while?"

"Six months," he muttered. "Give or take."

Now her eyes bugged out. "Seriously?"

"I've been busy," he muttered. "And six months isn't that long. Anyway, we might want to slow it down, or this is going to be the worst and shortest hookup you've ever had."

She stared at him. Then she laughed. "I like you."

"I like you, too." He reached for her. "And believe me, I'd love to show you. Slowly. That okay?"

"Um . . . sure." Slow wasn't her usual speed. She only had her hookups a couple times a month when she was lucky, and less than that since she'd started working two jobs. So she tended to look at them as cram sessions, more about stamina than finesse.

"I've never liked rushing," he said, picking up her coat and putting it down on the second bed before peeling off his own leather jacket. She watched as the muscles in his shoulders and chest bunched and flexed, and her mouth went dry. "I want to get a good look at you."

She felt like her blood was boiling. His slow perusal of her form, combined with his outstanding kissing, made her feel crazed with desire in a way she hadn't felt in longer than she could remember. He revved up her hormones and made her cross-eyed with overwhelming sensations that buffeted her from all sides.

She wanted sex, *now*. She wasn't the "slow-montage-of-seduction" type. Given the guys she'd been used to hooking up with, she'd learned to be selfish. She'd graduated from the hard, fast, punk-rock school of fucking—get yours, before he gets his.

So she ripped off her sweater, tossing it by her jacket, then sat down on the edge of the bed, grateful she'd worn the Aunt-Sally-styled Dr. Martens with the zipper. Even if he claimed to like slow, the tedious unlacing of a real pair of Docs was hardly what anyone could consider sexy.

He stroked her shoulder, magnifying the sensations skittering through her a hundredfold—a feverish combination of searing heat and shivering chills, wherever he touched her. It created a longing so powerful it made her knees buckle as she swayed toward him like a plant toward sunlight.

She stood up, shucked off her jeans, leaving her only in her underwear. She grinned when she saw he was staring at her rack. She'd worn her matching black lace panties and push-up bra—and there was plenty to push up. His breathing went shallow.

Slow, my ass, she snickered to herself, as she grabbed the hem of his T-shirt and tugged it over his head. As she got a good look at him, she found herself slowing down instead, stunned into submission.

The guy had a chest that belonged on a goddamned romance novel cover, chiseled and cut. The muscles she'd seen, under his shirt?

Even. Better. In. Person.

She couldn't help it. Her mouth dropped open in appreciation.

He acknowledged her approval with a tiny grin, then stretched out onto the bed next to her, reaching for the ribbon at the nape of her neck. "You mind?"

She shook her head, still speechless, still frozen. Any second now, she told herself, she'd get back in the saddle and give this guy the ride of his life. But for the moment, she was too busy devouring him with her eyes. He tugged at the ribbon, undoing it, releasing all the curls she'd kept trapped behind her. Then he gently wiggled his fingers into the mass, massaging her scalp, running his fingers through her hair. She hummed with appreciation and trembled—actually *trembled*—with pleasure as she felt his fingers work their magic. She tilted her head toward him like a flower toward sunlight. He framed her face, then moved forward, his mouth molding to hers.

Slow kisses. Drugging kisses. Deceptive ones, all slow and sneaky, starting off gentle before sinking in and rocking her like a left hook. She made a small moan and pressed forward, wriggling against him, her body half-covering his. That's when she felt the denim of his jeans underneath her thigh. She made a little sound of impatience at the barrier to his flesh.

"Slow, remember?" he whispered against her lips, nibbling at them. Then he shifted, and she found herself flat on her back, his body looming hard and hot above her. "We've got plenty of time."

She made another sound, this time one of desperate protest. She felt greedy, desperate, shaking for him. But he was stronger. Not in a scary way. In an impressive way. She could push, she could plead, but he'd keep on with his implacable pace, irresistibly wearing her down.

It felt out of control—and, if she had to be honest, it was fucking incredible.

He moved from her mouth, letting her take a deep gasp of breath as he inched down her throat, pressing heated kisses against her pulse, her collarbone, the tops of her breasts. When he leaned down and took a nipple in his mouth, suckling through the lace, her hips shot up reflexively, bumping against his denim-covered hardness.

"Oh, my God," she rasped, grasping his shoulders and digging her fingertips into the muscles there, pulling him toward her. In response, he moved the cup of her bra away, grazing the delicate skin with his teeth.

She swore her eyes crossed.

"Oh, my God."

She felt his chuckle along her skin as he shifted to her other breast, teasing, sucking. Her legs moved restlessly, her hips pivoting to brush against him. She felt like she was losing her mind.

"Jake," she crooned, as her fingers twisted into his hair.

His mouth skimmed lower, kissing and licking, trailing down her stomach. She giggled a little when he kissed her belly button. Then she felt his fingertips brush the top of her panties, starting to tug them down as his mouth moved even farther south . . .

"Whoa," she said, bolting. He yelped a little, since she'd inadvertently tugged his hair. "Sorry. You don't . . . that's not necessary."

He was poised at the juncture of her thighs, having wriggled a bit lower. He was grinning slowly, his eyes slumberous, sleep-sexy. *Here's a mental picture I'm going to keep for vibrator duty*, she thought.

"I want to," he said, starting to bend back to the task, but she tugged his head up again.

"You're too far ahead already," she said. "This has been all you, serving me. We need to get even."

"What, is it a competition?"

"More like . . . quid pro quo," she said, tugging him back up so they were face-to-face. She looped her arms around his neck, kissing that marble jawline of his, feeling the scruff of beard that was starting. She gave him a quick lick, her tongue tracing the tiny hollow where the hinge of his jaw met his neck, just below his earlobe.

"You like being in control, huh?" He chuckled, and it was a fun, carefree sound. "Why am I not shocked?"

She bit her lip. Then she bit his, causing him to snort out a surprised laugh. "You'll like me being in control, too," she promised.

"Bossy," he teased.

"Maybe." She looked into his eyes. "Let me?"

He sighed, then leaned back on the bed. "I'm yours."

That sobered her more than anything he could've said. For the tiniest moment, she was thrown. This guy probably had groupies—*God*, she hated that term—and may well have slept with thousands of women, for all she knew. Just because he'd had a six-month break didn't mean the guy was a monk. She was sexually active, and perfectly okay with that fact. But this guy may well have been sexually *voracious*, with a wide and assorted variety of experiences. From women who probably took frickin' continuing education classes in "getting your freak on." His body had probably been rocked and his mind blown by more people than she could easily name, in ways she'd only seen in porn.

She was confident, sure, but even for her, this was intimidating.

She faltered in her exploration, frowning. She didn't want to be just another lay, for whatever reason. She wanted to be memorable. She wanted to affect his life the way he was currently affecting hers, because she knew that even though they hadn't had sex yet, she wasn't going to forget any of this. It was blazed into her psyche, something she both marveled at and even regretted, because she knew other men were going to have a tough time measuring up. She wanted him to feel that way about her and other women. Normally, she wouldn't care, but tonight was different. Somehow.

She wanted tonight to be different. For both of them.

So she took a deep breath, then rested her forehead against his for a long moment. She stroked his chest, his shoulders, his arms, memorizing the feel of his skin.

He'd startled her with his attention to all her details. She realized she needed to flip the script, and take a page out of his book. Her first instinct had been to devour him, but she knew that was the wrong tack to take: it was her own impatience and eagerness and sheer desire. If she just leaped in there and started mauling him, she'd be no better than those douchebag guys who were more intent on "giving it to you *good*" than actually making sure you had a good time. She didn't want to be that guy.

Instead, she studied him.

She breathed in the scent of him, where his neck met his shoulder. Smoothed her palms over him, pressing kisses over his sternum, his pecs, his clavicle, his chin. Tiny sharp bites. Caressing kisses. Investigative touches.

Who would've guessed a guy this big was ticklish around his sides? Or that he had sensitive earlobes, where a well-placed nibble would make him shudder and clutch his arms around her waist?

She felt—hyper real. Everything was emphasized. The smell of him, like clean winter air undershot with hints of something expensive and musky, like sandalwood or amber. The feel of his skin, velvet over the corded steel of his muscles. The sound of his growls and low moans. Even the taste of him.

He was touching her, tasting her, as she explored, distracting her in the most delicious way as the combination of her discoveries and the passionate responses he was drawing out of her simply overtook her. She wasn't in charge anymore, didn't care that she'd lost track of what she was trying to achieve. She didn't have anything to prove right now. She was just indulging in the feelings that crashed through her.

It was different than any sexual or sensual encountered she'd ever had. That might freak her out later. Right now, she was in over her head and she didn't give a damn.

She reached for his fly, smoothing her palm over the long, hard length straining against the fabric. Then she paused, her hands on the button. She glanced at him, asking permission silently.

When he nodded, she couldn't help it. She smiled, and if it were anything like the hungry, sensual smile he had . . .

Oh, yeah. This was going to be good.

She undid the button, undoing the zipper tooth by tooth. Now it was his turn to growl impatiently. It felt like a drug. She could get addicted to this slow jam business.

She kissed him, nipping at his lower lip, licking his upper lip. Then she peeled down his jeans, shoving them off his hips. He took them the rest of the way off. Now they were finally even: down to underwear only. His boxers were plain navy cotton, his cock tenting them like the big top at a circus.

She felt her body tense. She couldn't *wait* for the main event.

She crawled on top of him, her panties brushing against the hard length of him, and her body shivered, going wet in a rush. She let his covered cock stroke between her thighs, and she cradled it gently, weaving from side to side above him, the lace of her bra whispering against his muscular chest. He reached up, removing the silky barrier, then cupped her bare breasts. She arched, pressing herself more fully into his hands even as it made her hips and thighs fit more snugly against his erection.

"You feel so . . . fucking . . . good," he ground out, his hips rising to meet her as his hands kneaded her breasts gently, but insistently.

She leaned down for a hungry kiss, smiling against his lips. "Not so bad yourself," she replied breathlessly. "This slow enough for you?"

He grinned back, then pulled her to him, his cock pushing insistently at her entrance, separated only by thin films of cotton and lace. "I'll show you slow," he promised in a growl against her throat.

"I'm looking forward to it," she said. Then she pulled away, slipping out of her panties. Now she was completely naked. She pulled down his boxers. His erection was everything she'd hoped, and then some, thick and straight and . . . yum. She stroked it, and it strained against her palm.

She needed to grab a condom. She wanted him inside her, now.

She gave him one more kiss, feeling the hot iron of him brush against her stomach. She was going crazy. "Let me just grab a . . ."

She froze as she heard her phone ring. Not just any ringtone. It was "Carry On Wayward Son." That meant Rachel's phone.

That meant trouble.

CHAPTER 3

Jake felt taut as fucking piano wire. This woman—holy hell, she was like lava, molten hot and sinuous. He had never in his life wanted a woman as much or as badly as he wanted Hailey.

Calm it down, he warned himself. At this rate, he'd come as soon as he entered her. So much for slow, he thought, grinning.

He heard her cell phone ring, let out a low growl. They probably should've shut their phones off. He hadn't thought about it, hadn't thought of anything but her. And now . . .

She'd been graceful in her movements, like a dancer. But the moment that phone rang, she grabbed for her cell like she was slapping out a fire, with an instinctive, clumsy haste. "Hello?"

CATHY YARDLEY

The heater chose that moment to kick on, drowning out the other side of the conversation, but he saw Hailey's expression fall slack, her eyes glittering with resolve. "All right. Don't worry. I'll be there in a few minutes."

She didn't even look at him as she clicked off her phone. She was up and off the bed in a flash, snatching up her clothing, putting it on like a firefighter who had just heard the alarm.

Just like that, it was as if he didn't exist. She moved like a machine, all her previous grace and sensuousness gone.

"What happened?" he asked quickly, standing up and reaching for her. "What's wrong?"

"I have to go. Now." Her deep violet eyes that had been so hot just a moment ago were now hard, cold. "Where did you put my bra?"

He pointed numbly toward the other bed, where he'd tossed it. "What's going on?"

"Nothing you need to worry about." She shimmied into her underwear, then tugged on her jeans. He felt a moment of loss as she put her bra back on. "I just need to go."

His body ached like a son of a bitch, but he wasn't a complete ass. "Is there anything I can do to help?"

"I got it." Each word was clipped, like she'd chipped it off an ice block with a pick. Then, seeing that he wasn't going anywhere, she shrugged. "Family stuff," she added, but the look on her face suggested something more.

What kind of "family stuff" happened at eleven o'clock at night, he wondered. Something that would . . .

Wait a second.

"Do you have a kid or something?" he blurted out. A sick kid would be the reason a woman would shut down and go into emergency mode.

"Or something," she said. The look of derision on her face was venomous. "And what if I did? Have a kid. Kind of a boner killer, huh?"

"I wouldn't care," he said honestly. He imagined any kid of Hailey's would probably be awesome, and was momentarily intrigued. "I'm just trying to figure out what the hell is going on. You were really into it, and now you're racing out of here like there's a hostage situation . . ."

"It's family stuff," she repeated tightly, with the silent *and it's none of your business* so clear, she might as well have held up a sign. She slipped into her boots as she pulled her sweater back on, then sat on the edge of the bed to zip them.

He grimaced. Then he sat next to her. "Are you in trouble?"

"Oh, Jesus," she muttered. Her movements were choppy, frantic. "No, we don't need any rescuing, thanks. This isn't a problem you can fix. I just need to go, okay?"

He felt anger bubble up in him. "What the hell is with the attitude? I'm just trying to help!"

"And I'm just trying to leave!" She said, yanking her coat off the other bed and pushing her arms through the sleeves. "I don't have time to hold your hand and reassure you. Don't like my attitude? I'll be gone in a minute, so no worries, you don't have to deal with it. Good luck with the convention and the show and all that."

That was the worst thing. Her tone. He'd gone from "incredible object of desire" to "obstacle and distraction" in the blink of an eye. She was also palpably anxious about that phone call. Whatever could scare this powerhouse of a woman had to be pretty goddamned bad.

He knew, instinctively, that she could probably handle it herself. But he found himself caring, and wanting her to know that maybe she didn't *have* to.

"Wait. *Wait*, damn it," he said, holding the door as she unlatched it.

Her blue eyes gleamed, her arctic gaze going from his hand, to his eyes, then back to his hand, with growing fury. "You do not want to try to stop me from leaving," she said, her voice icy.

"Just give me one second to throw some clothes on," he said, keeping his palm flat against the door and stepping closer to her. "I'm going with you."

She moved like lightning, slamming him against the wall, surprising him. "I need to get to my sisters," she said in a low growl. "Do you understand? They need me. *Right. Now*. Do *not* fuck with me on this!"

He let her shove him away from the door frame, worry, anger, frustration, and—yeah, sexual tension, he admitted—swirling around in him in a toxic cocktail of emotions. "Damn it! Why can't you accept some help? Why do you have to do this all by yourself?"

"Asking if I needed help? That was considerate. Your hand on the door, though? *Telling* me you're going with me?" She glared at him as she opened the door. "Why the *fuck* do you have to make this about *you*?"

His jaw dropped. "About me?"

But she didn't stop to answer his question. Instead, she was already moving, striding down the hall like the Terminator, like she'd kill anything that got in her way. She broke into a sprint about halfway to the elevator bank.

He watched as she disappeared into the elevator, then grumbled, realizing he was buck naked and standing in a hotel room doorway. Security cameras were going to *love* that, he thought, rubbing his hand over his face as he locked the door.

He gritted his teeth, then headed to the mini-bar, grabbing a small bottle of tequila. How did he always attract the crazies, he thought, downing half of it with one swig. Cheating ex-girlfriends. Persistent groupies. That damned stalker. And now Hailey Frost, Queen of Hot and Cold. He was probably better off without her.

Why the fuck do you have to make this about you?

Her words rang in his head, and he grimaced, finishing off the tiny bottle. Try to be nice, he thought defensively, and it bites you on the ass.

65

Asking if I needed help was considerate. Your hand on the door, though?

He frowned, grabbing another mini bottle. He didn't open it immediately, though. Instead, he rolled it around between his hands, sitting on the edge of the bed.

The thing was, he'd *liked* Hailey. Sure he was attracted to her, but there was more than just that flash burn of sexual combustibility. There was a warmth to her. She was fun to talk to, clever, quick, with equal parts of heart and snark. And there was a palpable passion when she talked about how much she loved her little town. She was a mystery, too, one he was dying to unravel.

"Goddamn it," he grunted, opening the second bottle.

He'd held the door because he wanted her to listen. He wanted to go with her, to help her. To fix her problems and erase the tension that had flooded through her. To learn more about her, delve deeper into her life.

She was right, he thought.

He'd made it about what *he* wanted. He hadn't listened to her at all, hadn't backed off when she obviously needed him to. She wasn't posturing—she was *telling* him, and he'd bulled through and *made it about him*.

He rubbed his face.

When he got the chance, he thought, he'd apologize.

That is . . . *if* he got the chance. Because there was a really good possibility that he'd screwed up his one and only shot at Hailey Frost.

·♥ · ♥ · ♥ · ♥ · ♥·

Please, God, let her be okay. Everything else—the almost-sex, the stupid scene with Jake, the whole thing—disappeared beneath the weight of that one thought.

It was lucky Hailey was just up the hill from their house. She was never a slow driver to begin with, but adrenaline and fear made her roar down the road like a Valkyrie before screeching to a halt in front of the dilapidated Victorian that was both her home and her sister's business.

Her half-sister Rachel opened the door, obviously waiting for her. Where Hailey was the hell-raiser, Rachel was the librarian—quiet, staid, studious. She and Hailey shared indigo eyes and full lips, but that's where the similarities shifted. Where Hailey was overblown, Rachel was perfect: perfectly symmetrical, perfectly proportioned. Stunning without being showy, sensuous without being overt. She was petite, about five foot three, with a slight but definitely womanly frame. She also had a face like an angel, like something carved out of marble. Right now, she looked like a luminous statue, somber and beautiful.

"Cressida?" Hailey asked quickly.

"She's in her room," Rachel said, her eyes filled with concern. "In the closet."

Hailey stepped in from the cold night air, peeling off her leather coat as Rachel shut and locked the door. "What the hell happened?"

Rachel sighed. "She tried to go outside while I was working. Vickie was driving by on her way to the store tonight, and saw Cress lying there on the front steps. Vickie said it seemed like she'd been there a while, given how cold she was." Rachel's voice sounded like jagged glass. "I worked late, which meant I stayed late at the library studying. I didn't . . . I wasn't . . ."

Hailey felt her stomach clench like she'd been punched hard in the gut. "Jesus."

"I rushed home, got her back upstairs." Rachel's face looked like it could've been carved out of porcelain, but her eyes were pure agony. "She's . . . Well. Balled up on the floor, beside her books. She hasn't talked in a few hours, though, and . . . I wasn't going to call you, but I was so worried. Maybe she should go to the hospital . . . ?"

"Fuck. No, she hates hospitals. I'll make sure she's all right." Hailey gripped Rachel's thin hand. It was like ice. "You okay?"

"Just wish I could help her more," Rachel said. "I'm sorry I called. I know tonight's your, um, night off, but I didn't . . ."

"Don't ever apologize for something about Cressida," Hailey said, and then let out a little huff of breath when Rachel made a tiny, almost imperceptible wince. "I love you, Rache, you know that. But Cress and I . . ."

"I know." Rachel squeezed her hand, then nodded to the upstairs bedrooms. "Go on."

Hailey bolted up the stairs, barely knocking on Cressida's door, more out of habit than anything. She opened it, grateful that Cressida hadn't locked it, and then stepped in, closing it behind her.

The room was neat as a pin, with deep blue walls and black-and-white artwork in white frames. An intricate-looking computer set up with two screens was on the Ikea desk, and the bed was made with a cheerful quilt. All in all, it was a cute, cozy room. But she couldn't see Cress anywhere, and that caused a moment of panic. She stood, silent, listening for any sound over the frightened pounding of her own heart. The closet door was closed, and Hailey could hear the soft, almost panting breaths inside.

"Cress?" she said, leaning against the closet door. "Cress, honey, it's Hailey. Are you okay? Let me see what's going on."

"Hailey?" Cressida's voice sounded reedy. "Damn it. Rachel shouldn't have called you."

"Well, thankfully, she's more scared of me than she is of you," Hailey said, trying to joke. Trying to shake the chill of fear out of her voice. "Hon, can I open the door?"

It took a long minute before Cressida finally sighed. "Okay."

Hailey opened the door. There, crammed under the clothes that were hanging up and a bunch of books on

69

a shelf, was Cressida. She'd obviously been balled up, scrunched against the corner. Since she was normally about five foot six, that couldn't be comfortable. Her ivory face, sprinkled with freckles, was covered by her long, red hair. She was buried in bedding, her willowy body obscured by a patchwork quilt.

The closet was Cressida's panic room, her retreat. The smaller the space, the more comfortable she felt.

Hailey didn't hesitate. She folded her taller five-eight frame in the closet doorway, tucking her boots under her. "What happened, sweetie?"

Cressida's already pale skin looked like vellum, showing the tattoo-like blue veins at the corners of her eyes and in the column of her throat. Her hazel eyes looked like moons, round and luminous. She looked like a living ghost.

"I tried to go outside," she whispered.

Hailey did a quick check. She didn't seem to have frostbite anywhere, from what she could see. Her temperature wasn't feverish, and though she was pale, Cressida didn't seem to look too pale. Hailey took her hand. "Jesus, your fingers are like Otter Pops," she said, quickly taking Cressida's hands in her own and rubbing them, just like she had so many years ago in the foster home, the first time Cressida had had a panic attack. "What made you want to go outside today? And why didn't you take a coat, sweetie? I mean, it's March and all, and it was, what, thirty-seven degrees out, but it's still not *that* warm."

She was still joking. Trying to joke. But her voice was hoarse.

"I did the books," Cressida said. "The accounting. We're in the red, by like, a lot."

Hailey swore under her breath. "Well, that sucks. So you decided, well, I'm having a bad day enough as it is, so I'll just push my agoraphobia while I'm at it?"

Cressida's look was mournful, reproaching. Hailey bit her tongue.

"If we can't stay here, Hales, then I'm going to need to figure out how to leave the house," Cressida said, her voice matter of fact.

"We'll stay here." Hailey's voice was like a drill sergeant's. "Don't worry. I'll figure it out."

"I'm tired of forcing you and Rachel to figure it out," Cressida said, her voice breaking. "I hate feeling like . . . like an *invalid*. A burden. Something you guys need to 'take care of.' It's killing me."

Hailey didn't know what to say to that, so she squeezed Cressida's hand harder. "You are *not* a burden," she finally answered. "You're my sister."

"Not your blood."

"Who gives a shit?" Hailey blurted out. "You were there for me when it was the worst. You took care of me. You were the only one who loved me when literally nobody else cared if I lived or died. You are my sister, and if you say one more word about it, I will fucking pound you."

Thankfully, Cressida gave her a watery smile at this one. "Bring it on, bitch," she murmured, the words sounding so at odds with her ethereal appearance, Hailey couldn't help but laugh.

"So, no more pushing yourself to try and get out of the house. We'll jump off that bridge when we come to it, okay?"

Cressida's mouth pulled into a tight line. "We may be coming to it soon," she said softly. "We're falling behind on key payments—not just the rent. We're always a month behind on utilities, and sneaky stuff keeps cropping up. Stupid stuff, like the furnace filter or when that pipe busted and we needed Pinky's to come out and fix it. We're just not making enough business. We need a windfall, to dig out from under, and then we need to have a better, more consistent client base."

Hailey felt pressure behind her eyes. Rachel was the businessperson, not her. She was just a blackjack dealer and former grifter, who loved her sisters. She knew that a business inside their home gave Cressida something to do as well as a source of income—and something else, like write-offs or credits, or something else official and accountant-sounding. But that was about all she could understand without her head aching. "We will make it work," Hailey said stubbornly.

Cressida didn't look convinced, but let it drop.

"Have you eaten anything?" Hailey said instead.

"Not hungry."

"That means no. Feel up to going downstairs for dinner?"

She saw it—the flinch, the curving of Cressida's spine, and quickly changed tack. "You know what? Why don't you get comfy pj's on, I'll get some grilled cheese sandwiches together, and we'll camp out on your bed and watch some River Song episodes of *Doctor Who*."

Cressida smiled. "Sure. Thanks. But I'm feeling more like a little *Supernatural*. Go hunting with the boys."

"Then we'll watch that," Hailey said. "Watching two sexy guys like Sam and Dean? Not a hardship."

"Speaking of sexy guys," Cressida said, before Hailey could make it out of the room. "You were going to stay over at the casino tonight, weren't you?"

Hailey gritted her teeth. A thought of Jake, spread out naked and resplendent on the bed, had her body tightening.

Cressida nodded. "I figured you had a guy. Tell the truth: we interrupted something, didn't we?"

"No." At Cressida's piercing gaze, she relented. "Nothing that couldn't be interrupted."

"He wasn't that good, huh?"

"He was . . ." She froze for a moment, trying to encapsulate Jake Reese, then shrugged. "Not bad."

That is, it was "not bad" in the same way that the Empire State Building was "sort of tall" or the North Pole was "kind of brisk."

73

"I'm sorry," Cressida said, sounding genuinely disappointed. "I know you've been tense lately. You could always go back. Really, I'm fine."

Hailey thought of how they'd left things. "No. He started getting a little stupid after that. Got a tad bit pushy."

"Not literally, I'm assuming," Cressida said, with enough concern for Hailey to know it was a real question.

"He'd still be nursing his balls if it was literally." Grandma Frost had signed her up for martial arts classes when she'd first gotten to Snoqualmie, and she knew enough street fighting from her scraps in Los Angeles that she protected herself as a matter of course. She also didn't get herself into situations where she'd need the skills if she could help it. "No. He just wanted to know what was going on, which was none of his business. Then he tried to play hero, and got a little too alpha for my tastes."

"Oh." Cressida frowned. "That sounds . . . ugh."

"Not my bag," Hailey agreed. "Pity, too. He had potential."

Understatement, yet again. She sighed.

Cressida shook her head. "Too bad you can't just get one guy you can count on."

"I'm strictly catch and release, you know that," Hailey said dryly. She leaned forward, giving Cressida a quick hug. "Go on, get comfy. I'll bring up the sandwiches."

She went downstairs, where Rachel was waiting. "How is she?" Rachel asked softly.

"She'll be okay." She went through the old kitchen, grabbing the loaf of bread, pulling cheese slices and butter out of the fridge, and pulling out a dented pan. "She tried to go outside because she did the books." She took a deep breath, then looked at Rachel. "Why didn't you tell me how far behind we're falling?"

"She's worried we'll have to move, isn't she?" Rachel said, avoiding the question.

Hailey pinned her down with an expectant stare. Rachel sighed.

"We're staying afloat, but yeah, it's been a struggle."

"I can give you more money . . ."

"You're giving us everything but the money you pour into Charlotte's gas tank as it is," Rachel protested.

"I'll . . . damn it. Figure out something."

"I've been thinking—maybe I should drop out of school. Just for this semester," Rachel said, holding up her hands protectively from Hailey's nuclear glare.

"Damn it." She started to assemble the sandwiches, then gestured to them in invitation, quirking her eyebrow at her sister. Rachel shook her head. "How much trouble are we in?"

Rachel fidgeted with the mug in front of her. "If we don't start getting more customers in, we won't be able to keep this place. She's right on that front."

"So we get more customers in," Hailey said. "You've been running those online ads and things. You had the interview with the local paper."

75

"All small bumps, nothing that would drive a lot of traffic, especially for just a bookstore. The used bookstore in North Bend just closed because they couldn't make ends meet, and they didn't have our living expenses on top of it. Or our landlord's crappy maintenance," Rachel said darkly. "What we need is a game changer. A big event or something. I'm working on doing some joint stuff with the local chamber of commerce, but most of the opportunities will be in the summer. We need something now, and something that will drive a more niche clientele."

Hailey got the butter frothing in the pan, then slid the sandwiches in. "Let me know what I can do, and I'll do it."

"If I did know, I'd tell you," Rachel answered, her expression thoughtful. "I think turning it into more of a fandom place might help. It's not like you can't get books on Amazon—we're in Seattle, for God's sake, in their backyard. So it's difficult to just be a bookstore without a niche. I'm thinking we can cater to . . . well, girl geeks, for lack of a better term."

"Sounds good to me," Hailey said. "What does that mean?"

"We order fan stuff, not just books," she said. "We can still have the used books, but we can get more female-centric comics, and fandom related stuff . . . maybe signed stuff, or items from Think Geek, or something. Even Etsy-styled stuff. Remember that *Hobbit* necklace Ren . . ." Rachel paused. "That I got in high school?"

Hailey blinked. Rachel *never* brought up her high school flame, the one true love of her life. She must be really rattled to let that slip. "Okay. So we make Frost Bookstore a fandom store. What do we need?"

"We'd need some items to really make that work. And we'd need a big draw, to get the right crowd in, to convince them to drive all the way out to Snoqualmie instead of the city." Rachel rubbed her temples. "Let me make some calls. I'll see what I can do to work fast. We need to get some more sales, and soon."

Hailey flipped the golden-brown sandwiches, then slid them onto plates. "Rachel, I know how hard you're working," she said, feeling a bit impotent. "I'm sorry you're hit with all of this."

"She's my sister, too," Rachel said quietly. "Ever since she came home with you, she's been part of the family."

"I know." But it was different. All three of them knew that. Rachel, the half-sister Hailey hadn't even known existed until she was twelve, didn't have the same formative experiences Hailey and Cressida had. The two of them had been through the trenches, apart and together. But since Grandma Frost had brought Hailey and Cressida home from Los Angeles, Rachel genuinely loved and valued them both as sisters.

"If we'd only been able to win that fan contest, the one Tessa tried to help us with, we could've had one of the *Mystics* stars come," Rachel said.

Hailey felt a pang.

Funny you should mention . . .

She thought about Jake, how she'd left him at the hotel. How he'd acted.

No. Wasn't worth it.

"Especially if we could've done something for this week, or next weekend, what with the convention they're running," Rachel continued, oblivious to Hailey's line of thought.

"We could've gotten some of that crowd over here, maybe, and you know some of those people would be local. We could build up our mailing list . . ."

As Rachel continued thinking out loud, Hailey felt guilt prick away at her.

Yes, Jake was overbearing about her leaving tonight. But she'd been sharp, too, out of fear and defensiveness. Maybe, just maybe, he was trying to be gallant. Maybe he'd seen the urgency, and he wanted to make sure she accepted his help.

Yeah. When in the history of ever *has someone simply tried to help me out?*

Well, maybe this was the first time, she thought, and wondered if it was hope or desperation that prompted the thought.

Hailey cleared her throat, interrupting Rachel's monologue. "If one of the actors did an appearance here, you really think that would help?"

"Are you kidding? It'd give me something to spin for P.R.," Rachel said. "It'd be a big draw. We've got some good fandom-related stock. I could organize the displays to show the paranormal romance that's like *Mystics*. And we could send out stuff, get people's contact info, start building off that client base." Rachel's slow smile was self-mocking. "But let's be real. They aren't going to be open to an eleventh-hour pitch from a tiny indie book-store. And unless you have contacts I'm not aware of, I think it's a hopeless cause."

She winced. It would mean humbling herself. Possibly even groveling.

It's for your sisters.

How much worse had she endured, to keep Cressida safe?

How much worse *would* she put up with?

"Give me a day," Hailey said. "Let me see what I can do."

· ❤ · ❤ · ❤ · ❤ · ❤ ·

The next day, Jake sat in the "green room" of the ho-tel—which was neither green nor a room, from the looks of it. It was a partitioned section of the ballroom where they were doing the majority of the panels, and the sales floor where they were selling *Mystics* memorabilia and other fan items. It was close to where he needed to be, but it was still separate, with its own door, guarded by a security guy—a bouncer, basically. His co-stars, Simon and Miles, were lounging at a table, joking about their own kerfuffle with the hotel the previous night.

"They finally dug us up a room at an Airbnb in Sammamish," Simon said, his eyes alight with mischief. Simon was like a grown-up Tom Sawyer, mischievous and boyish. He tossed a football to Miles, who was more like a young monk, with a wiry physique and silent, pensive expression. Miles caught the ball easily while only barely paying attention, a testament to how often the two pitched it back and forth. "I have no idea how they thought that place 'slept four,' since it just had a queen bed. Barely fit me."

"You sleep like a break-dancer, dude," Miles pointed out. "I had to camp out on the floor in self-defense. You throw more elbows than Karl Malone."

"You love it," Simon said, blowing Miles an air kiss. Miles rolled his eyes.

"You know, they're going to joke about you two sleeping together," Jake said.

"Not the first time," Simon agreed easily.

"We'll talk about it during the panel," Miles added, with a gentle grin of his own. "The slash fan-fic will be posted within the hour."

The two had been best friends for years, meeting as starving actors in Los Angeles. Simon had helped Miles get the gig on *Mystics*, as a matter of fact. Jake admired their easy camaraderie.

To be honest, he envied it.

"How about you?" Simon pressed, turning a chair around and straddling it, surveying Jake curiously. "No offense, but you look like hammered shit. Did they stick you in a tent or something?"

"Nah. I got a room in a little town about fifteen minutes from here." Jake shrugged.

"Oh?" Simon glanced at Miles. "Was it a rat hole or something?"

"It was nice," Jake protested, then realized the trap as Simon waited eagerly. "I just had some trouble sleeping."

"The fun kind of not sleeping?" Simon pressed, wiggling his eyebrows.

Miles chuckled, shaking his head. "Leave the poor guy alone, Si."

Jake cleared his throat. The truth was, he'd had a hell of a time getting to sleep after Hailey left. Not because he'd been left at the brink of satisfaction—okay, not *just* because of that, he privately amended—but because of the way they'd left things.

He felt like a total ass.

Hailey was different from other women he'd met. She wasn't intimidated by his fame or his father or his lifestyle. She took shit from no one. She was a problem solver, a force of nature.

Hotter than a Carolina Reaper. Probably just as lethal as the ghost pepper, he ruminated. They didn't have a Scoville scale to cover her level of hotness.

He hadn't ever reacted to a woman he'd just met the way he'd responded to Hailey. Her smile, her quick wit, her badass attitude and unbelievable responsiveness.

Then she'd gotten that call, acted weird and panicked. Wouldn't talk to him about why. He probably shouldn't have jumped to conclusions, but damn it, in his experience, if someone was too good to be true, it was because they were lying through their teeth.

I'm a terrible actress, but I'm a hell of a liar.

He sighed. Was she?

"You seem preoccupied," Miles said, smiling softly. "I heard what happened at the VIP."

"What happened?" Simon asked. Miles ignored him.

"They should've had a more experienced handler for you," Miles said. "You could sue that woman for assault."

"Whoa. What?"

Jake told Simon the story: the boob-signing, the pocket rip, making a break for it.

"Jesus," Simon said, shuddering. "I love our fans, don't get me wrong. But that's fucked up."

"Seriously. That doesn't sound like *Supernatural's* fan stuff at all," Miles agreed.

"Don't worry. We'll protect you this weekend," Simon added. "Hey, on an unrelated note: did your contract get renewed yet?"

"We just heard back yesterday," Miles said. "You'll probably hear back soon."

Jake had actually managed to put that out of his mind, in the wake of the VIP kerfuffle and the subsequent Hailey fallout. Now, he felt a knot in his stomach.

"I haven't heard yet," he said, hoping he sounded more casual than he felt.

Miles and Simon frowned.

"Maybe you should call your agent," Simon suggested.

Jake felt even more freaked out. He walked to the other side of the room, ignoring Simon's and Miles's story-swapping, remembrances from their days as early actors. He hit the contact for Susie.

"The room situation's all straightened out," she said, in lieu of a greeting. "I gave them the heads-up to keep your room number private, in case that looney woman tries to show up again and leave you presents. Oh, and make sure they have an impressive fruit basket and turn-down service and a bottle of aged Scotch waiting for you, or I will have somebody's balls."

He grinned. "You take good care of me, Susie."

"Bet your ass," she said fiercely. "Not that yesterday was a good example. I'm sorry, kid, that was a fiasco all the way around."

"I'm fine. I managed," Jake said, then cleared his throat. "Say, Susie . . . did the producers get back to you about renewing my contract yet?"

There was a noticeable pause.

"I saw that we'd been picked up for season three by the network," he rambled nervously. "Production should start up this summer, filming by July. I'll feel a lot better when the ink's dry on my renewal."

Susie sighed. Jake could almost picture her face: the picture of a middle-aged New Yorker in L.A., dressed sharp as a razor, stylish caramel-colored haircut over shrewd brown eyes, signature red lipstick on a mouth frowning with regret.

"I'm just going to come out and say it. They're not thrilled, and there's been some pushback."

Jake froze, glancing at the other guys, who were too engrossed in their own stories to notice. "What? Why?" he blurted, his voice low. "I haven't done anything bad. I'm not in the tabloids every week. I've been lying low for almost a year!"

"That could be part of the problem," Susie said, surprising him further. "Listen, it's great that the show's starting to pick up steam. But there's your Q Score to consider."

Jake boggled. "What does that even mean?"

She sighed again. "I blame myself," she said. "I should've pushed you harder on this front. I mean, you're Kurt Windlass's kid, I figured if anyone would be familiar with the cutthroat world of Hollywood publicity, it's you. Didn't your father set you up with his publicist?"

"That was a few years ago," Jake said, his voice tight. "So it's publicity related?"

"It's, well, recognizability, for lack of a better word," Susie explained.

"And I'm not recognizable?"

"You don't have a lot of brand recognition," she admitted, her voice apologetic. "I mean, if we ask people on the street, 'Who is Jake Reese?' you're pretty much known as either the underwear model or Kurt Windlass's son." She waited a beat. "If they recognize you at all."

Now it was his turn to sigh.

She hemmed a little. "You know, it's not too late to change your name . . ."

"I'm not Jake Windlass."

"Of course you're not," she soothed, obviously expecting his response. "And it's admirable that you don't want to cash in on your father's fame to further your own career."

That wasn't quite the reason, but he let it lie.

"But I'm having a tough time getting the producers to sign off," she said. "It's an uphill battle. The other guys are more bankable. They had that show together before, and if you got half the social media hits that Simon got, I wouldn't be having this conversation."

"Miles doesn't do a lot of social media," Jake pointed out, feeling confused.

"Yeah, but he's friends with Simon, so he gets a residual effect," she said. "And he's a fan favorite. Your part isn't written like his."

He grimaced. He could do more, he knew it. If they'd just give him a chance.

Susie cleared her throat, pressing forward. "If we got you more recognizable, it would help—not only with the contract renewal, but with other projects."

"Other projects aren't even on my radar right now," Jake said. "I just want to lock up next season. Hell, several seasons, if they keep getting renewed. I love this show, Suse. What do I need to do?"

She let out another sigh. "These things take a little time, but of course, there's always a way."

Jake sighed, not wanting to get into that argument again. "What are you suggesting, then? Orchestrating some abuse problem that I can go to rehab for? Or some other crazy scheme?" He tried to force a laugh, even though his stomach knotted. "Really. It all sounds crazy. The tabloids can come up with a lot of that crap on their own, you know."

"Nothing that radical," Susie assured him. "There's train-wreck publicity, and then there's the P.R. that actually helps your career. Like the charity stuff you do . . ."

"That's not for publicity," he said quickly.

"I know, you sweet kid. But there's no shame in it. Look at Chris Pratt, Russell Wilson," she argued. "It's not just about you boosting your image. It helps get the name of the charities out, too."

"I'll think about it." He rubbed at his temple. "Anything else?"

"A girlfriend, the right girlfriend, could work wonders."

He groaned. "No."

"What? Publicity setups can be effective, and they cut those deals all the time. Sure, they don't always work—that Taylor Swift and Tom Hiddleston fiasco, for example—but sometimes they . . ."

"Wait, that was fake?"

She laughed, a gravelly smoker's laugh. "You are so cute. What are you, twelve?"

"So you're saying I should get a fake girlfriend," he reiterated. He hated when Susie teased him for being naïve.

"Let me see who I can come up with," she said. "Talk to you later, sweetie."

"Susie, no—damn it!" She'd already hung up.

He felt a tap on his shoulder, and spun. It was one of the convention people, looking annoyed. "You're on," the guy hissed, covering the microphone of his headset. Jake quickly apologized, feeling guilty, and followed him out the door.

The panel was ready, and Simon and Miles had already made their way onto the "stage," such as it was. There were three chairs, and three microphones, and that's it.

It was a different thing than filming on-set. The energy was like a wall. There had to be a few hundred people out there, mostly women. They wore *Mystics* T-shirts, and a few were cosplaying. Some wore his characteristic leather jacket, others were dressed as Druid priestesses or wore Templar armor.

"This question is for Simon," said one of the fans, dressed as what he recognized was a Templar seminarian. "You're best friends with, and share a house with Miles. What is his most annoying habit? And what is his most endearing?"

Simon rubbed his hands together, and Jake couldn't help but laugh, especially when Miles hid his face behind his arms.

"His most annoying trait is the healthy food. He's constantly trying to make me eat new vegetables . . ."

"Hey, you liked fennel bulb," Miles gave a muffled protest.

"And his most endearing?" Simon's eyes gleamed with glee. "He sleeps with a stuffed panda bear named Mr. Bobo."

Miles emerged, pretending outrage. "You *swore* you wouldn't bring him up!"

"They wanted to know!"

"How about you, Jake?" the fan teased, but her smile was gentle, more playful than lecherous. He wondered if she was trying to make sure he didn't feel left out, and he felt his chest warm. "Sleep with anything endearing?"

"Miles," he said. "I just wish he wouldn't make me dress up as a stuffed panda."

The crowd roared with laughter, Simon started clapping, and Miles high-fived him. He grinned back, the annoyance and nerves from his talk with Susie forgotten.

He could see himself doing this for years—like *Stargate: SG-1* or *Doctor Who*—if given the opportunity. He loved the show's take on sci-fi and fantasy. He loved that, even though they hadn't done much with his character, the writing was great, alternating between humor and pathos, like so many of the shows he loved. And he even loved the conventions. Granted, this was their first, but he knew they would be booked in other conventions—panels at various Comic-Cons, stuff like that—and he was all in. He just frickin' loved this stuff.

For the rest of the panel, he mostly sat quietly, as the other two fielded questions about future arcs, and some things about *Double Negative*, the old show they'd been on. On *Mystics*, Miles was the brains, the scholar; Simon was the con man, the guy who charmed his way into anything. Jake was cast as the muscle, the action guy, so his arc tended to be . . . well, sort of flat.

He frowned as he thought about that. He really should have Susie arguing about that, as well—but since it seemed hard to keep him on the damned show, it didn't seem like the right hill to die on.

As his eyes scanned the room, he stopped short as his gaze locked onto a pair of deep violet eyes, staring right back at him. Her dark walnut hair was done up in pin curls, cascading behind a high ponytail. She had lips the color of a good Bordeaux and lashes that went on for miles. He couldn't see the outfit, but he guessed it was something brutally sexy. Maybe that was just because of the woman wearing it, though.

She came, he thought, and couldn't stop a smile from creeping across his face. Did that mean she'd forgiven him? Or did she just want to give him another piece of her mind?

"Jake?"

He shook himself. "Sorry. What?"

Simon grinned at him knowingly. "Question for you, dude. Stop staring at the ladies."

There was an appreciative giggle that rippled through the crowd, and his smile spread sheepishly. "Sorry about that. I was . . . distracted."

He gazed at Hailey again. Her perfectly arched eyebrow went up, and those full lips quirked in a knowing little lopsided grin.

"What was the question?" He looked over, trying to see who was at the microphone stand.

It was a guy—already a bit of an anomaly at the female-skewed crowd. He was wearing a *Deadpool* T-shirt and a serious expression. "Mr. Reese, I'm Ty Connors, from the AllThingsMystics blog," he said, with just a trace of self-importance.

"Great to meet you," Jake said. "What's your question?" He braced himself for something technical, or some tiny detail. Fortunately, he could nerd out with the best of them—he'd had long talks with several of the writers, discussing the backstory of the world. And he just had a memory for that sort of thing. He found himself looking forward to it.

"Is it true that your contract isn't going to be renewed?"

Everyone gasped. Jake froze. "What?" he finally croaked.

"Inside sources say that you may not be continuing with *Mystics*," Ty said, looking down at a small notepad, then glancing back up at him. "Is that your choice, or theirs? And are they planning on killing the character off, or simply re-casting it?"

CHAPTER 4

Sitting in the audience, Hailey saw the look of pain and shock pass over Jake's face the moment that stupid blogger asked him about being fired or replaced. She could've smacked the blogger for asking the question, but that was the way of it: controversy drove the news, such as it was. Admittedly, Jake leaving the show would be of great interest to the fans.

Jake stammered, looking over at Miles and Simon with a quick, baffled expression. "I . . . ah, I have no idea. I haven't heard anything like that from my agent." He looked momentarily at a loss. "I sure hope that's not true. I mean, I love this show, and I'll do whatever it takes to stay on it."

The crowd cheered, Hailey louder than most. Personally, she thought his performances were just as strong as Miles's and Simon's, if not stronger—the writers and producers underestimated his character and didn't give him much to do, but he had some sly humor and great delivery.

Granted, she was a little less charitable toward him after his epic fuckwittage when she'd had to leave last night, but it didn't discount the fact that she enjoyed his character.

She prayed he'd be more Rick, less fuckwit, now that she had to face him again. God, she hated asking for favors.

It's for Cress, and Rachel, she scolded herself. *So suck it up, buttercup.*

"Okay, that's it for questions," a man with a headset and a convention T-shirt said, holding up his hands defensively when the crowd booed. "Hey, the guys will have another panel tomorrow! And don't forget, we've got other events this week, including the cosplay fashion show and the dance party. Later this afternoon, we'll have two mini-panels, with the women of *Mystics,*" this drew an enthusiastic cheer from the priestess fans, "and the villains of *Mystics,* the Illuminati." Fewer people cheered at this, and a few jeered in response. The guys walked off the stage, waving, and headed to what had to be the green room via a door at the back.

Hailey wasn't here for any of the panels. She had used the VIP badge he'd left at the front desk to get into this one, grateful that Jake had done as promised before their "romp turned fuck-up." Now, she was going to see how

93

far it could get her. She waited for most of the panel attendees to file out, heading for food and restrooms. Then she walked up to the security guard who stood sentinel at the green room's door.

Unfortunately, she wasn't the only one who was looking for entry. "But I just want to see Jake," a woman—not much more than a girl, maybe twenty?—said, holding up her VIP pass like it was a weapon. "He'll be really pissed if he doesn't see me. Did you hear what those bloggers were saying? He's probably really upset!"

"What's your name?" the security guard asked, deadpan.

The girl frowned. "Missy. Missy Bailer."

"Your name isn't on the list, Miss Missy," the security guard said, keeping a straight face.

"My name isn't on the list, either," an older redhead said, looking at the guard with an obvious seductive pout. "But I'm sure he'll want to see me."

Good grief, was that the woman from the pocket-ripping brigade? Hailey shuddered. That lady had "predator" written all over her, from the hungry glint in her eye to the way she kept stroking her neckline.

The guard remained implacable, not looking at either woman. "Sorry. If your name isn't on the list, you don't get entry."

The redhead flounced away, while "Missy" tried even harder to convince, cajole, or bribe the man into letting her back into the green room. Hailey felt her stomach clench. Maybe she should wait until Jake was leaving, heading back up to his room? Assuming the hotel had fixed that problem and he actually *had* accommodations this time. But there were still other women, clustering around the green room door. They were probably there to see the other two actors, as well . . . it was going to be a crush, an absolute shit show.

Hailey stood straighter, doing her best "of course I belong here" strut. As if she didn't care, one way or the other if they allowed her access. Her goal was to get in, and see if Jake was amenable to helping out the bookstore. She'd back off if it didn't work, or press forward if it did.

One way or another she'd get to talk to Jake tonight, and ask about the appearance. There was more than one way to catch a fish.

The security guard gave Hailey more of a look than the others. "Hey, I know you," he said.

She blinked, then her eyes narrowed. "Do you?"

"You deal."

Missy stared at her, obviously assuming that "dealing" meant drugs. Hailey couldn't tell if the woman was appalled, or wondering if she should've bribed her way in with a dime bag.

"Blackjack dealer," he continued. "Up at Snoqualmie. Yeah?"

Hailey nodded, grinning. "You play? What's your name?"

He shook his head. "I'm Rico. I worked security there, few years back, before moving over to this hotel," he said, grinning back. "Don't tell me you're a fan?"

"I am actually," she said. "But I was supposed to, erm, talk to Jake Reese. My name's Hailey Frost."

His grin widened to a beam. "You're on the list."

"How do you know?" Missy demanded. "You didn't even look on your phone or on a paper or anything! How do you know she's on the list, and I'm not?"

"Because hers is the only name on the list for Jake."

"Thanks," Hailey said, leaving the girl to splutter. She walked down a dark hallway, before stepping into the little side room they'd set up. It wasn't that fancy looking—just a hotel's back room, with a table set up with some food and drinks, and a couple of chairs. The *Mystics* guys were there, in their full glory. Simon was just as good looking, with those piercing green eyes. Miles was tall, resembling a poet or a Renaissance painter with his trimmed beard and his longish hair pulled back at the nape of his neck.

"It's bullshit, man," Simon was saying to Jake. "You should talk to the producers. No way they're replacing you!"

"My agent told me they don't want to speak to me directly," Jake responded, rubbing his face with his hand.

No matter how they'd left things last night, Hailey couldn't help but feel her heart clench at his stunned expression, and the devastation in his voice. The show meant more to him than she'd realized.

Miles grumbled. "They're not going to fire you. I don't even know where the guy got that information." He was standing close to Jake, giving him one of those hard pats on the shoulders that guys give instead of hugs.

"I have to boost my Q Score," Jake said, still sounding mournful.

"What the hell is that?" Miles asked, obviously baffled. She knew the feeling. She wasn't sure if she'd heard it correctly, because she had no idea what they were talking about.

Simon, on the other hand, shook his head. He seemed much more knowledgeable, and shrewd. "Really? Your Q Score? What are you, a video game? A movie? A bar of frickin' soap?"

Hailey couldn't help herself. She snickered at Simon's histrionics, letting out the laugh as a sort of pressure-release from all the tension she was feeling, both for the bookstore and for herself. All three of them looked over at her.

"Well, hello," Simon said, his eyes gleaming with interest. "Who have we here?"

"Nobody's supposed to be back here," Miles said, almost simultaneously, standing protectively in front of Jake. Simon flanked him. It actually made her feel better, to see the other two looking out for him.

But Jake had gotten a glimpse of her before they'd created their human wall. "Hailey?" Jake stood in a fluid motion, his eyes lighting. "I didn't think I'd see you today. I'm glad you're here."

"Yup, here I am." She hated that her voice sounded a little hesitant. "Thought we should talk."

"Um, well, it's time we went up to our rooms. Get ready for tonight's VIP dinner," Miles said, then nudged Simon.

"I don't have to go anywhere," Simon countered, walking up to her and holding a hand out. "Simon. Nice to meet you. Hailey, was it? You seem familiar."

She grinned. Apparently, the tabloids saying the guy was a total man-whore weren't wrong. He was charming, and obviously loved women.

"You do have to go somewhere," Miles said, grabbing Simon's shoulder and shoving him toward the door.

"What? I wasn't even going to change my clothes."

"You have to do the thing," Miles said. "Remember?"

"What thing?" Simon protested.

"The thing where you don't cock-block your friend," Miles hissed, shoving him toward the door. When the door opened, Hailey could hear women shriek.

"Ladies!" Simon called out, the smile clear in his enthusiastic tone. "What have we . . ." It was cut off as the door closed, leaving her alone in the room with Jake.

She turned to him, hands in her pockets. "Um, I wanted to talk."

"I'm glad. I didn't have your number, and I really, really wanted to apologize," he said, surprising her. "You were right. I was an asshole last night. It wasn't any of my business, and you were obviously in a hurry. I thought maybe you were just not thinking clearly, or you didn't think you could ask me for help, but I crossed a line with the he-man crap. The more I thought about it afterward, the more I realized you had something serious going on, and the last thing you needed was my interference."

She felt a bubble of relief—and guilt. "It's okay. Really."

"I guess that I've just been burned a lot," he said. "I know, that's not a good enough excuse. But I hope you'll give me another chance, let me make it up to you."

The guilt intensified, which was weird. He was handing himself to her on a platter. She couldn't have gotten a better response from him if she'd schemed it herself.

"Do you forgive me?"

"Well, yes." She frowned, then shrugged. Best to be honest. "I do want something from you, though."

He froze. Then grinned. "I want something from you, too." He started to reach for her.

She evaded, holding up her hand. "No. I mean, not that I'm not interested there, too," she admitted, as a quick memory of the previous night—and what they'd almost done—flooded her mind. *Damn*, was she interested. "But I do want something else from you. That's why I'm here, actually."

Now his expression looked like a cross between eagerness and wariness. "What can I do?"

"I've got . . . well, my *family's* got a bookstore," she said, slowly.

How much to tell him? She didn't want to spill the whole thing. Cressida's life was hard enough, and the trauma behind Cress's circumstances wasn't her secret to tell, anyway. But she could share some details.

"Our landlord raised our rent in January. The bookstore was barely making it beforehand, but now we're running in the red and getting behind on bills."

God, the shame of it was like drinking battery acid. She swallowed painfully.

"We're, um, thinking of rebranding it, making it a fandom bookstore. You know, one that caters to geeky genres and a really strict niche. For women, though. Geek girls."

He shrugged, his previous warmth starting to chill. "How, exactly, do you need my help?"

"If you could do an appearance before you go back to Vancouver, it'd be huge," she said. "It would make a noticeable difference. Especially if you could announce it during this conference. It would go a long way toward helping us build our financial solvency."

"So. You want me to do an appearance, because your family business is failing."

She nodded.

He took a deep breath. "And did you know about this before or after you and I almost slept together?"

It was as effective as a slap. "It has nothing to do with what happened last night. Why I left, I mean." At his skeptical glance, she narrowed her eyes. "Trust me, buddy, if I were trying to run a number on you, I would've hit you up when I had your pants off."

That surprised a bark of laughter out of him, but he was shaking his head, and she felt her heart drop. "Sorry. I'm not supposed to do any non-sanctioned appearances."

She felt disappointment and anxiety start to bubble in her chest, but she pushed forward doggedly. "Why not?"

"I'm in contract negotiations," he said, and he just sounded tired. "And frankly, I'm trying to boost my Q Score, I'm trying to save my job. I can't afford to blow it."

"Couldn't you ask them?" she pressed. "It's charitable. Could be good publicity."

"My agent wouldn't go for it," he said.

She felt a burn of frustration. "The agent works for you, doesn't he?" she said sharply.

"She, not he. Was that all?" he asked with some challenge of his own.

She groaned, seeing the opportunity slip away. This was the best, and quickest, idea that she'd had. She wasn't going to lose the chance now. She was going to help Cressida.

"Maybe one of the other guys could help me, then?" she asked, keeping her voice level.

"I'll ask." He stood, gestured to the door.

This sucked. Well and truly sucked. Before the panic, and the stupidity, of last night, she'd really enjoyed the time they'd spent together. Now, seeing him closed off and hurt because of her question, she felt—well, she wasn't sure *how* she felt, only that it wasn't good.

"What are you going to do about that Q Score of yours?" she asked, unwilling to leave just yet.

"Hailey, you don't have to ask. I can't imagine it's that interesting." He shot her a sardonic smirk. "I mean, do you really care? You've got enough on your plate, right?"

That made her stiffen. "I do want your help, but you were the one who acted like an ass first. Yeah, I'm asking you for a favor. You can't, or won't, no problem. I'll figure it out, believe me."

There was enough snap in her voice to have his eyes widening. She tried tempering her tone, but then thought: *fuck it.*

"I'm not one of those fawning groupies," she said, and her voice took on an edge. "If you don't want to talk about it, if you want me to go to hell, that's fine. But goddamn it, I genuinely asked."

He sighed, then rubbed his hands over his face. He looked exhausted. "Well, it seems like I'm about to be fired from this job."

"I heard the question. The blogger."

"I really like it, working on the show," he said. "If they want me to do the VIPs, even when they rip at my clothes,

I do it. If they want me to dress up like a Labrador and dance the Macarena, I'd do it."

She nodded ruefully. *I know those feels, bro.*

"But I don't know how to . . . do that . . . publicity thing," he said. "Not well, obviously."

"Here's a silly question: can't you hire a publicist?"

He frowned. "I had one for a while. Or rather, my father assigned one to me."

"What? It didn't take?"

"She wanted me to be someone I wasn't," Jake said, and she could see the memories clouding his face. "I was supposed to be seen. I went to a bunch of parties. I hated it. I didn't care about anything they were talking about. I got drunk plenty of times, but I wasn't into drugs. And the stuff I was interested in, nobody else was."

"What are you interested in? "

"I don't know. Hiking, surfing, camping. And just talking about things." He looked frustrated. "My publicist said she couldn't work with it, wanted me to be something I wasn't. I cared about more than just who was sleeping with whom, and getting my next part." His shoulders hunched, and his frown made him look like an angsty gunslinger. "My agent thinks if I got the right girlfriend, it might help."

"So do that," she said. "Easy-peasy."

He shook his head vehemently. "For one thing, it feels wretched. Bit too much like being a hooker."

She felt one of her eyebrows pop up. Damn it, she hated it when people who'd never actually *been* sex workers talked about things like they were. She'd known plenty in L.A., and lots of them were sweethearts. "Oh?"

"Besides, I did try it once before," he admitted.

Her eyes went wide. "What, you were a prostitute?"

"No!" he yelped, letting out a burst of surprised laughter. "The setup girlfriend thing. Two girlfriends ago. She was trying to be the next America's sweetheart. I was doing the modeling thing," he said. "I thought she was pretty cool. Until I found her naked, straddling another actor."

"Oops." Hailey winced.

"In my house."

"That's gotta hurt."

Jake shrugged. "In my bed."

"Okay, stop," Hailey said, chuckling a little. "Next thing you'll tell me they got married."

"No, but she did get into his next movie. I don't know if those events were related, but I didn't stick around long enough to find out." He sounded bitter. "Anyway, I had another girlfriend after that, but she also just wanted to get a part on the show that I was on, which tanked. Then I got this gig. Been with *Mystics* for two years, and I love it. Working with Simon and Miles, the writers, getting to be a Knight Templar with magic powers fighting evil, centuries-old aliens fuckin' *rocks*."

She grinned. The smile lighting his face as he described the show was infectious.

He sobered. "I don't want to lose it." He paused. "And I'm not sure why I told you all that."

"I have one of those faces," she said, easily, and was rewarded when he smiled. "So, anything else you could do?"

"I could go on a huge binge, maybe crash a car, go into rehab," he joked, shaking his head. "Or, you know, skinny-dip in a hotel pool. Maybe get involved with a married co-star."

"Or one of your guy co-stars," she said. "The slash fans would eat it up."

"Much as I love those guys," he said, "I don't, you know, *love* those guys. And I don't think either of them want to help my career that badly. I'm not their type, either."

She smirked, nudging him gently. "Well, all you're looking for is a story. Something the fans want to see. Something to get them talking."

And then it struck her.

The perfect con.

"You're trying to become an integral part of the fans' lives. Why don't you date a fan?"

He looked at her in horror. "One of those women yanked the pocket off my jeans," he said. "*Denim*. That takes some significant strength. That lady must've had arms like an orangutan."

"I'm not saying date that one, specifically!"

"With my luck, I'd get involved with someone who then keeps me chained in her basement."

"Be nice," she said. "You have to respect your fans, especially if you want them to respect you. It's a great show, and you're great on it."

"I know. Sorry. I'm being a dick," he admitted. "I just . . . I can't just proposition some fangirl, and ask her to keep mum about why. It wouldn't be fair to her, either."

Hailey grinned, seeing the game laid out in front of her—a way to help both of them.

"I've got the perfect solution," she said, her smile slowly widening. "Pretend to date me."

· ❤ · ❤ · ❤ · ❤ · ❤ ·

Jake stared at Hailey, a surreal feeling of numbness hitting him.

"You want me to *pretend* to date you," he repeated, as if that might make it make more sense.

"Look, it's not that complicated," she said, her indigo eyes flashing with excitement. "You haven't been dating anyone, and there's some curiosity. You let it leak that you're dating a fan, someone you met at a convention. The first *Mystics* con, in fact. You're trying to keep it a secret."

"I must be really bad at it, then," he muttered, still trying to wrap his head around the concept. "Because if I keep it a secret, it's not going to help my Q Score much."

She rolled her eyes, sighing. The deep breath did nice things for her breasts, which were already straining against her blouse. It was a black blouse with lots of cherries on it, he noticed. Of course, he noticed more than the cherries.

"Flattering, but eyes up here, buddy," she said with an indulgent smile. "The things that spread are always the things that are supposed to be secret, trust me."

"So you're a publicist, too?" he asked. "Is that what you do for your bookstore?"

"God, no," she said, shaking her head. "Business is all Rachel's wheelhouse—that's my sister. Well, half-sister," she added absently.

"So how do you know this will work?"

"Because I used to run cons."

He blinked. "Run cons? Conventions?"

"No. Cons. Confidence games." He must've looked as puzzled as he felt, because she rolled her eyes. "Con artist. Get it?"

"Like *The Sting*, or *Ocean's Eleven,* or something? You're a grafter?"

"Grifter. Nothing so sophisticated," she said. "And I said 'used to.' Past tense."

"What made you stop?" He felt like he'd fallen down a serious rabbit hole. Or perhaps someone slipped him some 'shrooms. He wouldn't put it past Simon, prankster that he was.

"Juvie," she answered, with a shrug. "After that, Grandma Frost found me, brought me up here from Los Angeles. I didn't really need to run any after that." She rubbed the back of her neck, and he could see her gaze go soft, obviously remembering. "Besides, Grandma said if she caught me conning anybody in town, she'd beat me with a broom."

He tensed. "Seriously?"

"She didn't mean it. Probably," she amended. "It didn't matter, though. I didn't need to anymore. But the point—which we're going a little far afield from," she emphasized gently, "is that this isn't really that different from running a con. You're just trying to get people to behave a certain way, think a certain thing. Trust me. People are interested when fans hook up with famous people, because in their hearts, they'd like to think it's possible. And people spread secrets because they want to show they know something before other people do. That's just human nature."

She sounded so matter of fact. "But it's still a lie," he couldn't help but point out.

That indulgent look was back. "I'll let you pay for dinners, if it makes you feel better," she said.

"I hate lying." He grimaced. "I just hate being fake. Not being real."

"Okay, I hate to point this out," she said, "but you're an *actor*. You fake things for a living."

"It's not faking, it's acting," he said, then realized how ridiculous that sounded. "I'm portraying a character."

She leaned back against a wall, surveying him. "I suppose your previous publicist tried to convince you that you were just playing a role?"

He sighed. "Yup. Tried that. The thing is, I get to play pretend all day, for my job. But I don't want to live my job. My life is my reality."

"Well, you're going to have plenty of reality if you lose this job, right?"

He winced. Trust her to get straight to the heart of it. "If you put it that way."

"Listen. I think I can help you. I'm not saying I can work miracles or anything, but I think this is something I can pull off," she said, her face almost shining with intensity. "If I screw up, and it doesn't work, well, you lose the job. You don't have to help me. But if it does work and the contract goes through . . . will you tell your agent you'll do the appearance?"

He frowned, but felt himself being inexorably drawn in—like the Millennium Falcon toward the Death Star. If the Death Star was a smokin' hot gothabilly brunette. "What would it entail?"

She smiled, a sly, catlike smile of victory. He felt his body tighten, even as he reflexively threw his guard up. She had a hell of a smile. He could see how she would be dangerous—she could probably rob him blind and he'd help her pack that beast of a car with all of his belongings if given the chance.

So why was he feeling vaguely excited? He hated publicity, but the way she talked about running a con made it sound less like perpetrating a fraud, and more like just having a good time. Playing pretend, having fun.

Kind of like working on *Mystics*.

Of course, maybe his enthusiasm had to do with the fact that he'd be able to be around *her*. Sure. That could be it.

"Trust me. Nothing too strenuous," she said. "The key here is to whet curiosity. You're attracted to a fan. You're dating a 'civilian.' Once the press gets ahold of it, we'll work on making more . . . memorable things for them to write about."

"Define 'memorable.'"

"Oh, you know. PDAs, maybe double cosplay. Public sex. The usual."

If his eyebrows jumped up any higher, they'd hit the ceiling. She immediately started laughing.

"Oh, my God, the look on your face," she said, around a giggle. "Relax, there, chief. I think you've already got sexy in the bag. I'd say focusing more on fun is probably the key here. Go for goofy."

"Goofy?" he repeated, still reeling from the "public sex" comment. *If only I didn't picture it quite so vividly . . .*

"Yeah. You're funny. They don't take advantage of that enough, in my opinion," she said, and he felt unaccountably warm. Not sexy-warm, this time, though. More like hug-warm.

"You think I'm funny?" He knew he was fishing here, but he couldn't seem to help himself.

"Yeah. I've seen some interviews, and when you're a little more tired, or you're with the other guys, you loosen up. And you're funny as hell."

He smiled.

"That. That smile," she said. "Keep doing that, and you'll be on every magazine on the planet."

"So, just pretend I'm dating you and smile," he said, shaking his head. "Just that easy, huh?"

"Again: what do you have to lose?"

He sighed. "When you put it that way, not much, I guess. But if they find out it's a hoax, they'll crucify me. Us."

"I'm not a public figure. That's not going to be a problem," she said, shrugging. "But you've got a point. We'd probably need to spend a lot more time together to really sell it."

His eyes narrowed. "Like, how much more time?"

"I don't know. You're only going to be here for what, a week? That's not a lot of time," she said. "When is the contract deadline?"

"By the end of the week."

"One week. Not a big deal." He wasn't sure if she was trying to convince him, or herself. "We fake a grand romance, the fangirls get to dig into the idea that Jake Reese connected with an ordinary woman . . . you get your contract, our bookstore gets a nice boost of publicity. Win-win."

He was about to protest that nothing about Hailey could be considered "ordinary" when her words sunk in. They were faking this. It was a transaction—just like Susie wanted, an orchestrated ruse. He gets something, she gets something. It's just business.

The thought of having sex with her—with anyone—as a business transaction made his stomach turn. He knew women who felt they didn't have any choice but to have sex with a director in order to score a role. Men, too, now that he thought about it. He knew his father had abused his position as an A-lister to get women in the sack. They probably thought they were getting a good deal out of it, or it was "just business."

Suddenly, the idea of striking a "bargain" with Hailey made his stomach queasy.

"One condition," he said. "If we're going to do this—I don't think we should sleep together."

She blinked. "Sorry, what?"

"We can pretend to," he said. "If the—*con*—requires it. But I don't think we should, um, muddy the waters."

She stared at him for a long, silent moment, and for the briefest second, he thought he saw hurt shining in her eyes.

"Because you don't trust me," she clarified, her voice even and steady as a rock.

"No! It's not that," he said quickly, then frowned. "I mean, it's true, I've only known you for a day. But I don't mean to be hurtful, I just . . ."

"Don't apologize for protecting yourself." She cut him off. "Not ever. That's just being smart."

He stared at her. Her voice, her expression, was fierce. And not in anger—or at least, not anger at what he'd said. It seemed she was angrier that he was apologizing.

"This is business," she continued. "Good fences make good neighbors, that sort of thing. So it's a smart idea. We'll run the con, you'll do the appearance, and that's that. No sex."

"That's that," he echoed.

He could still feel the jolt of electricity. He could smell her—that fantastic smell, like night-blooming jasmine and hard candy. Her skin was soft, her eyes hot.

Absolutely no sex, he reminded himself.

"Deal?" she said.

She held out her hand. He took it. For a second, their gazes locked, and it felt like his heart skipped a beat, then picked it up again, pounding double-time. That furnace blast of awareness tore through him, making his body tingle.

"Deal," he answered, forcing his voice to remain steady, and shook her hand.

· ♥ · ♥ · ♥ · ♥ · ♥ ·

Hailey was still thinking about their deal later that night. Jake had wanted to start brainstorming, but she'd needed space and time to think out their game plan.

Besides, tonight was girls' night.

Their friend Kyla was curled up in a wingback chair, her feet tucked under her, an art pad and pencil in her hands. Their friend Tessa and her boyfriend, Adam, were cuddled on one couch, while their other friend Stacy sat on the floor, using the coffee table as a desk, leaning back against her boyfriend Rodney's knees as he perched in a chair behind her, glancing over her shoulder. "Girls' night" would need another name if the boyfriends kept coming over, Hailey mused.

Briefly, she imagined what it would be like if Jake were there. Just as quickly, she shook the image off. *Not the point here, Hailey.* She had to stay focused. After Cressida's little jaunt outside, they were all on edge, and Rachel had called an all-hands-on-deck gathering to discuss how they could turn things around. They'd discussed the re-branding. Kyla, cosplay queen and artist extraordinaire, had whipped up some quick pencil sketches of a revised logo and sign, while Rachel did rougher diagrams of how displays might work.

"Frost Fandoms," Rachel said, pointing to Kyla's most recent sketch. "I love it!" Kyla simply winked, heading back to the kitchen.

"So a memorabilia shop?" Tessa asked, looking at the sketches and diagrams pensively. "Would all the books go?"

"Absolutely not," Cressida said. "At heart, we're a bookstore. Gram loved books."

"And books are an essential part of most fandoms, anyway," Rachel quickly asserted. "Percy Jackson, *Hunger Games, Ember in the Ashes* . . . just going through the YA fandoms, we'd be stocked."

"There are novelizations, too," Adam added. "I read all my brother's *Robotech* novels, back in the day. And I'm totally picking up the *Mass Effect* novel by K. C. Alexander and Jason M. Hough when it comes out."

Kyla walked in from the kitchen, bundled up in an oversized fuzzy gray sweater, jeans, and leg warmers, of all things. "Spiked cider," she said, putting a tray down.

"Oooh. That'll go well with the cookies I made this afternoon," Cressida said, getting up and making a beeline for the kitchen. Kyla looked at Cressida's disappearing figure, then leaned toward Hailey.

"How's she doing?" Kyla whispered.

"She's hanging in," Hailey responded, keeping her voice low. "She's playing tough, but . . . damn it, Kyla. We've got to make this work."

Cressida came back in, and Kyla simply nodded. "Don't worry, we got this," she told Cressida and Hailey both. "I've got costumes you guys can display and sell, and I'm going to make smaller cosplay stuff, cheaper stuff, that'll go more quickly. *Mystics*-related stuff, too, to capitalize on the convention."

Cressida gave her a grateful smile, and Hailey hugged Kyla's shoulders.

"You're getting paid for those," Rachel said pointedly. "You work hard on your costumes. You deserve to get paid."

"You guys are family," Kyla said easily, with a wave of her hand, her smile bright as sunshine and sweet as lemonade. "Don't worry about it."

"I wish I'd gotten my act together around this sooner," Rachel said sadly. "We could've gotten a booth at the Mystics convention, selling stuff."

"Next year," Kyla said, patting Rachel's back.

Everyone else looked awkwardly at each other. Nobody needed to say what they were thinking: *if the bookstore was still around next year.*

Hailey cleared her throat. "I'm going to be heading to the Mystics con this week—I scored a pass from a guy I met at work." Which was not technically lying. She'd tell them about Jake when she had the details more clear in her head. "I'll hand out flyers. We just need to make sure we have enough cool stuff to stock it, and set up some displays. That's what you've been working on, right, Rachel?"

With that, their attention snapped back to the issue at hand. Rachel handled herself like a pro. She'd already discussed it with Hailey that afternoon, and Hailey was completely on board.

After an hour or so of brainstorming and writing details, while Stacy and Tessa talked social media planning, Hailey took the opportunity to retreat to the kitchen herself, just for a second, to decompress.

Cressida stepped in behind her. "What's up?"

"Felt more like cocoa than cider," Hailey hedged. "You okay?"

"I was going to ask you that," Cressida said, leaning against their heavy, battered pine kitchen table. She stared at Hailey expectantly.

"Just winding down." Which was true. The bargain she'd just made with Jake had her dialed up to eleven. She felt like her system was still revving, needle in the red.

How the hell am I going to make this work? I know nothing about publicity or acting careers. Or those score things. Or . . . well, anything.

She'd never tried to pull a hustle with this little foundation work before—and she hadn't been on the grift for years. She'd been too eager, very "let's make a deal," and jumped the gun. Hell, when she'd made her spiel, she'd even convinced herself she could pull this off. Now, with the buzz of adrenaline wearing off, and with the gang discussing all the plans they had for the bookstore, she was struck with the very real question of exactly how she was going to do what she'd claimed—and how she was going to get Jake *here*, to do the appearance and launch the whole pursuit properly.

She quickly added tequila to the cocoa, as well as chili powder, a trick she'd learned from Tessa. It wasn't as good as Tessa's—it never was, even though Tessa swore she wasn't keeping secrets—but desperate times called for desperate measures.

Cressida quietly shuffled around the kitchen, popping milk in the microwave to make herself a nonalcoholic version of what Hailey was drinking. Wearing Pusheen the cat pajamas and slippers that looked like Godzilla feet, she looked like she did when Hailey met her, all those years ago—like she was still about twelve, and a skinny, gangly twelve, at that.

"So what's *really* going on, Hales?" Cressida asked quietly.

Hailey winced, glancing quickly out at the living room/store, where the war room was still in full effect. "What makes you think . . ."

Cressida held up a hand, stopping her. "I could tell as soon as you walked in this afternoon that something was going on."

"How?"

"I could feel your energy."

Hailey narrowed her eyes. "Really."

"Okay, I could tell because you kicked your badass boots off and they're all sloppy and a mess in the hall-way," Cressida admitted, stirring hot milk into the hot cocoa powder in her mug. "You never do that. You baby your footwear. Ergo, you're obviously worked up about something."

This was the problem of knowing someone for as many years as they'd known each other. Cressida was her Jiminy Cricket, the angel on her shoulder, the one who knew her better than anyone.

The one who called her on her bullshit. Like she was now.

"Well . . ." Hailey started.

"Oh, shit," Cress said, stirring the cocoa and plopping down on the opposite chair, staring at her. "You've got that look."

"First the boots, now the look," Hailey shot back, rolling her eyes. "You caught me. I'm planning to rob Fort Knox."

"No, but you're up to something." A shadow passed across Cressida's sky-blue eyes. "You're not doing any-thing—you know."

"No, I'm not doing anything illegal." The words came out clipped, and she felt the quick one-two punch of anger and fear of getting caught, followed up by a hard hit of guilt. She wasn't doing anything criminal, admitted-ly, but she was still doing something . . . shifty.

119

CATHY YARDLEY

Of course Cressida picked up on that. "Not *technically* illegal?"

Hailey sighed. She should've known that she couldn't hold anything back from Cress. Best to just come clean.

"I'm working on getting one of the guys from *Mystics* to do an appearance to help promote the bookstore," Hailey whispered, then braced herself.

Cressida's cornflower-blue eyes went wide, and she did a quick check to make sure the others weren't listening. "What? How?" she hissed.

"That's the hustle. Nothing technically illegal. Nothing even illegal adjacent," Hailey clarified. "I'm . . . well, I'm going to help Jake Reese improve his K score, in exchange for helping us."

"His what?"

"K score. I think," Hailey said. "The thing that says how popular he is."

Cressida smirked. "Q Score. You're thinking Q Score."

"Whatever," Hailey said, embarrassed. *You can't even get the name of the score right! How is this going to work?* She shook off the thought. "Anyway, if I can help him improve his standing, then he'll ask his agent to do the appearance."

She could practically hear the gears shifting in Cressida's brain. "You don't know anything about publicity. And you don't even know what a Q Score is. How, exactly, are you 'improving his standing,' Hales? And why haven't you told Rachel yet?"

Hailey sighed. "I'm, erm . . ." She took a deep breath, and said it quickly, like ripping off a Band-Aid. "*Pretend-ingtobehisgirlfirend*."

If Cressida's eyes got any wider, they'd pop right out of her head. "You're . . . pretending . . . to be his . . . *girlfriend*." She repeated it slowly, softly, as if convinced she'd misheard something.

"Yeah."

Cressida went silent. The gears kept whirring away.

Finally, she nodded, with a slow sigh. "You're running a con. You're helping him run a con."

Hailey relaxed against the chair. There was no judgment in Cressida's statement, just observation. "This is why I love you. You get me."

"It's the star-falls-for-fan trope," Cressida said slowly, her eyes still misty and unfocused as her brain parsed out the details. "A shomance. Or rather, a promance—P.R. romance. Do you know how you're going to set it up?"

Hailey felt like a knot was untying in her chest. Cressida was on board, not naysaying. She could talk it out, talk it through. Just knowing she wasn't alone helped enormously. She should've turned to Cressida sooner, but it felt alien. It was her job to help Cress out, not the other way around.

"Not sure what my approach is yet," Hailey said, taking a sip of cocoa, and wincing at the tequila's bite. "I figure I'll stake out the paparazzi. There ought to be a few hanging around."

CATHY YARDLEY

"It'd be better if you got a fangirl to take a picture with her cell phone, or somebody from one of the *Mystics* blogs," Cressida mused, spinning the mug slowly on the table, lost in thought. "It'll seem more organic that way. Less staged."

"That's a good one," Hailey agreed, sipping the chocolate and letting the kick of tequila do its thing. "We'll work on getting the photos spread. I'll try to tell someone to *not* share it."

"Smart. Get the right fan, they'll share it even more that way." Cress sipped her own chocolate, sighing and grinning absentmindedly. "This'd be better with more whipped cream. So, once the story's out, how will you amp it up? It's not enough for the fandom to know. If he's trying to bump up a Q Score, he'll need more media covering it."

"That's where the paparazzi needs to come in," Hailey said. "It needs to go to those more viral places. TMZ, that crap. Boost the love element."

"Okay. . . ." Cressida was frowning now, biting her lip. "Still going to need something for them to talk about."

"I was thinking public sex."

Cressida laughed, then stopped abruptly. "Man. You're kidding, right?"

"Do you know me at all?" Hailey teased, trying to keep a straight face.

"Yes, and if you don't think I heard about that time you had sex on the Space Needle, you've got another think

122

coming," Cressida said. "I might be house-bound, but I see all and hear all."

Hailey let out a bark of laughter. "Shit. You do, don't you? How do you manage that?"

"I have an active online life," Cressida said primly, then smirked. "So yes, you'd do public sex in a heartbeat. But not for a scam."

"No, not public sex." Hailey frowned. "Although he's not the sort you'd kick out of bed for eating crackers."

"He is terribly handsome," Cressida said, then clamped down her mouth.

Hailey sighed. "Just ask."

"Were you planning on . . . I mean, is it a good idea . . ." Cressida's pale skin was scarlet with embarrassment. "How did you manage to convince him that this was a good idea, exactly?"

"I didn't take one for the team, if that's what you're asking." Hailey straightened her shoulders. "I haven't bounced a guy to get a deal ever, and you know that."

Now Cressida looked guilty. "I know. I'm sorry. I didn't think you would, but when it comes to protecting me . . ."

Hailey sighed. Cressida was right. If it meant screwing the Seventh Fleet to keep her family safe, Hailey would probably whore herself bowlegged. But she didn't want Cressida feeling more guilty, or worried. "It's not an issue, Cress. If it makes you feel any better, he already stated that clearly. Absolutely no sex."

Now Cressida blinked. "So he's gay?"

CATHY YARDLEY

Hailey burst out laughing. "Your confidence in me is appreciated. If his previous performance is any indication, though, he's definitely interested in girls."

"His previous . . . *oh, my God*." Cressida gawped. "*He* was the guy you were with last night? I interrupted you and *Jake Reese*?"

Hailey nodded, leaning back in her chair and grinning. "Yup."

"Oh, my God," Cressida repeated, her jaw dropping open. "Are you . . . I mean . . ."

It was so funny, to see Cressida so completely blindsided. Hailey chuckled.

"You talked to him about the bookstore. You're helping him out with his Q Score," Cressida said finally. "Was it . . . is this the start of . . . something?"

"Yeah," Hailey drawled. "It's the start of a scam."

"I mean, you've gotten together, you're helping him out," Cressida said, and she had that suspicious tone of voice again—the "calling your bullshit" tone. "Are you thinking, maybe . . . relationship?"

"Hell no," Hailey scoffed, taking a sip of her chocolate. "First, we didn't 'get together.' I left before the main event."

Cressida's expression was hangdog.

"It's just a con, sweetie. A business arrangement." She thought about what he'd said about "no sex" and the quick sting she'd felt. She told herself it was because she wished she'd said it first. "Even if we had slept together, you know my policy. Keep it hot, and keep it brief. I'll help him, he'll help me, and then we'll part company. He'll have a career, and we'll have a bookstore that's, God willing, running in the black."

"Hmm." Cressida's eyes went unfocused as she went into deep thought mode.

After a few moments, Hailey kicked Cressida's Godzilla toes. "If those gears in your head grind any louder, smoke is going to come out of your ears. What gives?"

"Nothing," Cressida said, with a slow, thoughtful, catlike smile. "So, do we get to meet Mr. *Mystics* Underwear Model?"

"At some point," Hailey said. "I haven't said anything to Rachel yet, though, until I can get the details laid out. I don't want to get her hopes up if he flakes, you know?"

"She's going to need to know to set up the publicity," Cressida warned her.

Hailey sighed, rubbing at her temples. "I know. Which is why I need to get the fake relationship hustle set up. The approach, the buildup, the payoff."

"It'll definitely seem more serious, and less like a hookup, if he meets your family," Cressida added. "Just sayin'."

"We'll save it for the appearance," Hailey said, then giggled. "You just want to get a shot at my boyfriend."

Cressida snickered, then made that "hmm" sound again.

"Okay. I'm going to work out a few more details of the con," Hailey said. "Want to help me sketch out the game plan, while the troops are figuring out the store stuff?"

"Do you like him?" Cressida asked instead.

Yeah. I really, really like him, Hailey thought . . . and felt a little knot form in her gut.

"What's not to like?" she said instead. "He's sex on a stick, and he can help save the bookstore. Two of my favorite things."

Cressida's responding smile was smug.

"But in a week, he'll go back to Vancouver or whatever, and that'll be that," Hailey added quickly.

No sex. One week. One scam. That was it.

I just have to keep repeating that to myself until it sticks.

CHAPTER 5

"Okay, this is your brainchild. What is it we're supposed to do?" Jake asked Hailey, feeling weird about the whole thing. He still wasn't quite sure why he was trusting this relative stranger to do his publicity when he didn't trust top A-list Hollywood power publicists to do so. Maybe it was because she wasn't from Hollywood. On the other hand, she was a self-confessed con artist.

That ought to give him pause.

Hell, maybe it was just to entertain himself. After all, it looked like his connection with the show was going down the toilet and he didn't have any other work lined up—by his own choice. He might as well do something to get his mind off of the pain in the ass his professional life was turning out to be.

Why not explore the real reason you're giving this woman a chance, huh?

He frowned at himself. The problem was, there *was* no logical reason. Yes, she was smokin' hot, but you couldn't swing a cat in L.A. without hitting some sculpted, manufactured "hot girl." It was more than that. Her personality. Her humor. Her intelligence and savvy. Whatever the hell it was, it was both potent and compelling.

And above all: he trusted her, when he rarely trusted anyone. The fact that he did after knowing her for such a short time unnerved him when he thought about it too much. Consequently, he didn't think about it at all.

"I did some research last night," Hailey said, breaking through his train of thought. They were sitting in his hotel room. She was drinking a large coffee with a metric crapton of sugar and whipped cream and stuff, while he manfully drank his black and wished he'd gotten a mocha-frappa-whatsit, so he, too, could enjoy something sweet. Especially watching the way she licked the whipped cream off her lips . . .

No, he chastised himself. *Stay focused.*

"Research?" he said, his voice cracking a little. He cleared his throat. "On what? Publicity stunts?"

"No, the convention," she said, rolling her eyes a little. Her eyes were very expressive. Especially with that bat-wing eyeliner she had going on. They were huge and a dark, almost purplish blue. "I know fans. And I hate to put it this way, but I know marks, and right now, the audience is our mark. We want them to spread the word that you're dating a fan. The goal is to get people talking, right?"

He nodded, still not sure where she was going.

She took a deep breath. "The mark is going to act in her own self-interest. Why does anyone gossip?"

"I have no idea," he said. "I hate gossip." He'd lived with enough of it in his life, being born a bastard son of a famous actor. And Hollywood was just one big grapevine of rumors and innuendo.

She leaned back against the cream-colored sofa, propping her booted feet up on the black lacquer coffee table. "People gossip because information has value. They want to show that they know something that other people don't know. Then they share because they want to show that they're not missing out on anything. Finally, they share with people who will care about the information—it makes them feel good to know they made someone else happy, because it improves their friendship level."

He stared at her. "You sound like a professor."

"I learned from the best," she said, and her expression turned hazy, almost sad. Then she sighed. "Anyway, we want to tell the story that you, hot studly actor, have gotten involved with a normal fangirl. The thing is, if we want people to talk about it, then we have to look like we're hiding it."

"Why?" he asked, puzzled. "If we want people to find out about it, shouldn't we be, I don't know, flaunting it or something?"

She looked at him, shaking her head. "Oh, my sweet summer child," she murmured. "That's the clearest way to tell people it's a fraud. This is classic misdirection. You want them to believe something? Let them think they figured it out on their own."

"Okay, Houdini," he said, sipping his coffee and wincing. "So, how do we do that?"

She bit her lip. She had great lips. He wished he could bite that full lower lip of hers.

"Yeah," she said. "Do that."

He blinked. "Do what? I'm just sitting here."

Her smile was slow and scorchingly sexy, and he felt his body tighten.

"You were sitting there looking like you wondered what I'd taste like dipped in chocolate," she purred, and it was like a punch in the chest. "You keep staring at me like that, and people will know something's going on."

"And where will you be?"

"In the audience, like any good fan," she said. "When's your next panel?"

He glanced at his watch. "Um . . . in an hour or so. What do you want to do till then?"

She shot a quick look at the bed, then gave a tiny head shake, one she probably wasn't even aware of. "We should probably leave the hotel room," she said quickly.

Taking in the bed—and remembering the last time they were together on one—made his body start to tense painfully. "That's probably a good idea. Where to?"

"We can't be too obvious, so wandering the convention floor holding hands is out." She got up, started to pace. "But we do need to be seen together. And we'll want to set up a couple of situations where we almost get caught doing something compromising. Get somebody to take a picture of us kissing, that kind of thing."

He frowned. "My publicist once wanted me to do stuff like that with a starlet," he said, feeling that gross sensation in the pit of his stomach. "I didn't even know the girl. She looked like she was a teenager. It was awkward."

"Well, I think I can say that nobody's going to mistake me for a teenager," she said, and he did it again . . . his gaze sliding over her.

Today, she was wearing a black pencil skirt and four-inch heels that looked like the world's sexiest 1940s secretary would wear them. She matched that with a sweater that was soft and fuzzy and matched her eyes, a perfect shade of midnight.

Damn, the woman was hot.

"There you go again," she said, and her eyes were gleaming. "That's the look. Want to go downstairs and give it a try? See if we can spark some attention?"

He was nodding before he knew what to do with himself.

They left the room, heading to the elevators. As the elevator doors closed, she surprised him by taking his hand. "This is how it would be, if you were really dating a fan and wanted to keep it quiet," she murmured, and he found himself riveted. "In public, we couldn't stop looking at each other, but we'd know we'd have to keep a lid on it. When other people were around, we'd have to keep it hidden, just wrap it up."

"But we'd be so attracted to each other," he finished, finally getting it, "we'd do a really bad job of it."

"Exactly," she said. "Really, a good con job is just like acting. You're playing a role, and getting other people to believe it."

"What exactly did you con people out of? And how'd you do it?"

There was more sadness in the pools of her midnight eyes, and she just shook her head slightly.

"Not now," she murmured, sidling up next to him. "We're on the job."

Just like that, he was riveted. She was tall and curvy and pressed against him. She smelled like jasmine again, exotic, sweet, and sharp. She nuzzled his ear, squeezing his hand.

"Nobody's here," he pointed out, noticing that his voice sounded a little strangled.

"Just getting you in the right place," she said, her breath tickling his ear, her chest pressed against his bicep. *God, the feel of her . . .*

Focus! He mentally slapped himself. This was business. A transaction. Hell, she'd drawn up a game plan like a goddamned football coach. She didn't *feel* anything.

He took a deep breath, his bloodstream rushing as he felt the heat coming off of her. Did she feel anything for him beyond the con?

The elevator door dinged, and she quickly stepped away. There was a slight touch of flush on her pale cheeks, and she stared at the elevator numbers like her life depended on it, as he stared at her.

Some giggling women stepped in, then gasped as they recognized him. "Are you . . . aren't you Jake Reese?"

He nodded, still looking at Hailey. She shot him a glance, then shook her head, nodding at the girls. He cleared his throat again.

"Yes! Yeah, I'm Jake," he said, smiling.

The girls gave Hailey a curious glance, but then focused on him, asking questions. He accompanied them out of the elevators. He answered a few questions, and signed a photo and a small journal. Then he glanced around.

Hailey was standing off to one side, smirking. She winked at him. He grinned back, walking over to her. She shook her head again, and he froze. What was he supposed to do now? They hadn't discussed past the initial "get noticed" step.

He watched as she weaved through the crowd, then went off to one side, to a hallway. He looked around, trying to be casual. He was stopped by fans every few steps. He signed dozens of autographs. "Sorry," he finally said. "I'll be at the panel in a minute though. I just need to, um, prep," he improvised.

God, he hated improv. He probably should've remembered that *before* agreeing to this idiocy.

He finally escaped to the hallway where Hailey was waiting. "How was that?"

"Not bad," she said, biting her lip again thoughtfully. "I think we've gotten some attention. Now, we just need to start that powder keg off."

"How do we do that?"

"By being obvious," she said. "But not being obvious."

"Obviously," he muttered. "Man, you're the worst director I've ever worked with."

She stuck out her tongue at him, and he grinned.

"No, we just have to . . ." She stopped, tilting her head. "Okay, here's our shot. Kiss me."

"Wha—"

Before he could do anything, she grabbed him, putting those pillowy lips right on his. His body, thankfully, wasn't as slow as his brain. It didn't care why this gorgeous creature was kissing him. It just wanted more, and it wanted it *now*.

He tilted his head, taking her lips in a strong, firm kiss just as she'd opened her mouth for a breath. He swept his tongue in, gliding along the soft satin of her inner lips. Her tongue moved forward, tangling with his, as he crushed her chest against him, pulling her hips taut to his where things were definitely getting harder.

"Um, Mr. Reese . . ." a girl's voice said. "Jake . . . I just . . . oh, my God! Oops!"

He barely registered it. Hailey tried to jerk away.

"Oh," she said, starting to turn.

"Not done with you yet," he growled softly, kissing her a few more times, feeling her fingers curl in his hair.

"Jake," Hailey said, looking embarrassed. Even blushing a little.

He turned to see three girls in *Mystics* T-shirts quickly clicking photos with their cell phones. "Is this your girl-friend?" one asked.

"Um . . ." He turned to Hailey, still feeling punch-drunk from the kiss. Aching to do it again. He tried desperately to get his head back in the game. Was this the way it was supposed to happen?

Hailey turned red. She truly looked like she was blush-ing right to the roots of her hair. Did she really think she wasn't a good actress? She was better than many of his previous co-stars.

"It's not . . . we're just . . ." she stammered, then glanced at him. For the first time since he'd met her, she looked uncertain. "Listen, nobody's supposed to know about us. Can you guys keep a secret?"

The girls giggled again, eyes wide.

"We just started, well . . ." Hailey trailed off. "It's new. And I don't know how his agent or publicist or anything

135

is going to feel about this, so we're just trying to keep it quiet, you know?"

"Why?" one girl asked.

Hailey shifted her weight. "Just . . . can you help us?" she pleaded.

They nodded immediately—well, two of them did. The third one looked just a little bit shrewd.

"So she's just somebody you're sleeping with," the third one said, sounding way older than she looked. And bitter. Surprisingly bitter.

"Absolutely not," Jake said, putting his arm protectively around Hailey's waist. She curled against him, snuggling in, as if taking comfort. *What the hell kind of comment is that? Who says something like that?* "It's not like that. I care about her."

The other two girls made a little "aww" sound. If possible, Hailey turned redder.

"Well . . . you'd better go, erm, get ready for your panel," Hailey said to him, then turned back to the girls. "Thanks for keeping this just between us."

They walked away, the girls quickly giggling off in the other direction.

When they were out of sight, Hailey's blush slowly vanished. "Where's your green room or whatever?" she said. "That's enough public for now. We'll get you ready for that panel, and I'll be sure to be out front or something . . ."

He stopped, stunned by how quickly she was able to recover. "You just . . . wow. That was all the con, huh?"

She sighed. "Well, yes. That's the point."

He didn't know why that upset him as much as it did. But it did upset him. She was turning it on and off like tap water. How was she able to do that so effortlessly?

Maybe the better question was—why couldn't he? His heart was still racing.

"It's not personal, Jake," she said.

"I'm sorry. I have to ask." He swallowed, unsure of how to proceed. "The cons you ran—were they on men? Were they . . . like this?"

Now she looked at him like he'd slapped her. "No," she said sharply. "Not like this. I was thirteen when I stopped, for Christ's sake."

"I didn't know that," he said. "I mean, we don't know each other very well, do we?" He grimaced. "Like you said: it's not personal. I was just wondering about your background."

Now she crossed her arms, her midnight eyes glinting. "I guess this is our first fight, sweetie," she said, her tone like poison mixed in honey. "Because we struck this deal, and if you're going to get judgy, maybe I just take a walk and you deal with your Q Score your own way."

"You're the one who wants to help your sister," he pointed out defensively.

He saw the expression drain away. Her normally expressive face became a careful mask.

"You're right," she said, her voice tight. "I'm . . . sorry. I—it's a touchy subject. I was a grifter, not a sex worker.

137

CATHY YARDLEY

Not that I have anything but respect for them, but again, I was a minor. And this isn't that kind of arrangement."

The suppressed pain in her words tugged at him. She obviously cared about her sister, enough to put up with his accusation and judgment. He'd bet she'd probably punch any man who suggested otherwise—but not if her sister's well-being was on the line.

Maybe it's an act, though, his rational brain counseled him. After all, she was one helluva liar. She was able to brush off their kiss while he was still gasping for breath.

If she could convince him that easily, without feeling anything—God, was he wrong to trust her? Was it all just lust on his end?

"What if there wasn't an audience?" he heard himself ask, surprising himself.

She blinked.

He leaned in, slowly, giving her plenty of time to pull away, not crowding her, not grabbing her. His lips barely brushed hers, a whisper of softness.

"If it isn't for show, how do you feel?"

She swayed toward him, her own lips brushing his, a mere slide of silk.

"You know I'm attracted, Jake," she said, and all he wanted to do was sink into that mouth and stay for a while.

She pulled away before he had the chance. "And you know that you're the one that made the rules. No sex," she said, her voice brisk again, the heat slowly ebbing away. "Because this is business. And as you just pointed out, I'm doing this to help my sisters. And I'd walk through fire to help them, so I'm not screwing that up . . . which means I'm not crossing any lines, and neither are you."

He winced. She was right. What the hell was he doing?

She smiled, but it didn't make it to her eyes.

"See you out there," she said, her voice rough. "*Sweetie*."

· ♥ · ♥ · ♥ · ♥ · ♥ ·

Jesus, Hailey, get yourself together.

Hailey sat in the third row at the panel. She was in a standard hotel room chair, the stackable kind, not the plushest seats in the world. But that wasn't the reason for her discomfort. No, the squirming was all her, still remembering Jake's kiss, the way he'd held her tight against him . . . the feel of that growing bulge, pressing against her stomach. *Yeah, baby.*

Was it hot in here, or was it just him?

She looked at her cell phone for the third time, and still forgot to really check what time it was. That's how flustered the man had her.

When was the last time she'd been truly flustered by a man?

Never. This was a first. That made her somewhat nervous.

It's just a con, she told herself. The guy himself knew it was strictly business. She was doing this for her sister, Cressida. And yeah, as noble as that sounded, and as important as Cressida was, she knew that it was also a bit of a cop-out. She was interested in this guy.

The crowd was predominantly women, all talking and laughing, waiting for the guys to come out. It was just going to be the brothers today—Jake, Simon, and Miles—in a more intimate talk. Different women were talking about which one they thought was the hottest. She grinned as she heard various lines from the show quoted back and forth to each other.

She sat close to the end of her row—near enough to the front of the crowd that Jake should see her, but far enough that she could walk out if she needed to. There were some photographers lined up against the wall by the door, cameras ready, angled toward the panel stage. Because this room was smaller than the big auditorium they'd been in yesterday, the rows were crammed, putting Hailey only a few feet away from the cameras. One of the photographers was a woman in jeans who looked very irritated and very bored.

"Do you even know what they're talking about?" Hailey heard the woman say, not too discreetly, to another cameraman.

He shrugged. "I don't watch the show."

"Neither do I," the woman said, then got on her cell phone. "Phil, listen, there's nothing here. I don't care if he

140

is Kurt Windlass's kid, this is boring! This is one step above pet fashion shows and sweet sixteens. And I'm up here in the middle of *nowhere*. I hear Ciara's up with Russell Wilson, something about the Sounders. I'm sure if I . . ."

She trailed off, looking pissed.

"Fine, fine, I'll take pictures of Kurt's choirboy kid," the photographer said, rolling her eyes. "But I swear to God, if I get something worth publishing, I'm going to sell it to the highest bidder and screw your job, Phil. I'm tired of being stuck out in the sticks."

The photographer was still cursing as she hung up. Hailey felt the tingle of prescience. This. This was an opportunity. Any good con woman worth her salt would see the same.

When the crowd burst into cheers, hoots, and applause, she got to her feet as well, clapping. The guys were all dressed casually, but all looked good. Simon looked almost predatory, turning on his charm like a spotlight. Miles was more withdrawn, shy. And then there was Jake, his eyes scanning the crowd as he grinned, this adorable lopsided grin that made him look boyishly handsome, almost mischievous.

His eyes met hers, and he nodded. Not warming up, she realized. He was still pissed about the whole job thing.

Damn it. There was paparazzi here. This was not a time for him to be prissy. He needed to sell the story—to set up the con. She couldn't do this by herself.

141

She'd have to loosen him up. Not easy, but not impossible, either, she thought, willing him to look at her.

The crowd started asking questions again . . . stuff about the show. "Simon, do you think your character is ever going to get a girlfriend?"

He shrugged. "Girlfriend, boyfriend, I'm open-minded," he said, to more whistles and catcalls. He winked, obviously playing to the slash crowd. "But you know how it is. Significant others don't last long on the show."

This brought up muted booing as they remembered his love interest in the first season had died brutally—drowning, for him to find. He made a sad face. The next question was for Miles, something about whether he was as bookish as his character.

As he answered it, Jake looked over at her, just for a second. She stared at him like her eyes were a tractor beam, and she was calling him in.

Get over it, she thought, taking a deep breath that put the girls up to their best advantage.

She noticed his glance slowed a little . . . and heated a little. *Better*, she thought. But again, she couldn't be too obvious. Damn it, she should've prepped him better. But how was she supposed to know the paparazzi would be following him here?

She had to get him to play along.

She cleared her throat, just a tiny bit. The audience by and large ignored her. But he caught it, she noticed. He stared, just a little longer.

"Sorry," she mouthed slowly, feeling a little stubborn.

She noticed him shrugging a little. Apparently sexy looks and apologies weren't going to get her anywhere. While the other guys were loose limbed and easygoing, he looked like a stick in the mud, a carved-out-of-marble tough guy with his arms crossed.

Well, screw that.

When next he looked at her, he paused, startled, then took a second glance. At least, she thought so. It was hard to tell . . . probably because she was crossing her eyes and doing fish lips. When she straightened her eyes out, he was staring at her, stunned.

She grinned, stuck her tongue out at him, and winked.

He looked startled, and then covered his mouth. She could see from his eyes that he was grinning.

"Jake," a voice asked, and he quickly shifted his attention. He was looking looser, though. *Well, that was something*, she thought.

"Yes?" he asked, a hint of warmth and a chuckle in his tone.

"Do you have a girlfriend?"

The crowd chuckled. "No. We're all single," he said, his tone suggesting it was obviously the standard line.

"Really?"

Now the crowd turned and looked at the person asking. It was the girl—the one from the hallway. She was grinning, a little cruel, somewhat smug, even as her friend hissed at her to sit down.

"Um . . ." Jake shot another glance at Hailey. Hailey quickly schooled her face to look surprised, maybe even a little panicked. "Yeeessss," he said slowly.

The moderator laughed. "You sure you're sure about that?" he asked.

Jake rubbed the back of his neck. "Um . . . let's just go with it's complicated," he said, and the crowd started whispering . . . and then he looked at Hailey again.

She could've sworn she'd seen all his sexy looks, but this . . . holy hell, the guy went straight to a DEFCON 1 *smolder*. She could feel it all the way to the toes of her Mary Jane stilettos.

She swallowed hard, even as she felt her nipples go hard against her bra. The guy needed to be registered as a dangerous weapon, she thought. He was a panty destroyer.

He winked at her.

Too obvious! She looked away.

The paparazzi had noticed, though, and was looking at Hailey thoughtfully. Hailey looked to the other side of the room.

Well, at least that was done . . . the photographer had taken the bait. Now, to reel her in.

She waited until the end of the panel, and stayed in her seat for a second as the crowd milled around. She saw people shooting her curious glances, but ignored them, keeping a casual, unnoticeable bead on the photographer. When most of the crowd had exited, she walked over to the green room door, where the bouncer was.

"Here to see Jake again?" he asked with a grin.

"I'll, um, wait for him here," she said, forcing herself to sound tentative. The bouncer spoke into the walkie-talkie thing attached to his shoulder, announcing her presence. The paparazzi was a few feet away, trying to blend in with a potted plant from the looks of it.

No wonder Phil doesn't trust you with bigger assignments, Hailey thought derisively.

Jake came out, giving her a hug that she shrugged off. "How'd I do?" he whispered in her ear.

"Not bad, but . . . come on," she said, tugging him away, toward the kitchens. He followed easily.

"Listen, I'm sorry I was hard on you earlier," he said. "I was just . . ."

"Shh," she said. "Play along."

Thankfully, he didn't need to be told twice. She kissed him hard, and he responded immediately.

It was getting easier, she realized. The way their bodies met and molded against each other. It was . . . God, she wasn't going to think something cheesy and cliché, like it was like coming home.

But it felt really, really good. Warm, and cozy, not just all flash and heat.

That is, until he gripped her ass and tugged her against the length of iron he appeared to have in the front of his pants, causing her to moan into his open mouth.

OH. MY. GOD.

She had meant to make sure that the paparazzi had followed them, but now, she could barely keep her head above water. His kiss was honest-to-God making her dizzy.

She felt his hand creep up under her sweater, his broad, hot palm flat against the skin of her back. She shimmied her hips a little as his mouth went to work on hers, then moved up her jawline, finding the sweet spot just where her jaw met her ear.

"Oh, my God," she breathed. "*Jake.*"

He sucked, with gentle but relentless pressure. She couldn't help it. She shifted against him, her hands in his hair, pulling him tight against her.

He spun her, his body pressing her against the wall. She felt as one denim-covered leg moved between her thighs, pressing against her skirt. She knew she was already damp.

He bit her earlobe, and she let out another moan.

"Anything else I should be doing?" he whispered.

"God, whatever you want, just don't stop," she said around a ragged breath as she clutched his shoulders. His chuckle was like dark chocolate, rich and sinful and delicious.

"We're in a hallway, baby," he said, trailing more kisses along her throat until she shivered against him. "But God, if we were in a room . . ."

She was ready to pass out. Yes. Yes, they need to get to his room, immediately.

Then, just like a switch, he pulled away.

"She left," he said.

She blinked heavily. "She . . . what? Who?"

He stared at Hailey for a long moment, then his smile was pure sunshine.

"The paparazzi. The one that was trailing you," he said. "I've seen her around a few times. That was why you dragged me in here, right?"

It took longer than she wanted to get her head together. "The . . . right! Right." She nodded, too emphatically. "That was the plan. Yes. The whole time."

"You okay?"

She shook herself. "Yeah. I have to go, though," she said. "I've got to, um, get to work. At the casino."

He stroked her cheek. "Okay. See you tomorrow?"

"Bright and early," she said, then almost stumbled as she took a step away.

"You sure you're all right?"

"Don't get cocky, kid," she muttered, "Bye." Then she was strutting back through the lobby, feeling people's eyes on her.

But she wasn't thinking about maintaining the con, or even upholding her image. He'd shaken her. All she could imagine was them in bed together. Then, he could be as cocky as he wanted. Hell, she'd encourage it . . .

No, she chastised herself. They'd already struck the deal. She wasn't going to fuck this up.

God, woman, get yourself sorted out!

· ❤ · ❤ · ❤ · ❤ · ❤ ·

The next morning, Jake was already on his computer. The room was nice—Susie had made management grovel, and he had a suite—but he was still having trouble sleeping. He didn't have to do anything until that afternoon, when he and the other guys would be judging a costume competition. He decided to take advantage of the break to see how his performance with Hailey went over. Just skimming TMZ and Perez Hilton, the photos had definitely been picked up—and they made his blood heat. The gossip sites had noticed as well. "Va va voom! Who's headed for Jake's room?" one article said. "Jake Reese has a new lady friend" another pointed out—rather obviously, given the clinch that the two of them were in.

If that didn't boost his damned Q Score, he didn't know what would.

He picked up his cell phone, dialing Susie. He doubted it would change the producers' minds immediately—although God, wouldn't that be nice?—but he wanted to make sure he was on the same track.

"Jake, sweetie," she said immediately. "How is everything? That hotel treating you right?"

"Yeah," he said, glancing over at the huge basket by his bed. "They even gave me this giant assortment of all my favorite candies. You put them on to that, I guess?"

"Are you kidding? I'm trying to keep your weight *down*, kid," she said, and he could picture her rolling her eyes.

"If not you, then . . ."

"Guess they must've talked to somebody in the convention," she said, "or one of those thirsty fangirls . . ."

He suddenly felt a pang, and looked at the basket with more suspicion. Then he dumped it in the trash.

"But I bet you've got more on your mind than your accommodations," Susie said, now with a trace of smugness. "Somebody's been busy, I see."

"That's why I'm calling," Jake said, stretching out on his hotel bed and crossing his ankles. "Well? Is this what the doctor ordered? Will this boost my Q Score?"

She took a deep breath. "It's definitely a step in the right direction," she said, but something in her voice sounded hesitant, sticking a pin in Jake's balloon of cheer.

"What's the problem now? I thought the idea was to become better known with the public," he said, trying not to sound petulant. "You told me yourself to get a girlfriend."

"There's a right way and a wrong way to do that, though. There's a big difference between a bankable star, somebody who can move you up the ladder, and . . ." Susie's voice sounded tight, tense for some reason. "Who is that woman, anyway? I know she's not an actress."

149

"How do you know she's not an actress?" Jake asked, knowing he was being difficult, but feeling incensed on Hailey's behalf.

Susie's chuckle was patronizing, and his hackles rose. "Hon, at that size? That age? Unless she's a comedian I'm not aware of, she's not going anywhere in Hollywood, and you know it."

He made a low growling sound. He had been going to let Susie in on their plan, but her attitude was grating on him. "She's sexy as hell."

"That is abundantly clear," Susie agreed, irritating him even more. "But again—we're thinking bankable. Your sexy girl isn't . . . well . . ."

"Isn't *what*?" Jake said, his voice low.

Another voice cut across Susie's, gruff and impatient. "Let me talk to him. Susie, give me the phone, let me talk to him."

Just like that, Jake's stomach dropped and his shoulders rose, pinching his blades together like he'd just been handcuffed.

Damn it.

"Jake," the voice growled. "What the hell have you gotten into this time?"

"Hi, Dad," Jake said, trying not to sound like the rueful fourteen-year-old he suddenly felt like.

His father was larger than life. A box office legend. Hollywood royalty, but not in a golden-boy sort of way. No, he'd been a hell-raising "man's man," an action anti-hero with plenty of rough edges. He'd successfully transferred from shoot-'em-up Westerns and cop dramas to psychological thrillers and political statement-makers, even garnering a few Oscar nods. When it came to the industry, few people were as revered—or feared—as Kurt Windlass.

Which made it hard to just look at him and see "Dad." Not, Jake supposed, that Kurt Windlass wanted to be a TV sitcom–styled father figure.

"Saw the pictures of you getting frisky with the bimbo," his father said sharply. "Did you pay her, or what?"

"Did I . . . No!" Jake snapped. "God, Dad. We're dating."

"You don't date women that look like that, kid," his father scoffed. "You don't kiss women you date like that, either."

"How do you know?" Jake asked, getting up and pacing. His muscles started tensing: fight or flight. Funny, how often his father provoked this response. "This is the twenty-first century. Women that look like that? Really? What kind of judgment is that?"

"Oh, don't pull that politically correct crap with me," his father answered, verbally waving away Jake's protests. "As far as Hollywood business is concerned, they're firmly in the fifties or possibly the forties, don't kid yourself. The reason that you hook up with young starlets is because Hollywood runs on sex, and people find young starlets sexy. You hook up with an actress that's recognizable because you multiply the star power. Christ's sake, son, this is Hollywood 101." He said it with evident disgust. "While I'm glad that you're finally getting your head out of your ass and trying to do something to boost your career, you're screwing it up. Why don't you let me hire Sheila back? Or some other publicist who actually knows what the hell's going on?"

Jake felt his stomach roil. He gripped the phone tighter. "The woman I'm seeing is a fan," he pointed out.

"Well, obviously," his father said. "Although I would've guessed pro, too. That chick—damn. Good to see a woman with actual curves, not those sticks the studio keeps pumping out."

"Watch it," Jake growled.

"So you hooked up with a groupie. Who hasn't? But that's not the stuff you want plastered all over the internet, kid."

"She's not a groupie. She's a fan of the show," Jake snarled.

"What show? That dinky sci-fi thing you're on?"

Now Jake had to fight not to throw the phone out the goddamned window. "*Mystics*, yeah. Anyway, we met here before the convention, sort of a funny story. I asked her to dinner, and we just clicked." Which was all very true. He smiled at the memory. "We're getting publicity, I admit, but hopefully that'll just help boost my profile enough to get the contract renewed."

His father went silent for a moment, and Jake wondered if he'd finally gotten through to the old man. As soon as Kurt opened his mouth again, though, Jake knew just how stupid he'd been to get his hopes up.

"Wait a minute. You're telling me you're actually trying to stay on that third-rate piece of crap? Are you kidding me? Susie, is he kidding me?"

Jake didn't hear Susie's reply, because his father was bulldozing forward regardless.

"Listen up, kid. You can do a hell of a lot better than a TV series on basic cable." His voice was the gravelly rasp that threatened bad guys in multimillion-dollar blockbusters. "Stop fucking around with groupies, and get it together, would you? Susie, see if you can talk some sense into him!"

With that, the phone was duly transferred over as Jake seethed.

"Jake?" Susie said tentatively, even as Jake heard a door slam in the background. "I am so sorry. He was just stopping by to talk about a new film that he's thinking of producing, and . . . well, you know how he is."

"Oh, I know," Jake ground out.

"That said—Jake, sweetie, he's got a point."

"Are you fucking kidding me?"

"It just looks like you partied, maybe, and found a groupie to hook up with," Susie said apologetically. "A distinctive-looking one, very beautiful, and I'm sure she's, erm, sweet and all that. But the narrative's just 'Jake is having sex with strange women' rather than anything we can work with."

Jake grimaced. *Goddamn it.*

"I genuinely like this girl," Jake said, and he meant it. "I'm not going to hook up with some twenty-year-old blonde whose star is ascending because she's on some high school drama on the CW. I like *this* woman."

"Enough to give up the show for her?" Susie snapped.

It was like a slap with a cold, wet towel.

"I see." Jake took a slow breath. "Got it."

"Sorry. That was blunt." Susie sighed, and he could hear papers rustling. Then she cleared her throat. "Your father means well, you know."

"Don't, Susie," he warned. "Just . . . don't."

Another pause, another sigh. "I'll let you know if I hear anything from the producers," she said. "In the mean-time—you might want to start thinking about plan B. I'm going to get some scripts together, see where I can have you audition, okay?"

Jake clicked off the phone. So much for Hailey's idea, he thought, then ground his teeth. No, that was unfair. The idea was to get him publicity, and she'd done that in spades. It was hardly her fault that people like his dad were painting her as a groupie. That it just looked like Jake was having sex promiscuously—that the story was becoming Jake partying, rather than falling for a fan.

He frowned.

Maybe that was the answer. Change the narrative.

Emphasis on *falling*.

He'd show them, he thought, quickly dialing Hailey's number. He'd show Susie, the producers. He'd shove it right down his father's throat.

Didn't think he could act? Thought that he needed some sleazy Hollywood publicist to create a fake story? He had the narrative. He knew just what the fans would eat up.

"Hey, Jake," Hailey said. He could hear the clattering of customers—she was at the coffee shop, he remembered. "What's up?"

"I figured out the problem," Jake said, without preamble.

"Oh? What problem is that?"

"We need to be in love."

CHAPTER 6

"We've got to *what*?" Hailey repeated, feeling stunned and almost dropping the muffin she'd just placed on a plate for a customer.

Stan came up next to her. "You okay?"

She looked. There was a huge line of people at the coffee shop. "Jake—listen, can you hold on? I'll call you right back." She hung up.

"Everything okay with that boy toy of yours?" Stan teased.

She was in *no* mood. She had only a few days left. Tomorrow was the last chance they'd have at capturing any of the convention fans, getting them to the bookstore. Which meant she had to help Jake get attention now. She made lattes as fast as she could.

"Hey, this isn't what I ordered," a man in a Huskies sweatshirt complained.

"Isn't it?" she asked apologetically, as she finished up another. "I thought you said double-shot decaf caramel latte, no foam."

"I wanted half-caf," he said, although she knew damned well that's not what he'd asked for. "And there's still foam."

That was milk, she thought, but she took it back. "Sorry. I'll get another one going for you," she said, her jaw clenching so hard she thought it would pop.

"Yeah you will," he snapped. "And I think I should get a refund. I've been waiting here for twenty minutes, and you can't even get the order right!"

That did it. She glared at him. "It was more like seven minutes, because we get busy. And I made a mistake, but you'll get it over. If it's that much of a problem"—she dug into her pocket, throwing a five-dollar bill on the counter in front of him—"go over to Starbucks or something. I hear they love to suck up to assholes."

Silence fell on the shop. She winced. Damn it. *Damn it!*

"Hailey?" The manager, Lizzie, cleared her throat, speaking nervously. "Can I speak with you in the back for a moment? Stan here will be happy to refund your money, and we'll get whatever drink going you'd like, sir. Thank you all for being patient."

Hailey felt shame burning through her, as well as anger. "I'm sorry, Liz," she said in a low voice, as Liz shut the door behind her. "I didn't . . . I've been kind of stressed lately."

"I know," Lizzie said. "And it shows."

That hurt. "I'm coming to shifts on time, and I'm working hard, though. I just . . . today . . ."

"I know you've been working hard, and I know you're working two jobs," Lizzie said. "You're burning out. I think you know that."

Hailey bit her lip. "I'll pull it together. I promise."

"I called Trina," Lizzie said. "You're off shift now."

"But we're backed up," Hailey protested. *I need this job!* "I know, I shouldn't have mouthed off. I'll apologize to that guy, okay? I'll make him three lattes. I'll make those little leaf designs. I'll . . ."

"Hailey," Lizzie said, her voice going a bit harder. "I really don't want any drama here. You're a hard worker, but it feels like you've got a little too much going on right now. Take some time off, until you can get it together, okay?"

Hailey glared. "Don't do that. Don't tell me that you want me to take more time off, to get myself together, when you just don't want to deal with me."

Lizzie's eyes were cool. She spread her hands. "You can take it however you want to, Hailey," she said, her voice irritatingly calm. "But I need you out. Now."

"Am I fired?"

Lizzie shrugged. "We'll call you when things calm down."

Hailey took off her apron, throwing it down onto the floor with a slap. "Fine. Just . . . fine."

"We'll mail your last check," Lizzie called after her. Hailey stalked out to Charlotte, feeling ready to scream. She put her head down on the steering wheel, feeling like slamming it. But she didn't.

I needed that job, she thought. Her sisters, the bookstore, they all needed that money. That God. Damned. Paycheck.

Now, she needed Jake's help more than ever. She had to fulfill that part of the bargain.

If she didn't get Jake some results, then he wasn't going to help her out. He could simply say he liked Frost Fandoms, do a shout-out at a panel. She just had to convince him to make an announcement soon, or they'd lose the opportunity to shuffle some of those convention fans to the bookstore. It would be a little clumsy, and it wouldn't have the same impact as saying, "I will be *at* Frost Fandoms," but it would have to do.

Sighing and crossing her fingers, she dialed him as she sat in the parking lot.

"You sounded tense," she said, after he'd barked out a greeting. "Like, bear trap tense. What's going on?"

"I talked to my agent."

"That's a good thing, right?"

"Ordinarily, yes," Jake said. "Not in this case. She saw the photos—they're all over TMZ and a bunch of gossip sites—but she said it's not giving me the reputation they're looking for."

She frowned. "What are they looking for, then?"

"Something more solid. Less, um, temporary."

"They're not looking for, like, an engagement, are they? Because I don't know that we can pull that off believably in just a few days." she joked, then faked a Scottish burr. "Damn it, Jake, I'm a blackjack dealer, not a miracle worker!"

She didn't know if he missed the reference, didn't find it funny, or was just so stressed he blasted by it. "We need to be in love."

She blanched for a second—couldn't help it. "Aha. I thought that's what you said before." She sighed. "So, fine. We'll be in love. No big deal."

"Yes, big deal," he retorted. "Right now, you could be anybody I slept with."

"Excuse *you*," she murmured, but he was too into his own head to catch it.

"It looks like you're just . . . well, a really hot rando. Maybe even an, um . . . professional." He sounded embarrassed. "That's not my opinion."

She shrugged, although the derision and disgust in his voice chafed. "You don't say."

He exhaled. "They don't know you at all. It was just the narrative. The pictures showed we were hot and heavy, but it wasn't emotional. It wasn't romantic. It just looked like a booty call."

He sounded contrite, although she wasn't sure if it was for the right reasons. Especially when he followed it up with, "I'm sure he meant that you looked like a groupie."

She gritted her teeth. She'd almost rather be called a hooker. "So your agent thinks I'm a prostitute and/or fangirl that you hooked up with," she reiterated, "and the problem there is that the story becomes Jake is hanging out with degenerates rather than Jake is dating a fan. Did I get that right?"

"That's not . . . it's . . ." Another sigh. "I'm sorry, Hailey."

"You damned well should be." She felt tears sting at the corners of her eyes, and blinked them back into submission. "Excuse the hell out of me for looking *temporary*."

"This really isn't about you, I swear. I'm overreacting to this whole thing. It wasn't just my agent," he admitted, his voice sounding growly and frustrated. "It was . . . well, shit. It was my dad."

His voice all but rang with the truth of that statement, pain naked in his tone. So that was the problem. She took a deep breath, pushing her hurt feelings aside. *I can't help Cress if I stomp away pissed off.*

Even if they had called her a hooker and a groupie. She gritted her teeth. She'd already lost one job today.

"So that's why you sound like something crawled up your ass and died," she said instead.

Jake let out a startled laugh. "Um, yeah. Again, I'm sorry. He sort of makes me want to rip my hair out."

She thought of his father. Everybody knew Kurt Windlass. If he was half as much of a hardass as he portrayed on the big screen, the guy was probably a drill sergeant. "That's too bad," she said. "Family can do that to you."

He stayed quiet. Obviously this wasn't a topic open for discussion.

"Okay, they do have a point," she reluctantly admitted. "We need the narrative to be that you've fallen in love with a fan, not you'll nail anything sexy that crosses your path."

"Well, you are sexy," he said, his voice warming. While she felt a little flattered, she knew he was just trying to shake off the talk of his father. Then he added, "The only reason I think they went the direction they did was because we have insane sexual chemistry. At least, I can say that it's never been like this for me before. You are a force of nature."

"I am aware of this," she agreed, glad he couldn't see the blush that was contradicting her bravado. "And I'm grateful for your vote of confidence, but now we need to go a little more public, apparently. There aren't a ton of paparazzi in Seattle, which is a good thing, but it also means that we need to stay somewhere the paparazzi will see us, but not seem obvious about it."

"It's got to be about more than sex," he said. "It's got to be about intimacy."

The way he said the word *intimacy* made her shiver, in a good way. "Right. Subtle, but accessible," she agreed. "And more romantic."

"Yeah, that works," he said. "But how are we supposed to convince anybody that we're in love?"

She frowned. *You got me, pal. I've never been in love.*

However, with Jake perilously close to freaking out, now was not the time to make that particular admission.

"Well, rather than being the sexy make-out show, we just need to go for something more classic," she said, with more confidence than she felt. "Romantic dinner or something, maybe?"

"That's kind of cliché, isn't it?" he hedged.

She sighed. "We don't have a ton of options. It's not like we've got a professional photographer that works for us, setting up press-perfect pictures for public consumption. We're relying on one lame member of the paparazzi who's just made her first break and will be looking for more."

"I was thinking more like a public declaration."

"No!" She rubbed her face. The guy would've been a terrible grifter. "What, do you want to look like a couch-jumping Tom Cruise?"

"You have a better idea?"

"I thought you hated faking it. Thought you hated lying," she snapped. "Now, you want to go all-in with this?"

That sunk home, she could tell from his little hiss of breath.

Jesus, Hailey, are you trying *to ruin all of your chances today?*

"Sorry. That was below the belt," she said. "And uncalled for. I . . . it's just . . . it feels like an overreaction. You want to prove something." *To your father*, she thought,

163

but didn't say it. "Trust me, I do a lot out of spite. I know what it looks like."

He let out a long exhale. She could feel the tension running through him, over the phone.

"I'm going to come over. We'll do something cute, something fun and, erm, couple-ish," she soothed, even as her own stomach knotted. "I'll wear something girl-friend-friendly and low key."

"And not too sexy?"

"Well," she drawled, "sugar, I just can't help that. I was born this way."

He laughed, and she thought she could feel some of the tension melting out of him.

"I must be out of my mind," he admitted. "This is . . . absurd. Absolutely bananas. Do you really think we can pull this off?"

He wasn't wrong. The knots in her stomach tightened and multiplied.

Can you pull this off?

She glared at herself in her rearview mirror. "Let me tell you something. You know how I said the bookstore is owned by my family? That we live there?"

"Yeah, you mentioned that."

"I've got a sister—well, sort of a sister—it's a long story. She runs the bookstore. It's really for her." She took a deep breath, then said quietly, "She's agoraphobic. I don't think I mentioned that."

There was a long pause. "No," he replied. "You didn't."

"Her name's Cressida, and she's awesome." She bit her lip, fighting back tears. "I'm going to come to the hotel, and we'll figure out a game plan. We're going to show the producers just how valuable you are. We'll get you that contract renewal. You know why?"

"No, why?"

"Because my sister is counting on me," she said, and let the full force of that passion, that dedication, come through in her voice. Convincing *herself*. "Because I don't let her down, not if it is humanly possible. If that means convincing the world that we're madly in love, on camera, then that's what I'll do. And trust me, the entire world—including you—will believe me. Because I've got too much riding on it, and I'm not going to fail. Okay?"

He paused. "This really means a lot to you."

"Well, *yeah*," she spat, before she could stop herself.

Thankfully, he laughed. "I mean . . . when you talk like that . . . it's like listening to a preacher or a president or . . . I don't know, Steve Jobs," he said, and she snickered. "Jesus, with persuasive skills like that, why aren't you in sales or something? Or actually in P.R.?"

"Haven't gone to college, don't really plan to go. It's hard for me to keep my attention on any topic I'm not passionate about, like general ed stuff." Not to mention the expense, but really, the thought of sitting in a chair like Rachel did, writing papers and putting up with a lot of bureaucratic bullshit, made her skin crawl. "So, do we have a deal?"

"You're on. You come here, we'll figure out something." He paused. "I want to help your sister, too. I'll figure it out, get over my neurosis, and make sure that I do the thing at your bookstore, okay?"

She felt a wave of relief. "I'll hold you to that."

"But that might not guarantee that your bookstore makes it," he pointed out, and it was like getting splashed with cold water. "Do you have a backup plan?"

She didn't, not really. Rachel had some . . . she needed to talk to her about that. But for now . . . "Just a good sale, getting a bunch of the convention traffic, would be a huge boost. It'd get us through the next month or two. Sometimes, that's as good as it gets."

He was quiet for a second.

"I'm not telling you this as a sob story," she said, feeling a pinch of pride. "I'm not just trying to guilt you into helping. This is an even trade, damn it."

"I know that," he said. "But you're a pretty cool woman, you know that?"

"I'm aware," she said, pushing the bravado. "See you in a few."

She clicked off her phone, then rested her head on the cold plastic of the steering wheel for just a minute longer.

"I can do this. I can do this, damn it," she told herself, turning the ignition and letting the engine roar to life.

She had to do this. Cressida and Rachel were counting on her. And if she'd get out of her own way, get over her pissy attitudes, self-sabotage and self-pity, she'd make sure it got done.

·♥ · ♥ · ♥ · ♥ · ♥·

Jake decided to have Hailey come up to his room to brainstorm. She sounded upset but determined when he'd talked to her on the phone. He knew this whole "fake relationship" thing was a long shot, but Susie still hadn't heard from the producers, and he was getting antsy. He had to do something. Besides, he was fascinated by Hailey. Attracted, without question. A little wary, too . . . partly because of his whole gun-shy approach to women, but partly because of her past. But just a little. His gut was telling him to trust her.

Of course, that might be his dick. They were in adjacent neighborhoods, after all, and sometimes his dick was louder.

She knocked, and he let her in. "Thanks," he said, glancing up and down the hallway to make sure the paparazzi wasn't there. They might've sent somebody more seasoned. Not that he was all that newsworthy, he thought. But the photos had been steamy, and sex sold.

She came in, sitting down on the bed. She must've come directly from work—she was wearing a pair of jeans that clung to her curves and a long-sleeved Seahawks shirt with the sleeves scrunched up. "Nice digs," she said, bouncing a little. Which caused other things to bounce, very nicely, on her frame. He forced himself not to stare.

Don't be that guy, Jake.

He sat on the small couch. "So, any ideas, coach?"

She stretched out, propping her head up on one arm. "I may have something."

She looked good on the burnished gold comforter, he thought. Which of course, reminded him of how close the two of them had come in his other hotel room, at the casino. His cock twitched. He steadfastly ignored it.

Working, buddy, he chastised absently. *Just business, remember?*

Too bad that was getting to be a harder and harder tenet to remember.

"Well?" he said, only sounding a little hoarse. "What'd you have in mind? Walk by the water, holding hands? Sharing spaghetti like *Lady and the Tramp*? I could buy you roses somewhere . . ."

"Slight pivot," she said, surprising him. "I'm wondering if maybe I got you on the wrong track."

He frowned. "Like . . . what, exactly? We should have promise rings and stay celibate or something?"

Her eyes widened, then she rolled onto her back, letting out peals of laughter. "God, no!"

"That's good," he muttered. No way was he thinking celibacy when he had someone as smoking hot as Hailey in front of him, even if sex was technically off the table.

If they were going to be in a "pretend" relationship, they were going to be "pretend" all over each other.

Remind me again why the "no sex" thing was a good idea.

He growled at himself softly, then forced himself to focus.

"I think you need to go hang out with the fans," she clarified. "Get to know your audience. And let them get to know you."

He blanched, thinking of the VIP fiasco. "I'm doing that on the panels, aren't I?"

"Not really," she said, surprising him. "On the panels I've seen, Simon's a raging extrovert, a showman. Charming as hell. Miles is Simon's straight man, and they've got the double-act down pat, but even then, he shares stuff about himself. Like his dog, Sarge, or his not-so-secret obsession with eighties music. You, on the other hand . . ." She surveyed him seriously. "You're pretty closed-mouthed. You're two-dimensional. There's nothing to grab onto."

"My jeans pocket would disagree with you," he muttered, squirming uncomfortably, but he sighed. "What should I talk about? I answer questions. And I don't want to talk about my dad, or Hollywood stuff."

"Good, because nobody wants to hear about that crap here," she said. "They want to get to know *you*. What's interesting about you?"

"How the hell should I know?" he said, getting up and pacing. "Seriously. I hike, I surf. I don't have any amusingly named pets, no weird hobbies. I am boring, white-bread, vanilla. There is no 'there' there."

He felt bitterness, and deep down, a slight sense of loss.

"I'm an underwear model, remember? Mostly they want me to stand around and brood."

She looked at him, silent for a long second. He waited. Then those ridiculously full lips of hers curved into a smirk.

"This a private pity part, or can just anybody show up?"

He winced.

"You are more interesting than you let on," she said.

"You've known me like a day," he shot back dismissively.

"A couple of days," she corrected. "And in that time, I figured out that you're more sensitive than you let on. You're funny. You like nature, and hate bullshit. You're honest. You won't have sex with me, partially because you don't trust me, but also because you're protecting me."

His eyes widened.

"Don't try to deny it. You know we've got a quid pro quo thing, and you don't want to mix sex into that. Know what that tells me?" She didn't wait for him to finish. "You're a romantic. You like sci-fi and fantasy, which tells me you have good taste."

He grinned at that one.

"You ran from some overzealous groupies, rather than cussing them out or being an asshole. You're not jealous of Simon and Miles. And you could've told me to take a hike, but you didn't. You were open-minded and gave me a shot, even though let's face it, it's a Hail Mary at best." She smiled. "You've got a good heart inside that great bod, Jake Reese. If more of the fans knew about it, the show would sign you in a heartbeat. So let's let them see it."

He swallowed hard. Nobody, not even women he'd dated, had looked at him this way. Read him this way. Said such positive praise in a no-nonsense way.

She got up, holding out her hand. "Let's go downstairs, and hang out with the masses a bit."

He took a deep breath, then stood up, holding her hand. "If I get mauled," he said, laughing shakily, trying to cover his suddenly raw emotions, "I'm blaming you."

"Poor baby," she cooed. "I'll protect you."

He leaned forward carefully, kissing her on the cheek. Her eyes widened.

"Thanks for the pep talk," he said, squeezing her hand.

Her look of surprise melted into something warmer—sweeter. Her smile made her look younger for a moment, less guarded.

"You're very welcome."

They headed down to the convention rooms. He felt a little nervous, but holding her hand like a talisman helped. He then discovered curving his arm around her waist and holding her to him helped even more.

"No hiding behind me, metaphorically speaking," she warned.

He chuckled. They went to the sales floor. He complimented several people on the fan-made art they were selling. There was an impromptu dance party going on in one of the other rooms, he noticed. Hailey tugged him over.

There were mostly women, he noticed immediately. They'd commandeered a small sound system, and were dancing around enthusiastically to the eighties alternative music that the show so often played. New Order, Talking Heads, David Bowie. He nodded in approval, clapping after a song stopped.

The women turned, staring at him, and he immediately felt self-conscious. "Private party, or can anybody join in?" he asked, echoing Hailey's earlier sentiment.

"Ooooh!" One woman squealed loudly, clapping her hands.

Oh, Christ. It couldn't be.

It was.

"Pocket-Ripper," he quickly muttered to Hailey as the woman came up and threw her arms around Jake. "*Help*."

Hailey took charge immediately. "You need to let him go. *Now*."

The other women in the crowd looked surprised—and a bit repulsed—at Hailey's sharp statement. In the lull in the music, he could hear them murmuring to each other.

Who the hell is she?

Why is she acting that way?

What's going on with the two of them?

Pocket-Ripper was wearing a *Mystics*' **All Knight Long** T-shirt and a smug expression, hanging on tighter. "What, you think because you slept with him you own him?"

"No," Hailey said, and he swore, it was like she was a theater-trained actor. She wasn't shouting, exactly, but every person in the room could hear every word she was saying. "I'm saying you need to let go of him because you were at the VIP event, and you assaulted him."

Now jaws dropped open, and the looks of revulsion turned to Pocket-Ripper.

The woman laughed nervously, but did release him, thank God. "That was . . . that wasn't . . ." she spluttered. "I'd had a little to drink, with lunch. It was a VIP event!"

"So you're saying you paid money, so you should get to touch whatever you want on him?" Hailey said coldly.

The woman turned to Jake. "Aww . . . he didn't mind. You didn't mind, right?" She sounded defensive. "I'm sure you've had worse."

"I didn't like it," he said quietly.

Since it had gotten quiet, all the other women heard him.

"Well, *excuse me*," Pocket-Ripper said, apparently feeling the heat of everyone's judgment. "I was just having a good time."

"That's not cool," said one of others, a tall woman with a *Doctor Who* T-shirt. "Not cool at all."

"That's sexual assault," another agreed. "What the hell?"

Pocket-Ripper spluttered. "Fuck you guys!" she said, storming off.

Hailey touched his arm, and he startled. He didn't realize just how tensed he'd been. "It's okay," she breathed. Then she turned to the others. "Sorry about that. So, are we dancing, or what?"

They laughed, and the music started up—this time Oingo Boingo's "Dead Man's Party," from the Halloween episode. They started bopping along.

Tall Woman walked up to Jake. "Sorry about that," she said. "I hope you don't think we're all like that."

Jake sighed. "No, of course not. The VIP event got a little out of hand."

"Sexual assault at a con or a VIP event, is *not* cool," Tall Woman said, shaking her head. "And considering your history, I'd think they'd be extra careful."

"What history?" Hailey asked curiously.

"The . . . you know," the woman whispered. "The stalker?"

Hailey turned to him, eyes wide. "You have a stalker? Should I be worried?"

Jake shook his head. "I haven't heard anything from her for a month or two," he said.

"Don't worry. We'll keep the baddies away," another woman said, bumping fists with Tall Woman.

"Thanks," he said, and meant it. They were nice, protective. He then wound up having a conversation with each of them. Tall Woman—real name Samantha—had come all the way from Nebraska. She was ordinarily a human resources rep for an equipment rental company, but she liked going to conventions, and she loved the show. The other woman was a dog groomer from Florida, also named Samantha. They were sharing a room, even though they'd never met before in real life. They both ran a fan site and Facebook group.

He took selfies with both of them. He then wound up talking to about twenty different people. He thought he'd hate it, but they all loved the show, and they were respectful and interesting. And just *nice*.

He wished he'd done this sooner.

He looked over at Hailey, who after defending him from Pocket-Ripper had left him to his own devices. She was shaking it to "Don't Go" by Yaz. And a damned fine shake it was. She winked at him, noticing him looking.

"She seems really nice," Samantha from Nebraska said.

"She is," he said, reluctantly turning away from his staring. "She's awesome."

Samantha from Florida gave her friend a quick look. "We don't mean to pry."

175

"You're not," he said, realizing this was probably the sort of opportunity that Hailey would approve of. "She's the best."

"How did you two meet?"

"After the VIP, strangely enough," he said, deciding to stick as close to the truth as possible. "That lady had just ripped my pants pocket off, and I was trying to hide. I dove into the coffee shop where Hailey was working and hid behind the counter."

"No way!" Nebraska Samantha said, laughing.

"True story," he said, grinning. "She agreed to give me a ride to the hotel. I bought her dinner to say thanks, and we just . . . hit it off."

It really was true. They'd had a great conversation, even before their too-short, almost-sexual encounter. Even with the craziness of their "agreement," he realized he liked talking to her. Liked hanging out with her.

He just liked *her*.

They were sighing. "That is so romantic," Florida Samantha said. "Would you mind if we shared that on our blog, and in the group?"

"Nah, go ahead," he said. "And if you want an interview or something, just let me know."

"Really?" Nebraska Samantha squeaked. "You'd be up for it?"

"Absolutely. Just email me."

She hugged him, then pulled away, red faced.

"It's okay," he said, and gave her a hug back, ignoring her soft *squeee*. Then he hugged Florida Samantha, and grinned at her red face. "Now, if you'll excuse me, I think I'd like a dance with my girl."

They were chattering excitedly when he walked up to Hailey, giving her a hug from behind. The English Beat was playing, talking about the "Mirror in the Bathroom." She was jamming, sweating, but she turned and gave him a brilliant smile.

"How're you doing, champ?" She leaned against him, and he felt her lush curves pressing him deliciously.

He kissed her neck. "Doing great," he said. "Thanks to you."

She turned around in his arms, kissing him against the mouth. "You're very welcome."

He stared at her for a long second. Then lowered his mouth again, gently, patiently, giving her plenty of room to back off.

Instead, she sighed, and leaned into him. Melted into him.

He closed his eyes, luxuriating in the feel of her against him, the sweetness of her mouth. He tilted his head slightly, his hands smoothing along her back. She had her hands crossed behind his neck, tugging him closer to her. Her lips parted slightly. He licked the fullness of her lower lip, nipping at it.

Despite the pounding beat, it might as well have been a slow dance. And they might as well have been the only two on the makeshift dance floor.

There was a long hoot, and he pulled away, momentarily stunned. The ladies were laughing, clapping, cheering.

They *weren't* the only two on the dance floor, he realized foolishly.

"Woot!" Nebraska Samantha yelled, as Florida Samantha whistled.

Hailey was blushing, but smiling broadly. "So, can you dance?" she asked, giving a fantastic shimmy.

He smiled back. "I do a mean Sprinkler." At which he grabbed his left foot, put out his right arm, and demonstrated his terrible skills. Her laugh blended with the others.

After a few more painfully awkward moves—the Cabbage Patch, the Running Man, and of course the Robot—he finally waved off, holding Hailey, who had collapsed against him, laughing.

"See you guys tomorrow," he called, and they waved back.

"That was fun," he said, as they collapsed together into the elevator. "I don't know if it'll help, with the contract I mean, but I'm glad I did it."

"You were great," she said, eyes shining.

They were alone in the elevator, leaning against each other, breathless from dancing and laughing. And looking at each other.

He leaned forward, testing. Tempting.

She met him halfway.

·♥·♥·♥·♥·♥·

She was kissing Jake. Again. Not in front of an audience. This wasn't for the con.

This was for them, and them alone.

His body pressed her against the wall of the elevator, and she had to fight the instinct to wrap her legs around his waist and just say "the hell with it." Her lips parted, and his tongue swept through, tangling with hers as his hands threaded through her curls, pulling them loose from the ponytail holder. She hooked a knee over his hip, and he held it closer, rubbing his hardness against her softness, making her growl against his lips.

She'd never needed someone like this. She'd had plenty of sex: fun, fantastic, varied. But she'd never felt like this about a person, specifically.

If she didn't fuck this man, she thought she might well die.

Isn't it more than that, though?

She silenced the tiny voice that whispered the traitorous thought. She'd only known Jake, what, seventy-two hours. She wasn't going to romanticize it. She wanted him. He wanted her.

He tore away when the door dinged, releasing her leg. He was breathless, his eyes blazing. "You're staying."

"I have to work a late shift," she said, her own breathing ragged. "In about an hour."

"Cancel." His voice was gravelly, and she shivered with need.

"Can't," she said, with real regret.

They stepped out of the elevator, and he grabbed her, kissing her hard, his hand holding her jaw as his mouth worked miracles. By the time he was done, she was trembling, her knees turning to water.

"Cancel," he repeated, fiercely.

"I need the money . . ."

"I'll cover whatever you're going to lose," he said.

That sobered her. "It's not like that," she said. "Not between us."

He let out a sharp breath. "No, it isn't," he agreed. "What's happening between us isn't a transaction. I don't know what the hell it is, but it's not that."

She felt a sugary warmth in the pit of her stomach. Whatever weird thing was happening to her, he felt it, too. She wasn't alone in this insanity.

"Take me to your room."

"An hour's not long enough for what I want to do with you." He nipped her neck, her shoulder, his hands smoothing over her sides, down to her hips. She moaned softly.

"No, it's not," she said. "But I don't want to waste whatever time we have together."

That sounded more dramatic than she'd intended, but she couldn't help it. She was on fire. Even if she only got fifteen minutes . . .

She'd beg. And she *never* begged.

He kissed her again, against his door, trying blindly to get the key card to work. She heard the beep as the lock unlatched, and he opened the door, stumbling the two of them in.

His hands were all over her before the door even closed. She wrapped her legs around him, as she'd wanted to, her fingers in his hair, her breasts pressed against his chest. "Jake," she breathed.

He was kissing her like she was his lifeline—like he would literally die if he stopped. The light was on, and they made it to the bed, landing on it. He pressed kisses down her collarbone, toward her cleavage. She arched her back, looking up.

Then she froze, baffled. Frightened.

"What the hell?"

He growled, then looked up, and froze, as well.

Abruptly, they rolled off the bed, looking around.

The room was a disaster. The bed had been slashed to ribbons, probably with a big-ass knife. A big fruit basket had been delivered at some point, and fruit was smashed into the floor, smeared onto walls. The large mirror on the wall was shattered by a champagne bottle. Jake's bags had been rifled through, clothes thrown everywhere.

"Jesus," Jake breathed, getting to his feet and moving her behind him as he looked around.

On the wall, above the headboard, somebody had spray-painted the words: YOU BELONG TO ME, RICK. DON'T FORGET IT.

"This happen to you before?" she asked, numb, on alert. She grabbed what was left of the champagne bottle by the neck, searching for anybody that might be lying in wait. Jake grabbed part of a broken lamp.

"Not like this," he said, searching the bathroom, the closet, under the desk. "When I was dating Chelsea Midas, somebody sent letters saying she was all wrong for me. Then somebody filled my trailer with flowers and balloons when we started filming the season after Rick's love interest died. But nothing quite this intense."

Hailey nodded, taking it all in. Whoever it was, he or she was obviously pretty pissed. And mentally unstable. She clenched her teeth together. That was worse. Everybody who'd ever spent some time on the street knew that mentally unstable was worse than mean, because mean still had logic and a sense of self-preservation.

The mentally unstable would set herself on fire just to burn *you*.

Jake called hotel management. They came, as did the cops. After talking to the manager, Jake sighed as the man finally made his last apologies and left, intent on "getting to the bottom of this."

"Shit. This is because of the pictures. Of you and me," Jake said, his face as stern and stoic as any of his father's action movie characters. "This is bad."

"Yeah, that'd be my guess," she said, more glibly than she felt.

"That clinches it," he said. "You're staying with me. From now on. Until we get this sorted out."

"Wait. What?" Hailey spun to face him, blocking out the angry graffiti. "Why would I do that?"

"You might be in danger, too," he said, his voice grim.

"I'll be fine," she said sharply, feeling resentment. He gets his room trashed by a stalker, and now he was going to assert his masculinity by ordering *her* around? Seriously? "Sure, Ms. Looney Tunes Stalker trashed your room. But there have to be security cameras all over the hotel. She couldn't have blended in that well. And it's not like she couldn't have confronted you in the crowd if she'd wanted to hurt you. This is deliberate. She wanted to warn you—us."

Jake got a stubborn look on his face. "The hotel manager said he'd look into it, but they hadn't seen anything yet. And there's nothing that says she won't escalate."

That clicked a new thought in her head—and a wave of concern. "She's more pissed at you than at me," Hailey said. "Are you getting any sort of protection? Bodyguards, something like that?"

Jake shook his head. "She hasn't gone directly for me before, like I said," he replied. "If it's who I think it is, she's sent messages, but I doubt she'd actually hurt me."

"That's completely ridiculous," she said. "Get a bodyguard, for God's sake."

"Only if you stay with me," he counter-argued. "If she hurts me, she won't have me. If she hurts you, she clears the way."

I'd like to see her fucking try.

"Damn it, Hailey," Jake said, his voice low and urgent. "I don't want to see you get hurt."

"I seriously doubt I'll get hurt," Hailey countered, even as a small voice in her head pointed out that odds were good that if this stalker came after her, there was a chance.

Nothing I can't handle, Hailey thought, feeling the familiar cold calm envelop her. That feeling of being cornered—of adrenaline, fear, and undiluted rage. *Been a while, but nothing I can't take.*

"There is another option," Jake said thoughtfully. "We can break up. Now, publicly. Say you were scared off. That takes you off her radar. Then you won't be a target."

Fear took on a new dimension. "We're not calling anything off," she shot back reflexively. She needed this too badly. The bookstore—her *sisters*—needed this too badly. She wasn't going to let some possessive fangirl screw with it. "I can deal with it, okay? I've got this."

"Oh, really?" Jake glared at her, doing that male "why won't you see reason?" scowl. "Ever had somebody in front of you with a weapon? Ever have somebody threaten your life?"

"Actually, yes, I have," she said. "And I'm still here, and he's in jail. So give me a little credit."

That seemed to throw him. "Who . . . ?"

She slammed down on the memory that crept up. Stefano in his wife-beater T-shirt, broken bottle in hand. Blood on the edge.

"Legacy of a misspent childhood," she muttered. He had a good point. This wasn't helping. She was falling back into old patterns. She *knew* better. "Okay. We're reacting. We're just making snap decisions. That's not the way to go about this."

"I agree." He crossed his arms. "That means you're coming with me. We stay together. And I'll hire a bodyguard. Okay?"

"I have to work," she said resolutely. "They're not going to find a replacement for a late shift, not this close."

"Fine." He took his phone out of his pocket, dialing blindly. "Susie? Remember when you wanted me to get a bodyguard?"

"What?" Hailey heard a woman yell on the line. Jake winced, holding the phone away from his ear for a second. "What the hell happened?"

"That stalker, the one that left all the gifts? She tore up my hotel room. I think it's because of the photos. I'll be

185

sending pictures of the room, and I've talked to the police, but I need you to send one of those bodyguards you recommended. Okay?" He paused. Susie was obviously talking, quickly, and though Hailey couldn't make out the words, she could make out the panic and concern in the woman's voice. "No, I'm all right. The room's destroyed, though."

More worried chatter on the line. Jake sighed.

"Can't stay here, and they're full up . . . yeah. I could go somewhere else. I'll figure out something, let you know." He hung up. "So. We need to find a new place to sleep, you and I."

Was it her imagination, or was he looking a bit happier?

"How far is it to Seattle?" he asked. "Like twenty minutes, right? I'm sure we can get a place there."

She groaned. "It's maybe twenty-five minutes, without traffic. With traffic, it's closer to an hour, sometimes an hour and a half . . . and there's usually traffic," she said. "It's in the opposite direction of the casino, and besides, you don't want to get caught in traffic tomorrow morning trying to get here."

Now it was her turn. She pulled out her phone, calling up the casino.

"Just give me a second," she said to him, and he grinned.

"Snoqualmie Casino and Resort, this is Amber, how can I help you?"

"Amber? It's Hailey," she said, thankful her friend was working the desk. "We got anything available? I want a room, in my name."

"Really?" Amber's voice held a smile. "Got a live one, huh?"

"You have no idea," Hailey said, rolling her eyes. "Got something for me?"

"As it happens, yeah. Small room, but the bed's big."

"Sounds perfect. Thanks, sweetie. We'll use it after my shift."

"Bet you will." Hailey hung up on Amber's laugh.

"Okay. You'll get the room at the casino."

"Perfect. You can stay with me," he said. "I'll make sure the bodyguard gets sent there."

She sighed. What was she getting herself into?

CHAPTER 7

It was midnight. Jake sat at a slot machine, absently plunking in quarters, watching Hailey at work at a nearby blackjack table. She was wearing black pants, a white shirt, a black vest, and a bow tie . . . which was a little odd when paired with her gothabilly makeup sensibilities, but he noticed that no one at the casino itself seemed to bat an eye. If anything, she was one of the more popular dealers.

"My shift's over at four," she'd said, then left him to his own devices. He hung out, playing some slot machines or drinking ginger ale at the nearby bar. Although a cold beer—or Scotch on the rocks—would have gone a long way toward taking the edge off his tension, he wanted to keep his head clear.

He didn't want her to be alone, unprotected, while she was working. She was doing her best to ignore him. She'd already talked to the pit boss. Jake wasn't allowed to play at her table, but they were doing her a huge favor, letting him loiter nearby. He knew it made security nervous, for a dealer to have "friends" anywhere near the gambling.

The bodyguard Susie was sending was supposed to meet them there, and talk to the casino's and hotel's security, to make sure they knew what was going on. Jake doubted that the stalker, whoever she was, was going to come all the way out here to start trouble, although what she'd done to the hotel room worried him. Up to this point, she'd been annoying with her love notes, sometimes infuriating in the way she'd infiltrate his house or hotel rooms to leave balloons or flowers. But he'd never felt anxious before.

That said, he didn't want to change his life for it, either. That would mean that the crazies of the world won, and he wasn't going to live like Howard Frickin' Hughes, just because a woman thought he was his character, and that his character was somehow her personal sex slave or something. He wasn't going to cower and hide.

"Winner! To the man in the blue polo," Hailey said.

"Woo! You're good luck for me, baby," the guy in the blue shirt said, winking at her and leaning forward. Even from this distance, Jake could smell the booze wafting off the guy. "Maybe you and I could get lucky later, huh?"

She ignored him. "Place your bets, please."

He wondered how often she had to put up with this. He knew that she was financially tight. He'd thought about how he'd felt, being essentially characterized as a cute ass and a pretty face, especially after that damned underwear ad. He thought he'd feel more like a stud, and instead felt more like . . .

Well, a girl, if he thought about it. If this was any indication of what women had to go through on a daily basis. Jesus.

"That's quite the vest you've got going on," the man kept pushing, starting to reach out for the vest.

"No touching," she said sharply. Jake stood up, angered.

The pit boss noticed what was going on, as well, and hurried over. "You're on break in ten minutes," the pit boss said. "Is there any problem here?"

"No, I'm fine," she said, although Jake could tell her expression was tight. "No problems." She kept dealing. The pit boss wandered away.

Jake found himself sitting at the table, next to Blue Shirt. She frowned at Jake, shaking her head subtly. He ignored it.

"You shouldn't be here," she hissed at him.

"Why not?"

"Because I *know* you," she said pointedly.

"I'm not playing," he said. "I'm just sitting here, hanging out."

"Hang out somewhere else," she said. "You can't be here."

Blue Shirt looked first at her, then at Jake, then back at her, his expression sour. "Figures. You like pretty douchebags, huh?"

Hailey ignored his question, dealing the cards.

Blue Shirt gave him a derisive look. "Because I bet I've got way more money that this guy."

Jake looked at the guy with amusement and disbelief. The guy had to be pushing fifty, maybe a bit older. The booze had obviously given him a puffed-up sense of importance. Jake bet that he probably had more than the guy's net worth in one single vehicle in his garage.

"No accounting for taste," Jake said mildly. Still, he felt like pushing buttons. He couldn't necessarily protect Hailey from the stalker, but he could shut this guy up. "Although I think that she's not going to get a whole lot of fun from a balding guy who probably drives, what, a Beemer and thinks he's Bill Gates."

"Shut up, asshole," the guy said darkly.

"Take it away from the table, gentlemen," Hailey warned, as the few other people playing nervously gathered their chips, looking for a quieter table.

"She's a whore," the guy said. "Everybody knows it . . ."

Jake was already angry, furious at the guy's attitude, frustrated at his inability to stop the stalker. That was the only way he could account for what happened next.

Jake popped up like a jack-in-the-box and decked the guy right across the jaw, dropping him like a lead balloon. Blue Shirt yelped in pain, then roared, coming up.

Unfortunately, two beefy guys with UW sweatshirts came up behind Blue Shirt, backing him up. They were friends of his, apparently, who had been drinking and looked eager to fight. Fortunately, several large casino security guards hurried over, as well.

"All right, you'll have to leave. All of you," the pit boss said, glaring at them both—and at Hailey. "Hailey, you're off shift now."

"This wasn't my fault!" she protested.

"*Now*," the pit boss said, but not without sympathy. "Talk to security on your way out. And next time, don't bring your *friend*, okay?"

She went to change out of her uniform, and Jake waited by the doors, pacing. He shouldn't have hit the guy, but he was asking for it, being such a dick. Hailey came out, her mouth in a thin line.

"They don't want you staying in the hotel," she said sharply. "They told me you're banned."

"Are you in trouble?" he asked.

"Bit late for that, don't you think?" she snapped back. "You might've thought of that before you pulled your little he-man routine!"

He winced. "Sorry. That was on me." He frowned. "They didn't fire you, did they?"

"No. They're decent people, and they know I'm clean—no record, no problems there. But they're looking at me in a way they didn't before." She sighed heavily. "I can't lose two jobs in one day."

He hadn't realized she'd lost the coffee shop job, and felt guilt hit him like an uppercut. "I'll find us another room, someplace else," he said, typing into his phone.

"Everything's booked, remember?" she said, looking tired. He felt impotent rage and guilt bubble in him in a toxic cocktail.

They walked out into the cold night air, only to find Blue Shirt and his drunk, belligerent, douchebag friends with him.

"Knew you'd be here, pretty boy," Blue Shirt said, trying to look menacing and just looking doughy and constipated.

"Ah, fuck," Jake said, stepping in front of Hailey.

"Looks like you'll get to find out who's the better man. Maybe you should've chosen your fuck buddies better, sweetie," Blue Shirt said to Hailey, as one of his friends brayed with laughter.

"Looks like we'll get to see what happens when you get your ass kicked by Doc Martens," she said instead, starting to try to push around Jake, who stopped her.

"Don't!" He bunched his hands into fists, eager to pummel the guy more. "I've got this."

"No, you don't, sir," another quiet voice said. A man stepped out of the shadows of the parking lot. He was wearing a black leather jacket and black slacks. He looked . . . well, nondescript. He had brown hair, wide cheekbones, and a boxer's nose. His build wasn't that tall, but

CATHY YARDLEY

was definitely stocky. He looked like the human equivalent of a pit bull. He stepped up beside Jake.

"My name is Vic Walsh. I'm working with you for the rest of your stay. I'm sorry I couldn't get here sooner."

"You're . . ." He nodded. "Oh. Right. You're Susie's . . . friend?"

"What, is he a hooker or something?" the other drunk brawler said, causing more donkey-like laughter.

Vic turned to the inebriated, snickering trio. "We're leaving. Now." He didn't have any inflection in it, just started walking.

"Listen, asshole," Blue Shirt said, grabbing a handful of jacket. "That bitch and your little friend were . . . *ack*!"

It was like a movie, Jake thought. Vic grabbed the guy's wrist and, in a blur of motion, had him sucking pavement in about two seconds. When the friends moved in, he nailed one in the nuts and had the other flat on his back, wind knocked out of him. They were all flopping there, gaping, like fish on the bottom of a boat.

Vic turned back to them as if nothing had happened. "I should speak to hotel security," he said quietly. "And may I suggest you getting to your room, and staying there? If nothing else, it would make my job easier."

"Unfortunately, your job is going to be a little harder. I, um, just managed to get myself kicked out of this hotel," Jake said, feeling embarrassed.

"All right," Vic said, unfazed. "We can—"

"I have an idea," Hailey interrupted. Then she sighed, rubbing her eyes. "Okay. This is a onetime-only thing. But for tonight . . ." She paused, taking another deep breath. "You can stay at my place."

· ♥ · ♥ · ♥ · ♥ · ♥ ·

I can't believe I'm doing this, Hailey thought as Jake and the bodyguard—Vic?—followed her up the stairs to the front door of Frost Bookstore and her home.

She'd never brought guys home, ever. She half expected Grandma Frost's ghost to come out on the porch and start whaling on her with a broom. Of course, she'd never had a bodyguard before, either.

She unlocked the door, and looked at Vic. "Um . . . are you sure you want to stay here? I doubt anybody's coming for him tonight. For one thing, nobody knows where he is, or where this is."

"As far as you know," Vic said, and she forced herself not to roll her eyes. "Besides, I'm on assignment. I'm here until he leaves town."

Right. That was soon. Another weird little blip went across Hailey's mind. Should she mind that he was going to leave by the end of the week? No. This was all for the bookstore. For her sisters.

"All right. I'll, um, get Jake settled into my room, and then I'll crash with one of my sisters." She blanched.

"Which reminds me. I'd better let them know that you're here. Um, both of you."

"I hate that we're putting you out," Jake said, and his face was full of genuine remorse. It warmed her, a little.

"No, no. This helps sell the story, anyway, right?" She winced when she saw Vic's curious look at her words. "Um, let me get you settled into my room."

Jake's smile was quick, and he looked interested. His sky-blue eyes shone.

"No hanky-panky," she cautioned him. "I don't bring sex home."

Jake's eyebrows jumped to his hairline, and then he started chuckling, quickly smothering it with his hand when she shushed him. Vic stayed stoic. He must be a helluva bodyguard, she thought.

"Um, Mr. . . . Vic," she said, wondering what she should do about the guy. "Did you want to bunk in with Jake?"

"If it's all right with you and your sisters," Vic said, in a low voice, "I'm going to camp here, on this couch. If anybody's going to break in, they're going to do it from this floor. At least your floors are already elevated. I'm going to do a quick check of your lowest doors and windows, and then I'll just set up down here. If anybody comes in, I'll know about it."

She wondered if he was going to sleep. "Um . . . okay."

He went back out the front door like a ghost. She led Jake up the first flight of stairs to the two bedrooms, hers and Cressida's. The attic stairs led to Rachel's room. "This is me," she said, pointing to the right. "The bathroom's right here, if you need it."

"I'll set my bag down and then get cleaned up," he said. "Thanks, again, for this. For everything. I'm sorry I was such a jackass at the casino."

"You were trying to be gallant," she said, her stomach feeling a little quivery at the thought. Good grief, a guy protecting her. Part of it was ludicrous—she fought her own battles, and generally kicked ass, thanks very much—but part of it was just . . . sweet.

When was the last time a guy had gone out of his way to take care of her?

Never, she thought. And that was unsettling.

"I'll . . . um, let my sisters know you guys are here," she said, hopping up the stairs and knocking on Rachel's door. "Rache? Rachel?"

"Hmrph."

She opened the door. From the light of the hallway, she could barely make out her sister, sprawled on her bed.

"I, um, have some guys over."

A slow roll. "Mmf?"

"Guys," Hailey repeated. "Um . . . a guy I'm seeing . . . and his, um, bodyguard."

Silence for a minute. "Wfr mummpher."

Then a low snore.

Hailey smiled. Rachel was a heavy sleeper, especially when she'd been working especially hard. Which lately seemed like always. Hailey took advantage of using

Rachel's tiny bathroom while Jake used the one down-stairs. She also borrowed one of Rachel's nightshirts. Hailey never wore nightgowns, but she wasn't going to sleep nude on her sister's floor, for God's sake. Rachel's nightie was a little snug, but she made it work. Then she went over to Cressida's door, knocking softly.

"Cress?"

Cressida was sitting at her desk, her headphones casually pulled down to her neck, her expression expectant. "Do we have guests?" Cressida asked, one eyebrow arching. "This is new. You don't usually bring a guy home."

"Well, this time, it's two guys, actually," she said, and then choked back a chuckle when Cressida's mouth dropped open. "Not like that, goob. I'm letting one guy sleep in my room, and the other's going to be camped out on the couch. They're fine, they're good guys," Hailey quickly reassured her.

"I'm in my home, my space. It's fine," Cressida said. "We do have the occasional male customer come into the bookstore, you know."

"When customers come in," Hailey muttered, worry for her sister and the stress of the day making her irritable. "I just don't want you to be scared, you know, because there are strangers."

"That's not how agoraphobia works, necessarily," Cressida said, her voice prim. "Don't worry, I'm okay."

"I'll hustle them out of here early tomorrow, I promise," Hailey said, feeling guilty. "I just couldn't think of where else to bring them."

"Are they in some kind of trouble?"

"Sort of." She sighed. So much for hiding it. She should probably explain who it was. "Remember when you asked when I'd bring Jack Reese home to meet you guys?"

Now Cressida's eyes opened wide. "Shut. Up!"

"I know."

"You had *better* not hustle him out of the house!" Cressida said, leaping up and grabbing Hailey's arm, hopping a little, like a kid. "Can I ask questions? Can I totally fangirl squee and get spoilers?"

"Okay, *no*," Hailey said, laughing.

"And who's the other guy? Miles? Simon?" Cressida was practically dancing with excitement.

"Actually, that's Jake's bodyguard."

"No shit. Better and better!" Cressida did a little shimmy. "This is so cool!"

"Shh!" Hailey looked out the door, but Jake was already in her room, with the door mostly closed. "I'm just going to get Jake settled, then I'm going to sleep in here on your floor. That okay?"

Cressida's eyebrows went higher. "*Shut up*, part two."

"I'm serious."

"Shut up, part three: *the revenge*." Cressida started giggling.

"I am not having sex in this house," Hailey said sharply, then abruptly wondered if her voice carried. It wasn't like the walls were that thick. "I mean it."

"Whatever helps you sleep at night," Cressida said, with an eye roll. "Sure, if you want to come in, go ahead. I'll have blankets and the foam roll-out if you want to use it. But if you don't, that's fine, too."

"Thanks," Hailey said, then gave Cressida a hug. "We'll talk tomorrow, okay?"

"Bet your ass," Cressida said, grinning.

· ❤ · ❤ · ❤ · ❤ · ❤ ·

Jake was wearing a pair of shorts and a T-shirt, out of respect . . . he normally slept in the world's rattiest boxers, but he found himself strangely self-conscious. He was still aching from their kiss earlier, and where he'd hoped it would lead. He felt badly about everything that had transpired since, though, and wasn't going to push his luck.

There was also the little fact that he was now *in her bedroom*. He didn't feel badly enough about what had happened to pass up this gem of an opportunity.

He wanted her, without question. But he found himself wanting to know more about her as a person, whether he got to have sex with her or not.

He looked around the room. It was small, even compared to his hotel room. It was painted a rich pumpkin orange. The bed was full sized, and the bed frame was beat-up pine, but the bedding looked cool—lots of swirling colors, dark and mysterious and sort of like an Indian bazaar.

On the walls, she had posters of punk rockers and pinups surrounding her: Bettie Page, Dita Von Teese. Siouxsie Sioux with Robert Smith from The Cure, hiding a mischievous smile. The posters were taped up, pastiche-style, like a big collage. There were also postcards: masks from Carnival in Venice, pictures of Montmartre and the Moulin Rouge in Paris. The demon-catcher image from *Supernatural*, and quotes from *Firefly*.

"'May have been the losing side,'" Jake read aloud, "'Still not convinced it was the wrong one.'"

God, he liked this girl.

The real focal point of the room was the clothes, though. The closet doors had been removed. The clothes weren't jammed in or anything, but there were a lot of them, obviously well cared for and in perfect order, which was more than could be said for the small "writing desk" thing that seemed more like a catchall for paper and pocket change and various detritus of the day.

The bedroom door opened, and he looked up. Then he stopped thinking, and breathing, for a long second.

Her hair was down, still wet from the shower. It spilled in maple ribbons over her shoulders, still wavy from the curls she'd kept it contained in earlier. Her face was naked, making her look younger, more vulnerable. Her full lips were a dusky raspberry color, naturally, and her indigo eyes were huge.

"Settled in all right?" she asked. "I'm going to go crash on my sister's floor tonight. I've got Vic set up on the couch. I just wanted to, um, make sure you were okay, and talk about how we're going to handle things tomorrow. Then I'll go to bed."

"I'm fine," he said. "Are you sure you're okay?"

"I'm tired," she said. "But otherwise, sure, I'm swell."

"I really am sorry, Hailey. About everything."

She smirked. "First a family emergency, then a stalker. It's like the universe is saying, 'Don't have sex,' you know?"

His whole body gave an emphatic *no* in response to that statement.

"Maybe it's just making us wait so we'll appreciate it more when it actually happens," he said softly. Because he felt in his soul that it *would* happen, force majeure be damned.

He watched a flush crawl up her naked face, and just a second of hunger in her gaze. She cleared her throat. "I'll try to get up early so we can get you to the con for your first panel and to deal with . . . you know, all of that . . ." she said, with a vague wave of her hand. "All that" being the stalker issue, and security, he assumed.

He stretched out on the bed. "I like your room."

She stiffened, stepping closer. "You didn't snoop, did you?"

"No, I didn't snoop," he said, smirking. "But now I'm going to want to, you realize. Because obviously there's something snoop-worthy."

She grimaced, coming in and closing the door. "Keep it down, will you? My sisters are trying to sleep." She growled, stepping closer. "And really, the only things you're going to find are a few sex toys, and maybe some candy bars. So don't even."

He stretched out, and felt something under his head . . . under the pillow. "Oh, really? Sex toys, you say?" he asked, reaching under.

He didn't even see her coming. She flew onto the bed, effectively tackling him. "That's nothing you need to see," she growled, snatching it away. But not before he could see what she held.

It was a notebook. "You keep a diary?" he asked, surprised.

"No," she mumbled, stowing it under the bed. "I mean, yeah. It's a journal. Kind of."

"Thought you were a hell of a liar," he teased, fascinated by seeing her truly flustered for the first time. "What is this really?"

She bit her full lower lip. "Story ideas," she finally muttered.

He blinked, then smiled. "You're a writer!"

"No," she protested. "Well . . . not really."

She was stretched out next to him, he realized . . . wearing a nightgown that clung to her curves. He felt his body tighten and forced himself to think about alien autopsies until he could get himself under control. She'd made it clear: no sex tonight.

There would be other nights, he comforted himself. Tonight was a fact-finding mission. He wanted to know everything he could about one Hailey Frost.

"What do you write? And when did you get started?"

She propped her head up on one elbow. "I like sci-fi and fantasy," she said. "When I was younger, I thought up stories all the time—it's a part of the con, or at least that's what I was taught. You make a simple story, you nail the details, and you believe it so hard that it doesn't feel like a lie."

He nodded, mirroring her pose so he was looking into her face. Without her makeup, she looked vulnerable. Still beautiful, obviously. But also open.

"When I moved up here, Grandma Frost had all these books. I hadn't been that big of a reader, but I couldn't earn TV time until I'd read for an hour. And when I was grounded—which was often—reading was all she'd let me do. I got hooked before I knew it." Her smile was gentle as she reminisced. "Then I found myself thinking of characters I'd play, if I were in a world like that. It sort of grew from there. I've never finished a whole book. I've barely completed a few short stories—don't have the time. And I've never shown anyone what I write."

"Maybe you'll let me read something of yours one day," he ventured.

She shot him a skeptical glance, some of her smartass armor coming back. "Really? You're a reader?"

He felt stung, but played up an exaggerated expression of offense. "Hey! Don't let the hot bod fool you. There's a mind up here."

"You read sci-fi and fantasy, I mean?" She looked intrigued.

He nodded. "I'm a huge fan."

"Sure you are," she said. "What are your favorite books, then?"

"I really like the Kingkiller series by Patrick Rothfuss," he said, muttering, "and it'd be really great if he could, I don't know, get to the third book."

He was gratified when she beamed at him. "I know, right? He said he wrote all three of them, that it was just a matter of revising . . ."

"And if that was the case . . . jeez, man, why take so long?"

"I know!" She was laughing softly. "I mean, I don't want to push—like Neil Gaiman would say, the man isn't my bitch or anything—but I am *dying* to find out what happens."

He smiled. "Is the fact that your family owns a bookstore the reason behind why you love reading?"

She shook her head. "The bookstore's pretty new. We've only had it for a few years. We set it up after Grandma Frost died. It's a way we could make some income for my sister Cressida. It's hard for her to find a job."

Cressida—the one with the agoraphobia. "But the bookstore's having trouble."

"Rachel—my older sister—she's the one who says we should pivot, make it more . . . niche, or whatever." She sighed, propping her head up on one arm. "That's why I came to you."

"And here I thought it was because of my underwear model bod."

"That was just a perk." She nudged him with her shoulder.

"I'm sorry you guys have had it so rough," he said, and was surprised by her bitter chuckle.

"If you think that's rough . . . oh, my sweet summer child," she said, her voice laughing, but her eyes warm and sad at the same time. "You've lived a lucky life."

"I have," he admitted.

They were lying there, not touching, just staring at each other. It was unnaturally quiet in the house—winter quiet, snowfall quiet, even though it wasn't that cold out. It was like they were the only two people on Earth.

"I wasn't planning on becoming an actor," he heard himself say. "I thought I'd be—don't laugh—a park ranger."

She laughed anyway. "A *park ranger*?"

"What? I like nature. I like hiking," he murmured, smiling back at her and turning onto his back. She nuzzled against him, resting her head in the curve of his neck. She was pressed against him, but he didn't want to scare her away. "I could probably do okay on that *Alone* show—you know, the one where they drop people off in the middle of nowhere with just a camera, and then see how long they survive. I could probably make it a good month or so."

He felt more than heard her chuckles, as she shook gently against him. "Okay, Nature Boy. What happened?"

"There was this girl."

She laughed harder. "There's *always* a girl."

He stroked a lock of hair out of her face, then stroked her shoulder, softly, tentatively, seeing if she was okay with it. She made a soft sound of pleasure.

"She was in the drama club, and they were doing *Romeo and Juliet,* and there was talk of a lot of kissing. I wasn't quite the brawny guy you see before you," he added. "And what I didn't know about girls could and probably did fill volumes. So I went for the play."

"And you got to make out with her, and thus the acting bug bit," she summarized, her fingertips absently tracing patterns on his chest and stomach, light and fluttery.

"Actually, no," he said. "She wound up hooking up with the lead, who knew quite a bit more than I did. And I'd committed to being Mercutio, which had a lot of talking and was really hard. But I liked it. Which was weird."

She lifted her head, looking into his eyes. "Then what?"

"I told my mom. I wanted her to come see me," he said. "She used to be a makeup artist in Hollywood, working with actors. That was before I was born, and before she'd moved to San Diego. Anyway, I thought she'd be proud."

"Was she?"

"She slapped me."

"She what?" Hailey's hand jerked against him. "Why?"

"You have to keep in mind: I didn't know who my father was," Jake said. "That's why I don't go by Jake Windlass. She was still pretty pissed at him. He'd been having an affair with her while he was married to his last wife, and having affairs with a bunch of other people, as well. She didn't even put his name on the birth certificate."

Hailey was quiet, thoughtful. The tracing fingers continued.

He sighed. "Anyway, after all that, she moved out of L. A., even though she was a decent makeup artist and was building up a clientele and a solid reputation. She told me that she didn't want that life for me. She apologized for slapping me, though," he added. "She never hit me otherwise."

"So you did the play," Hailey prompted.

He took a deep breath, feeling almost high on her scent—spice, night-blooming jasmine, the sexy scent that was pure Hailey. "I did the play," he echoed. "And yeah, I was bit by the acting bug. I wound up joining the drama club, and working with my high school teacher on monologues and stuff. Then I turned sixteen. I was working out a little more—that was for girls, not acting—and eating everything that wasn't nailed down. And then I turned into . . ." He gestured at himself.

Hailey rolled over, resting her chin on his chest so she could grin at him. "Bet Juliet regretted not making out with you then, huh?"

"Don't worry. We made up for it," he said, grinning back. "For a while, girls eclipsed any acting aspirations. But I still wanted to give it a try. My mom was still leery, so I took a ride with a friend and went to an audition in LA. The casting director took one look at me, and freaked. Then, apparently, called my father, saying that I was a dead ringer." He was quiet a minute, remembering. "Dad called me that week, came down to San Diego and visited. From there, he started . . . well, butting into my acting life."

She looked somber. "What about the rest of your life?"

"There is no non-acting life when it comes to Kurt Windlass," Jake said. "I'm not . . . bitter, or at least I'm trying not to be. But my dad's whole life is acting, being a successful actor. When he found out about me . . ."

"He didn't *know* about you?"

"My mom never told him."

He'd never told anybody about this. Not his friends, not girlfriends . . . nobody. Why he was telling Hailey—a professed con artist, for God's sake, somebody he might not even see again after this week—baffled him. Maybe it was the anonymity. Maybe it was just foolishness.

Whatever it was, it felt right.

"Anyway, from then on, he took an interest. He immediately claimed me, and strongly condemned my mother for not letting him know. I would've kicked his ass for it," he said, "but he gave her a ton of money to keep quiet, and he explained: it was for publicity. Otherwise, it would lash back on my career. My mom told me to go along with it."

"That's why you hate lying," Hailey said softly. "Why you hate publicity that's set up."

He nodded. "Probably. It definitely factored in. For the past nine years, he's tried pulling strings. He's the one who got me my agent. He hired the publicist—the one I mentioned before."

"Sounds like he's genuinely interested in making your career a success," she said, but her tone was careful—like she wanted to say something else. Her eyes were a little bit suspicious.

Jake stroked her petal-soft cheek. "He only has daughters."

"Sorry?"

"I have six half-sisters," Jake said. "And I'm his doppelganger. That was the thing that got the casting agent's attention, all those years ago. I was the spitting image of my dad."

"Oh." Hailey nodded. "Hence the interest. You're Mini-Kurt."

Jake blew out a breath. "Basically, I guess."

"Sorry," Hailey repeated. "It sucks. But at least he cares, in maybe a narcissistic way."

"He plays the part," Jake said, and it was like the floodgates of bitterness opened. "He plays the caring, gruff, hardass father, the one who knows what's best for me. When he was with my mom, he played the attentive lover. He plays for the paparazzi. He plays for studio heads. I don't even know if there's a real person behind all the angles anymore. And that's what he wants me to turn into."

Hailey watched him, thoughtfully. She pressed a kiss against his chin. "He doesn't know what he's missing," she said softly.

It warmed him, more than anything else she could've said. "Sometimes, he accuses me of picking the sci-fi projects and TV shows just to rebel against him, to choose a different way. Hell, I don't even think he's wrong. I don't want to pick movie roles because they're going to move me up the ladder. I don't need a ton of money, I do fine. I just want to do stuff I enjoy, and still have time for a life of my own, you know? I don't want to become fake."

"Like him."

"Like him," Jake agreed. "He's sold his soul to Hollywood, and now, it's all he cares about. The next acting gig. Moving up to director. Staying on the list of the most powerful people in Hollywood. I don't want to be like that."

He stroked her back, hugging her, snuggling her to him. Just taking comfort in her warmth and her presence and her listening.

"So . . . what were you doing when you were fifteen?" he joked, trying to shift the conversation.

"Going to juvie."

He dropped his smirk immediately. She'd mentioned juvie before. He held his breath, not wanting to do anything that might distract her or have her pull back self-consciously.

"My mom died when I was seven," she said, almost like she was bored—something that the almost anxious look in her eyes belied. "I got popped into the foster system, because nobody knew if she had any family anywhere. I didn't even know I had any living relatives. I was lucky enough to get placed with a couple on the grift. That's where I learned conning."

She gave him a little wobbling smile. He put both arms around her, stroking her back.

"They'd been really good, once upon a time. They were in their fifties. Frank was a big deal in the eighties, running long cons on coked-up businessmen. Abigail was this hourglass Amazon who used to be the best pickpocket on the West Coast. But after years of hard partying, and the recession in the nineties, then Abigail started getting arthritis . . . they were in a bad patch. So they got me."

Jake felt his stomach turn to frozen lead. "To . . . sell?"

"What? No. God, no," she said, and he started breathing again, warmth slowly seeping back into his system. "I was their distraction. Lost kid, giving her a chance to pick purses. That kind of thing. When I turned out to be good with cards, they would sometimes take me to poker games to show off—again, while Abigail cleaned them out while they were busy watching me." She paused. "You know, she's the one that got me into dressing the way I do. That's how she dressed when we worked a con. I always thought she looked like a badass."

"She dressed like that?" he asked, surprised enough to interrupt. "But it's so . . . obvious!"

She grinned. "That's the idea. Memorable. But a character," she pointed out. "When we went out as normal people, she looked completely different. Nobody knew what she really looked like, and they certainly didn't connect her with police descriptions."

"So it was a disguise," he mused.

Suddenly, it occurred to him: that's why she wore it. It was distraction. No one knew who the real Hailey was. And it made her feel like a badass: strong, undefeatable.

It was armor.

"They sound like they cared about you," he said instead.

"In their own way," she acknowledged. "But I knew the score, too. I was there till I turned eleven. Frank had tried this check scheme that went bad, so they had to run. They left me behind, so I got popped back into the system."

He must've made a sound, because she looked at him, shaking her head.

"I still ran a few things as I got shuffled to more houses, more families, even a group home at one point."

"Why did you keep moving?"

"The usual. I'd run away if things looked too sketchy, or they were too restrictive," she said, her voice casual . . . at odds with the bleakness she was painting. "One family actually put a lock on the fridge, so we couldn't eat without permission. We were hungry all the time, and they had like four fosters. It was grim. They kicked me out when I got picked up by the cops—I was trying to run the 'I need money to get home' grift, but I was still too young, and I couldn't get away before some concerned Samaritan called child protective services. Anyway, when I was fourteen, I met Cressida. We were both fostered in the same house, with the same monster."

Jake felt his blood run cold. Hailey's expression didn't change. She might've been telling him about a TV show she'd watched.

"Anyway—he hit us. Locked Cress in a closet, which was ironic, since small spaces are the only places she felt safe," Hailey said. "Cressida was supposed to be home-schooled because of the agoraphobia. I can't tell you her story, but actually, as fucked up as it got, the guy was actually a step up from when she was a kid. It became pretty obvious that he wanted to keep Cressida—like, past when she turned eighteen. He saw her as a cross between a slave and a pet. Cressida was the first person I trusted without reservation. She was my sister in all the ways that counted. And when I saw what was going to happen to her . . ."

Now, Hailey's eyes blazed like a butane torch.

"I wasn't going to let it."

Jake clutched her involuntarily. "That was what you were talking about, at the hotel. Facing somebody with a weapon."

"One night, he was drunk. Angry, because Cressida had dropped a fifth of bourbon and he was out. He came at her with the broken bottle. I got between them."

Jake held his breath.

"He passed out drunk before he could do anything worse. But it cemented it—we had to get out. We needed a lot of money in a hurry, so we could not only get out, but stay out of the system altogether. So I tried doing a big con."

"And you got busted?"

She nodded, then rubbed her cheek against him. "It was bad. I was a mess. Turns out the rich people I tried to fleece did a full background search on me. They knew more about me than I did." She chuckled mirthlessly. "But something happened. They found my grandmother—and she found me."

"Was Grandma Frost your real grandmother?" he asked.

She smiled. "Yes. The first adult that really looked out for me," she said. "She took me in, no questions. Got the lawyer that helped reduce my sentence and get my record sealed. And when I freaked out and told her I couldn't leave Cressida, she figured out how to take Cressida with us."

He pressed a tiny kiss against her temple, grateful for her grandmother—and for the stroke of luck that brought her, and her sister, to this place.

"And the rest is history," Hailey finished. "This is home."

She yawned again, her voice turning to a whisper.

"I'll do whatever I have to, to keep her here. To stay here."

And just like that, she was asleep.

He sighed, pushing another rogue curl away from her face. In sleep, without the harsh edge of her attitude animating it, her face was unguarded, gentle . . . tired.

How long had she been exhausted, working two jobs? Worrying about the bookstore, and her sisters?

He pulled the blanket out from under him, folding it over her like a taco. Then he threw on sweatpants and stretched out next to her.

She turned him on, but there was just so much more to her. He wanted to know all of it.

If she'll let me.

He ought to be more focused on the contract. Susie was emailing PDFs of scripts for movies and shows he should audition for. She was pushing, telling him to focus on his career. It made no sense that he was sticking with this one series, pulling out all the stops. And it definitely made no sense that he was fixating on a coffee shop waitress/blackjack dealer that he probably wouldn't see again once he left the convention.

His chest hurt.

It didn't have to make sense, he thought, stretching out next to Hailey and putting a gentle arm around her waist, pressing a soft kiss to her forehead. He was here, now, and he'd make the most of it.

CHAPTER 8

Hailey woke up in a rush. Light was coming in—she'd pulled the blinds, but hadn't closed the black-out curtains, she realized. Beyond that, though, something was just wrong. It took her a minute to figure out what, though.

She was in her room. That wasn't unusual. But she realized she should *not* have been in her room. She was supposed to be in Cressida's room, on Cressida's floor. Not . . .

Oh, fuck. She'd fallen asleep. Here. With *him*.

Jake.

Which brought up wrong, number two: *where the hell was Jake?*

She bolted up out of bed and headed out the door. The bathroom was empty. What the hell time was it? And where the hell was he? Had he left?

It might be better if he left, actually. She couldn't remember anything about actually falling asleep with him the night before. They'd been talking about things she never talked about with anyone outside of her family, not even the close friends she'd made. It was strangely intimate. Most of the guys she hooked up with . . . well, it wasn't like there was a lot of conversation going on there, beyond logistics and things like "more," "harder," or "my leg is cramping, switch positions."

Last night, she may have snuggled with Jake, just a little, smelling his clean, masculine scent, enjoying his body heat, listening to the low rumble of his voice. Was it any wonder she'd fallen asleep, surrounded by that kind of hypnotic comfort?

She heard voices coming from downstairs. Male voices. Jake was still here. Must be talking to the bodyguard.

She knocked on Cressida's door, thinking to warn her that their guests were up. Also, she wanted to explain about not showing up the night before.

And that she hadn't slept with Jake.

Well, she had, but it was only sleep.

God, Hailey, you are a mess. Get it together!

"Cress?" she said quietly, knocking again. She realized Cress might've had a hard time sleeping with strangers in the house—she might still be asleep, with headphones on. Better to let her sleep.

She headed downstairs, peeking. Nobody in the store. There were sheets neatly folded on the couch. She thought she heard argumentative voices. Was that Jake's voice rising? And . . . Cressida?

She bolted before she even thought about it.

"Are you kidding?" Jake said, hooting. "That movie is terrible. Seriously. It's like one of the worst movies in the history of bad movies."

"That's what makes it so good!" Cressida said. She wasn't angry, Hailey realized. She was giving as good as she got—and they were talking about entertainment. "Back me up, Hales. Tell this heathen that *Buckaroo Banzai* is a classic for a reason."

"John Parker, baby," Hailey responded immediately. "And Yoyodyne."

"But it sucks," Jake said, with baffled laughter.

Hailey rolled her eyes. "See? This is why you have no geek cred." She high-fived Cressida, feeling relief flood through her.

The bodyguard was sitting there, looking long-suffering but vigilant. He had an unnerving intensity. Probably why he was a bodyguard, she thought. Then she realized her own state of dishevelment. "I, um, ought to go get changed."

"Yeah, maybe you should," Jake said, although he didn't really look like he minded, either. His gaze on her was warm.

She motioned to Cressida, who followed her. "Sorry about last night," Hailey said, feeling embarrassed.

Cressida just looked amused. "What happened?"

"We were talking, and I guess I just fell asleep."

Cressida's eyes widened. "Really? That's it?"

"Yeah."

"You just . . . *slept* with him," Cressida repeated slowly.

"I guess I was more tired than I thought."

"And you were okay with that."

"I don't always have to have sex with a guy, you know," Hailey said, feeling a little stung. "I mean, he's hot, but I don't bring sex home. There was no way I was getting my freak on in Grandma Frost's house."

"No, I didn't think you would," Cressida said, worrying at her lip with her teeth. "But you kind of trust this guy, huh?"

"What? No!" That hit Hailey like a slap out of nowhere. "I don't even . . . I barely know him."

"You brought him home," Cressida pointed out.

"He didn't have anywhere else to go," Hailey argued, even though some part of her thought that they could've figured something else out.

"You trust him," Cressida repeated. "That's not a bad thing, trusting people. Trusting men."

Now Hailey goggled. Cressida, who trusted nearly no one? Really?

"I want you to be happy," Cressida said, connecting the dots for her. "I just . . . I don't want you to get hurt, is all."

Hailey's jaw dropped. "I'm not falling in love with the guy, for God's sake," she said. "I don't believe in instalove in books, movies, and certainly not in my own damned personal life. This is . . . it's a business transaction, basically."

"Come on, this is me you're talking to," Cressida said, rolling her eyes. "Don't con me."

"I would never con you."

Cressida crossed her arms. "Then don't con yourself."

Hailey huffed. "Whatever. I need to get ready. We have to get back to the *Mystics* convention."

"You're not working at the coffee shop?"

"No," Hailey said, feeling the pang of getting fired again. "I'm supposed to spend all day with Jake. We made good progress with his Q Score yesterday, I think. Or at least with his rep among the viewers."

Cressida was still staring at her.

"Cress, I love you, but stay off my ass, okay?"

Cressida sighed. "Okay. I will."

With that, Hailey headed for her room to get changed. Rachel came downstairs in a rush. "What's all the hubbub? I overslept. I'm going to be late," she said.

"Um, we've got people downstairs," Hailey said.

"Yeah. Hailey brought Jake Reese and his bodyguard home last night," Cressida added, with a smile.

Rachel smiled absently. "Sure she did," she said over her shoulder, putting a pair of earrings in as she headed downstairs.

Cressida looked at Hailey. "Wait for it. Three, two . . ."

There was a startled yelp. "*Oh, my God, you're Jake Reese!*" they heard Rachel say.

They high-fived again. If nothing else, it was worth it to have Jake stay over just for that.

· ♥ · ♥ · ♥ · ♥ · ♥ ·

Hailey felt imprisoned. Constrained, at the very least. Vic was a subtly badass third wheel, scouting the area intently, like a Terminator that resembled Tom Hardy. She was only alone when she went to the bathroom, it seemed.

Jake was able to either ignore or at least deal with Vic easily. "My dad has bodyguards," was his explanation.

"Yeah, well, I can imagine wanting to kill your dad, too," she muttered back, and he chuckled.

It was the last day of the convention: the day they'd pay off the con they'd been running. She'd been handing out flyers the past few days, and Jake had managed to score her space on the goodies table for a sign. It had helped somewhat, but it wasn't the game-changer Frost Fandoms desperately needed—not yet, anyway. She ought to be all business, helping him figure out how to sell the pitch: sweet and warm, just supporting his embarrassed "girlfriend" by mentioning her family's bookstore. She ought to have him practice.

The problem: she was swirling in a tidal wave of conflicting emotions, and she was scared she was starting to buy the hype.

223

CATHY YARDLEY

She enjoyed the atmosphere of the convention, and since they'd gotten rid of Pocket-Ripper, she'd loved the people they met. There was a feeling of camaraderie, of family. Like no matter who you were outside of the convention—an accountant, a stripper, a college student, a mom of six—in here, you fit in. You had the same love. There was no judgment. You were all *Mystics*. She liked that.

Now, she was looking at everyone as potentially some-one who would slash up furniture. A coward. A terror.

And then there was the sheer, compulsive draw that Jake presented. The kind that had her share a bed with him *and* share her stories, without sharing her body. She liked spending time with him, joking with him, talking to him. Her body craved his like chocolate.

He's leaving. This is fake, remember?

"C'mon," Jake said. "We've got one more panel today, with Simon and Miles."

That was also weird. She felt like she knew Jake, at this point, but Simon and Miles were unknown quantities, other than her tidbits of fangirl knowledge.

They walked into the green room. She fist-bumped Rico the bouncer/security guard guy as she walked in.

"You okay?" Rico asked, stopping her briefly. "Heard about the room. Don't worry, we've got our eyes out. Nothing's going to happen to you guys."

"Bet your ass," she said, and he grinned. "Thanks, though."

Jake smiled, nodding at the guy, and they headed in. Simon was there, telling a story to Miles.

"Hey," Miles said immediately, as soon as he saw them enter. "Are you two all right? The convention organizers gave us a heads-up."

Simon, usually jovial, also looked serious. "We heard what happened to your room—the knife work, the message," he said, shaking his head. "That is seriously fucked up."

"It was creepy," Jake admitted, giving one of those man half-hugs to Miles and then Simon in turn. "That's probably as far as it'll go though."

"Well, everybody's on high alert," Simon said, scowling. "Where you'd wind up crashing? You could've bunked with us, man."

Hailey was looking at Jake's face, so she figured maybe she was the only one who noticed how surprised—and touched—Jake seemed to be by the offer. He nodded brusquely to hide it, then flicked his chin toward Hailey. "Thankfully, Hailey let me, um, spend the night at her house."

"Oh, really?" Simon looked over at her. "Hailey. We met earlier. How are you holding up?"

They really were nice, she thought. "Hanging in there," she said. "We had Vic, after all."

They all glanced at the bodyguard, who stood casually off to one side, a cross between a Secret Service agent and a piece of furniture.

"He looks badass," Simon said.

"Don't talk about him like he's not there," Miles said in a low voice, rolling his eyes.

"Okay." Simon leaned back, addressing Vic directly. "Dude. You look like a badass."

Vic nodded.

"See? Badass," Simon said to them, gesturing to his proof. Miles shook his head in disbelief.

"He is a badass, actually," Hailey admitted. "You should've seen him drop these guys at the casino who were giving us a hard time."

"The casino in Snoqualmie? What were you guys doing there?"

"I work there," Hailey said. "Blackjack dealer."

"Shut up," Simon said. "Really? That's awesome. Why didn't you stay at the casino's resort? I hear it's nice."

"We were going to stay in the hotel," she explained, her eyes glinting. "It sort of . . . fell through."

"Fell through?" Miles asked.

She looked at Jake, who was staring at the ceiling, but still nodded. "I was working a late shift."

"This guy was hitting on her, being a total disrespectful, drunk asshole," Jake interjected.

"So Jake punched him," she said cheerfully. He sighed.

"He deserved it."

"And we all got kicked out," she continued. "It's been booked solid pretty much everywhere, and by then, it was midnight. And then Vic came. The drunk guy and his friend were waiting for us in the parking lot . . ."

"I could've taken them," Jake pointed out.

"But Vic was there, and he was like a frickin' mixed martial artist. I haven't seen anything like it, and I've known guys who could handle themselves in a fight."

They looked at Vic again for a second. Vic didn't look at them, but she could see a very tiny grin ghosting across his face.

"So, what are you doing later?" Miles asked. "Where are you staying, I mean? The convention's over tonight. You're not driving back to Vancouver afterward, are you?"

Hailey tensed. That hadn't even occurred to her.

What about their deal?

He hadn't heard from his agent, so she hadn't fulfilled her end of the bargain. So why should he help her?

She thought about falling asleep with him last night, after they'd talked. Just talked.

"I'm staying around tonight," he said, and she felt her shoulders drop a little in relief. "I'm going to stay at this lodge by the falls."

"Salish Lodge? Nice," Simon said. "Swanky. Did you know they used it in *Twin Peaks*?"

"I heard," Jake said, putting his arm around Hailey's shoulders. "Anyway, I don't want to leave Hailey alone until this stalker stuff's settled."

Hailey frowned. Did he have to make it sound like a chore, an obligation? "I'm staying at the Salish Lodge?"

"We could stay at your place again," he teased, nuzzling her neck. "But I don't think it's fair to have Vic bunk on one of those small love seats of yours, do you?"

"I suppose I can force myself," she joked back, feeling a little uncomfortable. "But you'll owe me."

He laughed, then straightened. "That actually reminds me. What are you guys doing tomorrow night?"

"We were planning on staying one more night," Miles said. "Then maybe hanging out in Seattle, hitting Pike's Place and doing touristy stuff or something."

"There are a couple of old haunts I wanted to show off," Simon said, with a grin.

"Think you could do a special appearance with me, instead?"

Hailey held her breath.

Simon looked at Miles, who shrugged. "Sure, I guess. What'd you have in mind?"

Jake smiled broadly. "How do you feel about bookstores?"

"Love 'em," Miles said immediately, warming Hailey's heart.

"They're okay," Simon said. "I read mostly on my phone, though, to be honest."

"Hailey and her sisters have a bookstore that's struggling," Jake said. "I'm doing an impromptu special appearance promotion tomorrow. I'm getting a bunch of memorabilia signed, too. It'd help if you guys could make it. All three of us . . . that'd be a hell of a thing."

Miles looked at Hailey, then nodded. "Helping an indie? Sure. I'm in."

Simon shifted the weight on his feet uncomfortably. "This is in Snoqualmie, isn't it?"

She nodded. "But you don't have to . . ."

"It's not that I don't like bookstores, or that I don't want to help you," Simon said, and to her surprise, he looked embarrassed . . . and guilty. "But I, erm, don't go to Snoqualmie."

"It's fine," she assured him. "Really. You guys don't have to do anything for me. I mean, you don't know me, or my family. There . . ." She fought to figure out the right way to say the words. "It's . . . there's . . ."

"There's nothing in it for you," Jake said for her. "But I'd consider it a personal favor."

Miles shrugged. "You had me at 'bookstore.'"

Hailey felt her heart warm. She gave Miles a quick hug. "Thanks," she said, giving him a peck on the cheek. He smiled back.

"Well, shit, now I feel bad," Simon grumbled. "I'll go."

She smiled. "Thanks, Simon."

"Where's my kiss?"

Laughing, she kissed and hugged him, too.

"I like her," Simon said to Jake, over her shoulder.

Jake wrapped his arm around her waist, tugging her to him, his smile warm, his eyes heated. "I like her, too," he said, nuzzling her neck. Just like he would've if he was her boyfriend, she thought. At least, she assumed.

229

And she felt herself melt against him, letting him hold her, talking with Simon and Miles as if it were the most natural thing in the world.

She cared about him. She felt more comfortable with him than she could remember being with anyone—any man, especially—outside of her family.

A helper came in. "Excuse me, gentlemen. The panel's starting."

They nodded. Jake turned to the guys. "Give me a second, I'll be right in," he said. They walked off toward the door, and Jake turned to her. "Stay with Vic, okay?"

"You didn't have to do the bookstore thing," she said. "I haven't helped you get your contract renewed yet."

He smiled, and stroked her cheek. She curved her face into the palm of his hand before she realized what she was doing.

"I'm doing it because I like you," he breathed. "Because you're awesome, and your family's awesome, and I want to help. Okay?"

She nodded.

He kissed her again, ignoring the helper's throat clearing and "We need you now, Mr. Reese" announcement. When he pulled away, his eyes were gleaming.

"See you soon," he said.

Her heart was beating so hard, she was surprised he couldn't hear it. She simply nodded, watching him walk away.

God, she thought, feeling overwhelmed. He was help-ing her. He was helping the bookstore. He was helping her sisters, she thought, as she heard him announce the appearance from the panel stage.

She owed him so much.

She wanted more. She wanted everything he had to give.

And that scared the hell out of her.

· ❤ · ❤ · ❤ · ❤ · ❤ ·

Jake wasn't sure how Rachel had managed to get all that *Mystics* memorabilia, but he, Miles, and Simon had duti-fully signed everything put in front of them. He'd made the impromptu announcement at the panel yesterday afternoon, and people had been excited. Well, maybe not the promoter, but the fans had been. Now, the place was probably a fire hazard, there were so many bodies crushed in there.

Vic wasn't thrilled, either, now that he thought about it. He was hovering by Jake and Hailey, who he forced to stay in proximity.

"I can't believe this many people came," Hailey said, for the fifth time.

"This store is adorable!" a fan said, coming up to Jake for an autograph. "How long have you two been togeth-er?"

"Not long enough," Jake said.

"Feels like forever," Hailey said, holding his hand. He struggled not to grin as she stared at him pointedly. He knew that part of that was because he was forcing her to stay safe. But the thought of someone doing anything to her—his shoulders tightened.

Not going to happen, he thought. Not ever.

He wasn't sure how she'd gotten past his defenses so quickly and so completely, but he cared about her. He wouldn't have wanted anyone to be hurt because of his actions, or because of him. But the thought of Hailey being hurt by anybody, for any reason, was enough to make him unhinged.

How could he care about someone so damned fast?

A bubbly, chubby, curvy blonde in a huge gray sweater and jeans came up, putting out more stuff. "We're selling cookies and stuff, too," the girl said to Hailey, giving her a hug. "How're you holding up? Need a coffee?" Then she winked. "Something stronger?"

"Nah, I'm okay. Thanks, Kyla," Hailey said, hugging her back. "How are you doing?"

"I sold three paintings." Kyla beamed. "And the T-shirts, the ones with the *Mystics* designs, are selling like hot-cakes. We're doing great!"

"Oh, that's fantastic!"

"All for the Frost Fund," she said, and then shook her head when Hailey's expression fell. "Oh, don't you start. You are family, sweetie. I've loved you and Rachel and

Cress like sisters for almost a decade now, so you're just going to suck it up."

"Yes, Kyla," Hailey said, squirming.

Kyla laughed, her face beaming. When she smiled, she looked like a movie star, Jake thought, slightly stunned. He was even more stunned when she gave him a hug.

"And you," she said. "Thank you! This is helping out so much."

"No problem at all."

"And you're taking care of our girl," she said with a contented smile. "That's nice. She deserves a good guy to take care of her."

"Hey! I take care of myself," Hailey protested. Kyla waved it away with a hand gesture.

"Since she's family, I'll tell you the same thing I tell all the guys who date family," Kyla said, her smile sweet as cotton candy. "Treat her right, and I'll love you like family, too."

He smiled at her. "Thanks."

She leaned a little closer. "Hurt her, and things . . . will not go so well. Just sayin'."

He was surprised, pulling back. But she still had that bubbly, happy smile. She even waved at Vic as she walked by. Vic, smart man, watched her carefully.

"Did she just threaten me?" he asked Hailey quietly.

Hailey was snickering to herself. "Um, yeah. She's protective."

He glanced at her. "Should I be nervous?"

"Do you watch *The Walking Dead*?" she answered. When he nodded, she smirked. "You know Carol? How she seems all sweet, baking casseroles and cookies and stuff, and then she kills like a platoon of guys all by herself? That's our Kyla."

He let out a low whistle. "Okay. Well. That's something to consider."

His cell phone vibrated. He glanced at the screen. "Shit. That's Susie. I have to take this."

She nodded. "Of course."

He headed to the kitchen, staying in sight of Vic, who glowered at him. "Susie? What's going on?"

"It's crazy!" Susie said. "Your Q Score is through the stratosphere, kiddo. First, those crazy videos of you dancing so horribly? They went viral!"

He groaned, rubbing his eyes. "Of course they did."

"But what really pushed you over the top were the stalker photos," she continued, surprising him. "The pics of your torn-up hotel room? They got on TMZ. You're getting on news—not just fan sites, actual *news*. They think they've got a suspect, by the way, and they're bringing her in now."

He leaned against the wall, feeling relief course through him. "Oh, thank God."

"I'd still keep the bodyguard for a bit, to be safe, but you're probably in the clear. Besides, you might want to kick that Hailey girl some money. She's a sympathetic figure—normal, fangirl, everywoman type."

"Yeah?" He glanced back into the crowded main room. Simon, for an inexplicable reason, had Miles in a head-lock. The fans were chattering and laughing, hanging out, looking like they were having a great time. And Cressida was manning the register with an expression of grateful ecstasy.

It was a good day, he realized, feeling better than he had in months.

"So, since my Q Score . . ."

"Is through the fucking roof," Susie said, with a raspy chuckle. "It's been like Christmas. We have serious movie offers. One from Bernardo Vacquero. You know him?"

She didn't wait for him to respond.

"He's only the hottest auteur on the planet right now—he did that Oscar winner last year, the indie that made huge box office numbers. Remember? The one about the guy who talked to machines and stuff?"

Jake made an indiscriminate noise. He didn't really re-member.

"Well, the lead of his latest film just dropped out. Drugs, something, I don't know. But it means that Bernardo's in the lurch, and he wants you to come down and take over!"

Jake stood, stunned.

"Lead in an Oscar-winner's film, Jake! With full studio backing!" Susie sounded like she was going to pee herself.

"Maybe I can fit it in on hiatus," Jake said, feeling more relief. That ought to please his dad. Lord knows, Kurt put a lot of faith in that gold statue.

That seemed to bring Susie up short. "You don't get it. The guy needs you *now*, Jake."

Jake frowned. "How long's the shoot? You know we're supposed to go back into production for the show in a few months."

There was silence on the other end of the line. "You . . . are you kidding?"

"No, I'm not," Jake said, grinning as Simon told the story about when the three of them were fishing in Vancouver, and Miles caught . . . well, Jake's line. Hailey was laughing along.

He was happy here, he thought. With these people. These fans. This show.

"I was hoping you'd have heard," he said. "Contract deadline should've been tonight. When can we find out about the contract for *Mystics*?"

Susie sighed. "I thought you'd be happier about this. It's a big break, Jake."

Jake felt a tiny sting of guilt, but held his ground. "I want this show, Susie." And everything that went with it.

Including the fact that Vancouver was only four hours from Snoqualmie.

"I'll do what I can," Susie said, still sounding disgruntled. "And I'll call you the minute I find out. But I can't promise anything."

"Text me the minute you find out," Jake said. "Please. And thanks, Susie, for everything."

"I just want what's best for you," Susie said. "But you want to give some thought to your future."

Jake hung up. Then he looked around. He liked the store. He liked Hailey's friends.

He really, really liked Hailey.

Give some thought to your future.

He was, he realized. And he saw *Mystics*, and Hailey, in it.

*

CHAPTER 9

Hailey couldn't believe how well the promotion had gone. Most of the merchandise they'd pulled together had sold, as had a bunch of books and Kyla's creations. She assumed that meant they had some much-needed breathing room. But the real revelation had been the guys. Jake had been amazing, schmoozing with people, charming them. Simon had been his usual gregarious self, and Miles had made everyone crack up with his dry wit. The stalker hadn't shown up. Cressida had been radiant.

It was one of the best nights of her life.

"Thanks so much for coming by," Rachel said to the guys, after the last fan had been escorted out and the CLOSED sign put up.

"No problem," Miles said, obviously a little smitten with Rachel. Not a big shock there, Hailey thought, hiding a smirk. Rachel was stunning. Most people were smitten with her. Simon had been staring at her all night, it seemed.

"Are you sure we've never met before?" Simon pressed. Rachel laughed gently, even as Hailey rolled her eyes.

"Really, dude? That's the best line you can come up with?" Hailey called out.

"It's not a line," he protested, and to her shock, he looked dead serious. "I swear, I've met her before. Somewhere."

"I really can't imagine where. Or when," Rachel said. "Did you ever hang out down here, at Mount Si?"

"Not really."

Rachel frowned, thinking, then turned a touch paler. "You didn't . . . did you know someone named Ren?" She paused. "Ren Chu?"

Hailey stopped smirking. Ren, the guy Rachel had been in love with. The guy who, ten years later, she *still* hadn't moved on from.

"Nope," Simon said, not realizing the import, and pain, Rachel was holding with that one name.

Kyla must've noticed, too, because she popped in. "You went to a private school, right? You didn't go to Mount Si High with us."

"I didn't really make it over here much."

"Private school . . ." Kyla mused. "Hey, did you know Mallory, maybe?"

Hailey was watching his face, and she saw the look of shock cross it. "Mallory Prince?" he said, and his voice *shook*.

"Yes!" Kyla smiled brightly.

"I . . . yeah. We knew each other," he stammered. She'd never seen him tongue-tied.

Well, this is interesting.

"Mallory's a friend of ours," Rachel said. "I've known her since high school."

"She was going to try to make it tonight," Kyla added. "But she got caught up with some client work. She said she might try to stop by after, though."

Rachel tapped her chin. "So, maybe we met . . ."

"That'd be it," Simon said quickly, before she could finish. He looked at his watch. "Hey, it was great meeting you guys, glad I could help. Good luck with the bookstore!"

With that, he vanished out the door. Miles shook his head, distributing hugs all around.

"Sorry," Miles said. "Snoqualmie makes him squirrelly, I have no idea why. If you need anything else signed, or anything, let me know, okay?"

"Thanks," Hailey said.

Rachel and Cressida went to the kitchen with Kyla, cleaning up. Vic exchanged a look with Jake, nodded, then went outside.

"So we're allowed to be alone now?" Hailey said, warming to the idea—alone with Jake, finally.

"The stalker's been arrested."

"Really?" She felt almost dizzy with relief. "Thank God!"

Then she realized: no stalker, no reason to stick around.

She swallowed hard. "Does that mean . . ." She cleared her throat roughly. "So are you leaving?"

"Not tonight," he said.

"Did you hear back from your agent?"

"Still waiting," Jake said, putting his hands in his pockets, looking at her seriously. "We've done everything we can. And I can't thank you enough. Even if I don't get my contract renewed, you've helped me more than you know. I'm getting all kinds of attention, new roles. Susie—my agent—is pretty stoked."

"That's great," she said weakly.

Where does that leave us?

He squared his shoulders, took his hands out of his pockets, and reached out, pulling her to him.

"Come with me," he said. "Spend the night. The deal's behind us, there's nothing between us but *us*. Spend the night with me."

It was like lighting dry kindling. She went up in a blaze. She leaned forward, kissing him with all the passion she'd been saving up. All the wanting, all the yearning.

"Yes," she breathed against his mouth. "Oh, God, yes."

He swept her up off her feet, and she laughed.

Cressida came out, smiling gently. "You two are off, I take it?"

"I'll have her home by morning," he said, nuzzling her. "Probably."

"I need . . ."

"You won't need anything," he said, eyes blazing.

He was right. They had everything they needed. And she'd waited long enough.

· ❤ · ❤ · ❤ · ❤ · ❤ ·

It was maybe ten minutes from Hailey's house to the lodge on the waterfall, but to Jake, it felt like ten hours.

After all of the waiting, and the bullshit, he'd finally be with Hailey. It seemed fated: after their first near encounter, then striking the fake relationship bargain, he'd had the weirdest week of his life with this woman. She was . . . there weren't words for how he was feeling.

All he knew was that he wanted to be with her.

He didn't believe in love at first sight. And he hadn't fallen in love with her—when he'd first seen her. But damn if he didn't feel strongly about her now.

Don't label it. Don't overthink it, he counseled himself, as he checked in and grabbed the key card, taking her to his room.

The door closed behind them. They had a balcony. It was too foggy to see the falls, but he could hear the roar of it outside. The force of it, the great rushing volume, felt like his bloodstream roaring in his ears. He turned to

Hailey, staring at her like she was fresh water and he'd been trapped in a desert for years.

She was wearing a dress today, midnight violet-blue, just about matching her eyes. Something with a flouncy skirt and a tight, fitted top. He wanted to rip it off her, but got the feeling she'd kick his ass if he did.

He grinned at the thought. She was formidable. He kind of loved that about her.

She smiled back. "Feels like it took us forever to get here," she said. "I don't know if I should jump you or search the room for stalkers or paparazzi or something."

"Nobody here but us," he assured her, stroking her cheek, like he had when they'd slept next to each other in her room. "Hailey . . ."

She kissed him. It wasn't the hot, frantic kissing they'd indulged in that night at the casino. It was . . . sweet. Tremulous.

"You have done more for me in a week than most people I've known in my whole life," she said. "I'll never forget it."

He gripped her arms. "I don't want you doing this—doing anything—because you feel gratitude."

Her eyes flashed, and she nudged him, hard, until he landed butt first on the bed.

"I feel grateful," she said. "But I'm not sleeping with you because of it. I'm sleeping with you because I want you. More than I've ever wanted anyone in my life, damn it."

Her disgruntled tone would've been funny, had it not been for the equally sharp desire, riding him like a damned jockey with a whip. "I know exactly how you feel."

Her deep violet eyes clouded. "I doubt that," she murmured, unfastening the tiny buttons, opening her bodice. "I can't get a grip on my feelings. I've never been like this."

"Me neither," he said, and tugged off his shirt in a fluid motion. "You're special, Hailey. Amazing. You're—"

"Shh," she said. Now that the dress was undone, she pulled it over her head, tossing it to the ground. She was wearing navy-blue panties and underwear, and looked like a stormy goddess. She smiled, those brick-red lips pillowy and pouting. "No more talking. Just . . . have me."

She reached behind her, undoing the bra, taking it off. Her breasts were amazing, more than a handful. His breathing went shallow. She shimmied out of her panties as well, then stretched out. Actually stretched, arching her back slightly.

His mouth went bone dry. God, he wanted her.

He stripped out of his pants and boxers, socks and shoes, desire making his hands clumsy. Her eyes followed his every motion, and she licked her lips, just the tiniest bit. It shot through him like an arrow.

Now he stretched out next to her, feeling her soft skin stroking against his own. She felt like hot satin. She writhed slightly, brushing against him. Her nipples were pebbled, hard and erect. Her breathing was shallow, too. He stroked his hands down her, cupping her breasts, feeling the span of her waist. He kissed where his hands had been, following the trail they'd traced. Then he reached down, between her thighs, parting the soft curls there.

She gasped, her hips jolting, arching beneath him. She was already wet. He sucked gently on her breasts as his fingers found her clit and pressed, gently at first, then flickering his fingers on either side of it.

Her corresponding cry of pleasure was louder, and she pushed her hips against him insistently.

He leaned down, kissing her stomach, kissing lower. She smelled delicious.

"Jake," she said, her eyes hazy and unfocused. "Wait . . ."

"Let me," he breathed against her mound, pressing hot kisses. "Please."

She watched him, wary. Then he saw her nod, and lean back, throwing an arm over her face.

He dove in, licking the top of her slit, working his way lower until he tasted her. She tasted like spice and sweetness, and God, he wanted her.

She cried out, her thighs tightening on either side of his face. He groaned, flicking her tight bud with his tongue, sucking gently but with gradual insistence. Then nibbling, ever so carefully, with his teeth.

"Jake, Jake," she moaned. "Oh, my God." She was panting hard, her head thrashing back and forth.

He pressed harder, sucking, circling, drinking her in. Then, as she was shaking beneath him, he pressed a finger inside her.

She was so fucking tight, he thought, as the orgasm hit her. His cock twitched hard, dying to dive into her, to feel her clench around him. She was incredibly responsive, and a pleasure to touch, to taste, her jasmine scent going to his head like some kind of drug. But it was so much more than her body. He *knew* her, and everything about her—her strength, her heart, her passion, her loyalty—seemed to be imbued in her every physical detail.

She was so fucking *perfect*, and he wanted all of her.

He wiped his mouth, moving up on top of her. She was hiding her face from him, so he licked one nipple, then the other, until she giggled, moving her arm. Her eyes were dilated. She looked shocked.

"I've never done that with anyone before," she said.

He felt strangely proud that he'd given her something no one else had, that she'd trusted him enough to let him do so. "Why not?"

She shrugged, hiding her face again.

"Too intimate," she finally said. He saw the blush covering her neck, her chest.

It was intimate. He wanted it to be intimate. He wanted to be intimate with her.

"How about you?"

His cock was all for it. But he didn't want a blowjob, not right then, because he didn't want to wait. "I just want to be inside you," he said. Close to her. He wanted to feel like a part of her.

She sighed, reaching for him.

He grunted and reached for a condom he'd dropped on the bed, tearing the foil, rolling it on. He positioned himself between her legs, his cock aching, straining. He stroked the broad head against the nub he'd just sucked, flicking at the bundle of nerves with a sure motion. The sensation made him groan and shudder.

She cradled him, her legs spreading. She arched her back, resting on her elbows. "Jake, *please*."

He entered her with one long, slow, deep movement. Then shuddered again. "Hailey," he groaned. "God*damn*, Hailey."

She whimpered, and shimmied her hips. The swirling, clutching movement nearly made his eyes cross.

She wrapped her legs around his, bringing him taut against her. "Go deeper," she said. "Give me everything you've got."

He was helpless to deny her. He withdrew, then drove himself deeper. Hearing her mewling gasp of pleasure drove him wild.

"Yes," she breathed, her hips pushing against his. "Yes."

He withdrew and plunged, again and again, while she angled her hips and met his every thrust. He lifted one of her legs, balancing it against his shoulder so he could go even deeper.

She grabbed one of his hands, putting it against her breast. He squeezed, gently. She tightened around him, and he thought he'd die from the pleasure of it.

It was like lighting a fuse of dynamite. He bucked against her. She was panting, grasping at the sheets, grasping at his hips. Her pussy gripped him mercilessly, and he pounded into her as she gasped and sighed and panted.

"Jake . . . oh, God, Jake, I'm so close . . ."

He was close, too. He was losing his grip. He wanted to draw it out, make it last as long as he could.

"Come with me," she whispered.

He felt her rolling, rippling release, and he couldn't have stopped if a gun was to his head.

"Hailey," he yelled, the orgasm shooting through him like a shotgun blast. "*Hailey*!"

They shuddered against each other, their hips spasming. It was like they'd blurred into each other, fusing. He wanted to feel this close to her forever.

He released her leg. "That was way too fast," he rasped, a bit embarrassed. He kissed her, hard, then took care of the condom, tossing it out in the bathroom. He felt weak, but also exhilarated, as he came back to bed, spooning her and nuzzling her neck. Their lovemaking had been white-hot, an explosion of passion. Now, curling up against her, feeling her soft skin and her heat and the way her breathing slowed, felt more like slipping into a perfect hot tub—comforting and encompassing.

"That's okay," she said, her eyes glowing with humor. "You'll make it up to me. Next time."

He smiled, then kissed her. He lingered, nibbling her lips. Licking her throat, softly. Pressing hot, tiny kisses along her jawline. Nipping at her earlobe.

She sighed. "You're good at that."

He was momentarily swamped with overwhelming emotion. "I could do that to you forever." He breathed against her, wishing more than anything for the opportunity to do just that.

"Would you want to?" she asked in a tiny voice, then threw her arm over her face again. "Gah. Never mind. Don't answer that."

He moved her arm. She looked embarrassed . . . and hopeful.

"What if I said yes?" he whispered back.

She kissed him . . . slow, and long.

"I don't know," she said. "But tonight . . . I'd believe you."

He kissed her. Then whispered again, against her lips.

"Yes, Hailey," he said. "Forever."

· ❤ · ❤ · ❤ · ❤ · ❤ ·

The next morning, Hailey was still reeling from the night she'd spent with Jake. She should be exhausted, but she felt strangely energized. Or maybe she was just afraid to go to sleep—afraid to lose any moment with this man.

It wasn't just the sex, she realized, as she watched him sleep. Like a creeper, she thought, with a bemused smile.

She'd never watched a guy sleep before.

In all the time they'd been together, he'd been thoughtful. Protective, even, she thought as she remembered his insistence on staying together after the stalker kerfuffle. But he'd still let her be her. He'd accepted her, rather than trying to get her to change her looks or her behavior or her beliefs.

She'd never had boyfriends, never wanted them. She was devoted to her family, to her own well-being. But with Jake—there was something else there. She didn't want him to be hurt. She wanted him to have what *he* wanted.

It scared the hell out of her.

She was closer to him, emotionally, than she'd ever been to any man, ever. She wasn't sure what that meant, what she should do about it.

Just have sex, she told herself, and she smoothed her hands down his back, watching his lips curve into a smile.

"You giving me a massage?" he said, his voice sleepy-rough and sexy. "I could use it. Damned woman, you wrung me out."

"You loved it," she said, feeling a shiver of apprehension.

Loved it.

He rolled over, kissing her. They'd only made love an hour before, but she wanted to again.

Wait. *Making love*? She frowned as she processed the thought.

She chastised her subconscious. Still, she couldn't call it something crude, a term that she would've used with any of the other guys she'd fucked and forgotten. It was so much more than just sleeping together, or having sex. She hadn't understood that before.

She'd opened up to him, trusted him, cared about him.

They'd been acrobatic, crazed. Now, after hours and lack of sleep, he was languid about it. He kissed her, like he could kiss her for days. He touched her like he was worshipping her.

She returned the favor, tasting him, savoring him. She reached over, getting a condom, teasing them both as she slowly rolled it over his length. Then she eased herself over him, fitting him to her. Glided over him with a sigh.

It was like waves against a beach, she thought, as they slowly moved together, ebbing and flowing, until the building sensual pressure made their breathing uneven, their bodies less graceful, more desperate. The orgasm caught her unaware, leaving her shuddering helplessly around him. His cock answered with its own release, pulsing inside her with frantic thrusts.

She collapsed against him, breathing hard. And kissed his chest, just above his heart, so softly that she doubted he'd notice.

He tugged her up, kissing her thoroughly. "Hailey . . . I . . ."

He looked confused, overwhelmed.

She knew just how he felt.

His phone buzzed, and he looked at her with regret.

"Welcome to the real world," she said, rolling off of him. "Go ahead. You should get that."

He picked up his phone. "It's a text," he said. "From Susie."

Her body felt cold without him warming her. She tugged the blanket around her. "What's the news?"

He tensed. Then looked at her, his eyes unbelievably cold.

"They . . . I didn't get my contract picked up," he said, sounding as stunned as he looked. "They're either replacing me or writing me out. Either way, I'm not part of *Mystics* anymore."

She felt the pain that he was showing. She hugged him gently. "I'm sorry. I'm so sorry," she said. "I know how much it meant to you."

He held her tight, and in that minute, she fiercely wanted to scream at those stupid producers. Or beat the shit out of them. Yeah, that sounded better. Anything to punish them for putting that look of pain in her man.

She stopped dead in her mental tracks.

Her man.

"What are you going to do now?" she heard herself ask, even as she steeled herself for the response. "Go back to L.A., or San Diego, I guess?"

He was quiet.

"I'm sorry," she said. "I wasn't able to help you at all, and you tried so hard. So *damned* hard."

"That's not true," he said quickly, his blue eyes cutting to hers, reproving her. "You helped me more than you know. My agent's gotten all kinds of offers since you helped boost my Q Score."

She should've felt happier about that, she realized. But she felt like a failure.

"In fact—there's a movie offer. For Bernardo . . . I forget the guy's last name. He won the Oscar last year."

"Oh, I know that guy!" Hailey said. "He's really hot right now, right?"

"So she says," he answered. "Anyway, the leading man for his latest production dropped out, and he wants me to step in. It'd be a lead role in a major film."

"That's fantastic," she said, hugging him hard. "That's wonderful."

He was still quiet. "It's in South America. Brazil."

She stilled against him. "Oh."

"I think it's a three-month shoot." He squeezed tighter. "And I'd have to leave immediately. Like, tomorrow."

"So soon?" she asked in a tiny, weak voice.

So that was it. That was all.

She was losing him.

He pulled away from her, so he could look into her eyes. She tried to get her shit together, so she didn't look so damned pathetic. She knew this arrangement between them was temporary. Feelings be damned, she *knew* this was just a bounce. A transaction. A short-term gig.

A con.

He kissed her. "I don't know what's going to happen after this," he said. "But I know one thing. You and I aren't done."

She couldn't help it. She smiled.

"That's why I want you to come to Brazil with me."

CHAPTER 10

Jake held his breath. Hailey was staring at him like she'd had an aneurysm, her mouth working wordlessly.

"You okay?" he finally asked.

"Brazil?" she repeated. "The country?"

He laughed. "Rio de Janeiro. Carnival. The big Jesus statue." He chucked her chin. "That place with the parrots from the cartoon movie."

She didn't laugh back. "What am I . . . I mean . . . how long?"

"For as long as you can," he said. "Shooting would be for at least three months."

She goggled.

"I want you with me," he said.

"Why?"

He laughed. "Oh, I can think of a few dozen reasons," he drawled, stroking her skin.

"One would be better," he thought he heard her say, under her breath. Before he could ask, she pulled away. "You can get sex from lots of women."

He frowned. He'd freaked her out, he could tell. Why, though? Yeah, it was fast, and it was unexpected. But she wasn't the type to be afraid of anything.

"Yeah, I can," he said. "And I've had sex with a lot of other people. So have you. I don't judge you for that, and I'd expect you not to judge me."

"I'm not," she said, her tone frustrated. "I'm just saying—you don't need to bring me with you for just sex." She smiled weakly. "They've got women in Brazil, I imagine."

"There are no women like you."

She was breathing, quick and shallow, and her pupils dilated. It was like passion—but it wasn't, he knew. It was fear, pure and simple.

"I can't be gone that long," she said.

"I'll fly you in as often as you want," he said. "It's kind of a long flight for just a weekend, but damn it, I'll take you any way I can get you."

"You've known me for just a week," she said, her voice reedy, completely unlike her usual husky, rich tones. "This is sort of ridiculous."

"I know," he said. "Ride with it."

"I . . ." She shook her head. "The sex is great."

He waited. "But . . . ?"

"You can have it when you come back," she said, her expression turning stubborn. "If you come back."

"If?" It hit him like an open-handed bitch slap. "I've never asked anybody . . . I'm taking you to a whole other *country*." Hell, when he'd had a girlfriend, it'd always been understood: he had his work, she usually had hers. He could go months without seeing someone he was in a relationship with, with the crazy meshing schedules of actors.

Hailey wasn't like that—didn't have that problem. And even if she was the next Jennifer Lawrence, he'd do whatever he could to keep her by his side.

"Yeah, you've got tons of money," she said, her voice a little bitter. "And this is a great opportunity . . . *for you*. If you want to get ahead as an actor, boost your career, I think you should take it."

That made him frown, for a different reason. It was something his father would say—only nicer.

She nodded, as if she'd made a decision. "I want you to take it."

He was still stinging from not getting the *Mystics* renewal. He was heartbroken, he admitted to himself.

Having Hailey with him would cushion the blow, he realized. Was that the real reason he wanted her there?

Don't try to make this reasonable, a little voice inside him scolded, insistent, just this side of clawing desperation. *This isn't about reason. You want this girl. You are crazy about her.*

Do not let her go.

"We'll figure it out. We'll wing it," he said quickly, as persuasively as possible. "We'll hang out on beaches. You could be topless."

She shook her head. "Tempting as that sounds . . ."

"We'll have sex in a plane," he said, his voice low, like a crossroad demon offering the bargain of her life. "In five-star hotels. In a tent on a beach, under the stars. Anything you want, any way you want. Just as long as I can have you."

"What do you want with me, though?" She shook her head. "What will people think?"

"That we're incredibly lucky?"

She smiled at that, but her eyes—she wasn't there. Not yet. "You want me to be an international fuck-buddy?"

"Do you really give a fuck what other people think?"

That seemed to bring her up short. "And who's going to look out for Cressida while I'm gone?"

He grimaced. He'd forgotten her family. "I can make sure you get back if she needs you," he said, trying to gloss over the trickiness of those kinds of logistics.

"That would be hours. Maybe days," she said, not falling for his salesmanship. "That'd be too long, especially if it's an emergency."

"She's a grown woman," he bit out.

"With a serious illness."

"And you're not her mother."

It was the wrong thing to say. He knew it as soon as the words left his mouth.

She pulled the blanket tighter around her. "She's family," she ground out. She got off the bed, heading for the bathroom.

"I didn't mean it," he said. "Not that way."

"You'll say anything," she shot back. "Just so you can keep fucking me. Is that it?"

"It's more than that," he said, his hand on the door frame of the bathroom. She washed her face, splashing cold water on herself, then pulled on the dress that she'd discarded on the floor the night before. "Don't try to reduce what we've got . . ."

"What have we got?" Her voice was impassioned and sharp. "A week? We don't even know each other."

"But we will."

"We have fucking," she said. "And a guy who's used to getting what he wants."

"We have a woman who I care a lot about," he said. "Who is scared enough to hide behind her sick sister to prevent herself from being vulnerable."

Her eyes went wide. He saw tears glisten there, and felt guilt crush him like a boulder.

But he meant it.

"We're done here," she said. And turned toward the door.

He felt his heart breaking.

"I'll call you a cab," he said.

"Don't bother," she said, and stalked out like she had that first night—never looking back.

· ♥ · ♥ · ♥ · ♥ · ♥ ·

Hailey had managed to keep it together until she got back home. Thankfully, she'd managed to make it past Cressida's room without Cressida waking up. She thought she heard Rachel moving around in her room, but Hailey slipped into her room almost silently, then collapsed onto her bed.

The tears started, and didn't stop. She cried, silently, hugging the pillow to her, stifling any sobs in it.

How can I hurt this much?

It was her own fault. She'd let herself get too close. This wasn't how she operated, for damn good reason. Lots of women would think she was crazy for passing up on a guy like Jake: rich, handsome, the best sex of her not inconsiderable experience. What the hell was her problem?

It would only get worse. She already felt addicted to him. Out of control with it.

She didn't want to get hooked on anything she couldn't keep.

You're hiding behind your sick sister.

Now, that accusation pissed her off. Still, she was thankful for it, since it underlined exactly what was wrong with the whole offer. She thought he just wanted sex, fun—stuff she wanted, too. If he'd simply said, "Let's hook up when I'm back in the area," she would've kept the door open for him. But he wanted to cart her off, keep everything on his terms—have her at his beck and call, without thinking about what was most important to her. It wasn't just a fun spur-of-the-moment fling anymore. It was . . . well, she wasn't sure *what* the hell it was, but it wasn't what she'd signed up for.

You don't need him, she convinced herself. Or tried to.

She changed into her rattiest sweats and comfiest T-shirt and crawled under her covers. After an hour, she fell into a fitful sleep. She might've slept until the next day—except she heard a loud, *really* loud, squeal coming from Rachel's room.

She was out of her bed like she'd been shot from a catapult, grabbing the baseball bat she kept by her bed. She sprinted up the stairs, throwing open the door.

She didn't see anything wrong, she processed as she choked up on the bat's handle, surveying for any threat. Rachel was just standing there with papers in her hand, laughing like an asylum inmate.

"Who? What? Who?" Hailey spluttered. "Rache, what the hell?"

Rachel laughed. "We did it. Two months, baby. Two whole months. And that's net!"

"What?" Hailey repeated, still looking around for unseen assailants. "What the hell are you talking about? I got, like, no sleep last night . . ."

"I'll bet," Rachel said, her voice still shot through with joy. "I'm talking about the sale. We sold all the books, and the extra stuff—"

"Wait," Hailey said, holding up a hand. "What extra stuff?"

"I got a bunch of memorabilia from the convention, and the guys signed it, along with some of the Mystics tie-in books I grabbed. We're sold out of everything." Rachel looked like she was going to explode, doing a little bouncing, spinning dance. "*Everything*!"

"And we made enough money to pay rent for two months?"

"Net!" Rachel repeated. She was wearing her work clothes. Hailey remembered absently that it was a Monday. Not that she had any job to go to, herself, Hailey thought. "I got up early to balance the books. We're doing better than I'd hoped. We've got to keep momentum up, but I think pivoting the business, shifting focus from used books to fandoms, is just the boost we needed."

Rachel's smile was incandescent. Hailey walked over, hugging her.

"Thank you, Hailey," Rachel said, hugging tighter before letting her go. "There's no way we could've done this without the guys' help. Tell Jake thank you from me."

"Sure," Hailey said, feeling a stab in the chest, thinking of Jake.

Rachel was too happy to notice her reticence. She supposed she ought to tell Rachel that they'd . . . what? Broken up? That the ruse was over?

Hailey shut down mulishly. Rachel would figure it out. Eventually.

"I'm going to grab some coffee and get to the office," Rachel said. "Where are you today?"

Hailey frowned. "Nowhere today. But I'm going to look for a new job, something to replace the coffee shop income."

Rachel's bright expression dimmed somewhat. "Soon, you won't have to work two jobs," she said. "We'll pull this around. I swear it."

Hailey shrugged. Truth be told, she'd rather be busy today. Maybe she'd help at the bookstore, and they were sure to have some spillover clients from the convention and yesterday's promo. If not, she might finally clean out the freezer. It spoke volumes about her state of mind that she was willing to scrub.

Rachel gave her another quick hug, then bolted for the kitchen. Hailey headed down the stairs to her own room more slowly. Now that she was awake—and frightened into wakefulness, at that—there was no way she was easily going back to sleep.

Cressida peeked her head out of her bedroom. "Everything okay?" For as long as Hailey had known her, Cressida was a perpetually light sleeper.

With damn good reason.

"Everything's fine. The bookstore's netted two months because of the sale." Hailey felt her heart ease, just a little, from the look of relief on Cressida's face. "So there's that."

But Cressida was more attuned to Hailey than Rachel was, and her eyes narrowed, scanning Hailey like an X-ray.

"What did you do?" she asked finally, her voice low and suspicious.

"I didn't do anything." Hailey crossed her arms.

"Get in here," Cressida said, dragging her in and shutting the door. "That bullshit might work on Rachel, but we've known each other too long. What happened?" She paused, then her blue eyes sparked. "Did Jake do something to hurt you?"

"No!"

Cressida's eyes glinted dangerously. "I will call Kyla," she said. "And Mallory, and Tessa. I will activate the whole damned phone tree."

"He didn't hurt me deliberately," Hailey amended. "And nothing physical."

But yeah, he did something. And yeah, she was hurting.

Worse, she did what she always did when she felt frightened and hurt. She hurt him back.

"We just didn't work out," Hailey finished, her voice quiet.

"Spill." Cressida sat on her bed, looking surprisingly fierce in her fleece pajamas.

Hailey sighed. "I didn't hold up my end of the bargain. He got canned from the show."

"Aw, shit." Cressida's expression softened. "I'm sorry, that sucks. I know how badly he wanted it."

"Yeah," Hailey said. He'd been so disappointed. Crushed. She'd felt that for him, felt terribly for him. She wanted so badly to fix it, and so damned *helpless* that she couldn't. "Anyway, it's not all bad news, I guess. His agent said his phone's been ringing off the hook since our, you know, story. He's got another job offer." She swallowed. "A film."

"Well, that's good." Cressida rallied.

"There's this hot director that's doing a shoot in South America. Main actor fell through—he wants Jake." Hailey took a deep breath. "It means that he's going off to Brazil. Tomorrow, I guess."

"You guess?"

Hailey didn't meet Cressida's eyes directly, frantically looking around the room instead. "It wasn't . . . it was just a con, Cressida. Just an act, remember?" She was trying to remind herself, desperately, she realized. "I don't do long-term. I barely do repeats."

Cressida growled. "That is such *bullshit*, and you know it."

265

"I have issues," Hailey said. "Okay? It's not like I'm *un-aware* that I am emotionally fucked up, especially when it comes to relationships. I *get* it. So yeah, I might have panicked when he asked me to go to South America with him."

"It's a film shoot, not the end of the world," Cressida pointed out. "Long distance might suck, but he'd be worth it."

"I think the opportunity could be huge for him," Hailey said. "Can you imagine? He'd become a huge star. Doing movies all over the world, traveling all the time . . . various shoots, stuff like that. And he owns a place down in Los Angeles."

Cressida's eyes narrowed. "Jesus, you're not even going to give it a chance, are you?"

Hailey shut down. "This is home for me, Cress. You, and Rachel, and the bookstore. You're my North Star, my constant. I do whatever I have to, to keep you guys safe." Her chin shot up pugnaciously. "I don't walk away from that. And I'm sure as hell not going off with a guy who thinks I could."

"You're scared, is what you mean," Cressida accused.

"What if I am? Jesus, aren't I allowed to be a little scared?" Hailey couldn't help it. She shouted. She rarely shouted at Cress, but Cressida didn't usually poke this hard. "Why are you being such a hardass about this?"

"Because you've got a great guy who's in love with you!"

Hailey blanched. "He didn't . . . we've only known each other for, what, a week? Christ, this isn't a TV show." She rolled her eyes. "He doesn't know me, I don't know him . . ."

She paused. Actually, he knew her better than most people. She'd trusted him, shared with him—more than she'd shared with anyone outside of her family or their little circle of friends. And he'd told her things about his past. They'd shared a lot in that week.

"I'm not saying I wouldn't be interested in finding out more. Maybe," Hailey tempered. "But . . . there are so many problems. Too many. I'm just getting used to the idea of being in a relationship at all, and this is like diving into the deep end."

"Do you do things any other way?" Cressida asked with a little smile.

"I don't need someone else to take care of my shit." Hailey stood up, pacing across Cressida's plush rug, the one she'd hooked herself. It was the Tardis in the French countryside, done van Gogh style.

"Besides, the bookstore's only got two months' worth of rent, and we still have a lot of bills," Hailey said quickly. "God knows what other expenses might come up, and I've still got a lot of work to do. I'm not jetting off to wherever and losing my income. I'm not letting him pick up the tab for everything. I'm not getting a goddamned sugar daddy."

"No," Cressida agreed. "You wouldn't."

"So that's that. Does it hurt? Sure. But I'll survive."

Cressida was quiet for a minute.

"I'm gonna go back to bed," Hailey said, mentally going over the books she could read to try and distract herself, when Cressida's voice cut through.

"Please tell me you're not giving up Jake because of the store."

Hailey blinked. "I'm 'giving up' Jake because we won't work out," she corrected.

Cressida's pale skin was hectic with color. "And you think you won't work out because you're tethered here. With the house, with the bills." Her eyes were almost glowing with emotion. "You're stuck here because of *me*."

Hailey rubbed her hands over her face. "Please don't make my breakup about you. Okay?"

Cressida pulled back as if slapped. Hailey hadn't realized it was possible to feel worse than she had, but surprise! Now she did.

"I didn't mean that," she said, and realized she sounded just like Jake. "I'm sorry."

"I am not an infant. I'm sorry the agoraphobia is so damned debilitating. It's not like I haven't tried—"

"Do *not* do anything stupid like go outside again," Hailey said, too loudly, too sharp. "I mean it. I am not up to that shit today."

Cressida's eyes went wider, and filled with tears. "Out."

"Shit. Cress . . ."

"OUT!"

Hailey stepped out, turning. "I didn't mean it. I . . ."

"You are a control freak, Hailey Jessica Frost," Cressida said, her voice so low and cold it sounded frozen. "I am grateful to you and your family for taking care of me, but I fucking *hate* that you feel like you can hide from your bullshit issues because I'm sick."

With that, she slammed the door in Hailey's face.

We have a woman . . . who is scared enough to hide behind her sick sister to prevent herself from being vulnerable. Jake's words haunted her.

"FINE," Hailey yelled, and went to her own door, slamming it and then throwing herself down on her bed. She hadn't cried in years, as far as she could remember. She might've teared up at a television show or two, but really, that wasn't how she was wired. Now, hot, angry, heartbroken tears poured out of her like a faucet—the second time she'd wept that morning, and now she was weeping like a damned Disney princess.

She had too many emotions, and absolutely no idea what to do.

$\cdot \heartsuit \cdot \heartsuit \cdot \heartsuit \cdot \heartsuit \cdot \heartsuit \cdot$

After the blowup with Hailey, Jake caught a Lyft back from the lodge to the convention hotel, where the convention was finally shutting down, packing away memorabilia.

He ignored lingering convention-goers, and caught Miles and Simon as they were checking out.

"Hey, dude," Miles said. "Great event yesterday. Glad we were there."

"I really appreciate it," Jake said. They were good friends, with each other, he thought. They were good friends of his, he realized. He really, really wished that he could've done more with them, with the show. He was going to miss them. He had a lot of acquaintances, but not a lot of people he'd genuinely call *friends* . . . people he'd ask a favor of, like he had of them.

That shook him, a little.

"Want to grab breakfast?" Miles said, missing his little epiphany.

"I want to get the hell out of this town." Simon grunted. "But I could use some fuel first before going back to Vancouver. We're skipping Seattle and just heading back. Four-hour drive, ugh."

Jake swallowed against the lump in his throat. "Breakfast sounds good."

"Come on," Simon said, clapping a hand on his shoulder. "I know a place nearby that's pretty decent."

They went to a local joint in Issaquah and thankfully weren't recognized.

"So, here's to a first successful convention," Simon said, raising his coffee cup. "Fingers crossed, it's the first of many."

"I'd love to go twelve seasons or more, like *Supernatural*," Miles admitted. "I think *Mystics* has legs. The writing's solid, the story line is different, and the showrunner's great. And we've got some great stuff coming up next season, by the way. I think my magic gets bumped up."

"I thought I heard Sarah mentioning something like that," Simon said. Sarah was the head writer, Jake remembered. Simon then glanced at Jake. "I heard that they've got some good stuff lined up for you, too. Miles and I have been lobbying."

Jake took a deep breath, pushing the egg scramble around on his plate. "You heard wrong, buddy. They didn't renew my contract."

"What?" Miles said, eyes bugging out. He was loud enough to have several other diners staring at him. "That's crap! I know that they like you on this show."

"That has to be the stupidest decision I've ever heard of," Simon muttered darkly. "Seriously. This is bullshit."

Jake felt his chest warm for the first time since Hailey had shot him down and stormed out. "It's been that kind of week."

"And you're just going to take it?" Simon leaned forward. He was normally the jovial one, the devilish one. Now, he was stern, almost somber. "Damn it, Jake. You can't let them just . . ."

"Let them?" Jake repeated. "It's their fucking show. What am I supposed to do?"

"Fight for it!" Simon snapped back.

271

"I've fought for plenty," Jake said, thinking of Hailey—of how he'd tried everything, only to fail and push her away. "Did it ever occur to you that sometimes, you just *lose*?"

"Not when there's no good reason!" Simon pointed at him with his fork. "You're great for the show. They're finally figuring that out. If you let them cut you, you'll both regret it. Are you really going to just slink away, tail tucked between your legs?"

"What the hell do you want me to do?" Jake snarled. "Go up to the producers, get in their faces, demand that they sign me? What, because I'm such a big star?"

Simon didn't back down an inch. "I'm not saying be a dick, Jake. I'm saying find out what the hell's really going on, and figure out a way around it! You're not even going to *try* talking it out?"

"Guys, I'm serious, this can't be right," Miles interjected, before Jake could address Simon's caustic remark. "I was talking with the writing staff. They really, seriously want to work with you. We were talking about adding more jokes. You're funny," he said, in his forthright, gentle way.

Jake couldn't help but smile. "Well, the deal must've fallen through after they had that conversation."

Miles's eyes narrowed. "What, exactly, did your agent say about the deal falling through?"

Jake sighed. "That I wasn't a big enough name. That I wasn't the right direction for the . . ." He paused, what Miles said finally clicking. "Wait. You said that they were going to *expand* my part?"

"Sarah said it herself."

Miles was tight with the writing staff, Jake knew. He suspected Miles might want to be a writer, himself. But that went against what Susie had told him—that they didn't think he was a good fit for the show.

"If that's the case . . ." Jake frowned. "What the hell did change their mind? It wasn't like I was asking for more money. I jumped through fiery hoops to show them how badly I wanted to be on the show."

What happened?

"You could ask them yourself," Miles pointed out.

"What?"

"They're over in North Bend today. That's what Sarah told me, although I think that was supposed to be a secret. That's not far, is it, Simon?"

"It's totally not," Simon said, grinning. "It's like fifteen minutes away. Do you know where they are?"

"Sarah said they were talking with the mayor," Miles said, surprising Jake further. "Probably going to do something like scout locations for an episode or something. Let me text their admin, see where they are."

"So, Jake," Simon poked, "you gonna go handle this, or keep being a punk?"

Jake shot Simon the finger, causing him to laugh. He threw some money down on the table. "I'm going to go handle this."

"Atta boy," Simon said, then reached into his pocket. "Here, take my car. Remember: don't be a dick, but don't walk away until you figure out what the hell happened."

"And get back on the show!" Miles added.

Jake nodded. He had nothing to lose. This was what he really wanted—and it would put him four hours closer to Hailey. He'd been a punk there, as well: he respected her decision, but he wasn't going to give up on her that easily, either.

This was the future he'd seen. And both were worth fighting for.

CHAPTER 11

Hailey could tell Cressida was well and truly pissed. She didn't come down to work in the bookstore, texting Hailey—*texting*, from her damned bedroom, not even to saying it to her face!—that she wasn't feeling up to it. That she "couldn't handle it." And yes, she'd added quotes, as an added slap, referencing Hailey's treatment of her as an "infant." Hailey was hardly in the mood to deal with it, but she didn't have the coffee shop shift now, and the bookstore was getting customers in. Which meant that there she was, manning the register.

She was re-reading William Gibson's *Pattern Recognition* for probably the fiftieth time. They'd gotten a wave of people in from the con, people who would be leaving that day. They were disappointed that the memorabilia had all sold out. Some had bought sci-fi novels, some romance novels, and lots had added their names to the mailing list that Rachel had set up on their website.

Hailey was hardly an optimist—okay, she was *never* an optimist. But this looked good. It looked promising. The town's population was growing like crazy, with lots of fandom-hungry kids. Seattle and the surrounding areas had more conventions than you could shake a stick at: Sakura-Con, Emerald City Comicon, and a bunch of new ones every few months. If Frost Fandoms could bring in the business from those, and keep it going, then Cressida could stay here as long as she wanted. They could all stay as long as they wanted.

But was this what she wanted?

She frowned, putting her book down, choosing to straighten shelves instead. Cleaning, she realized—which meant she was stressed. She compulsively cleaned when she was anxious.

She was used to taking care of herself and taking care of Cressida. She'd expanded that to taking care of Rachel, too, even though Rachel was older. Rachel had been alone with Grandma Frost for years, when their mother had run off to L.A. and Grandma Frost had refused to let her take baby Rachel with her. Rachel had never known their mother, but she'd led a nice, sheltered life here in the small town instead. She didn't know how horrible life could be. Not like Hailey and Cressida did. So Hailey did what she could to shield them both. She made sure that there was enough money in the till. She devoted her life to her family.

Was she hiding behind it, though?

She frowned. Worse . . . did she love Cressida because Cressida was physically incapable of leaving her?

What kind of fucked-up psychosis was *that*?

She dusted, hunting down every speck like they were war criminals.

Was that why she'd spiked the relationship with Jake? Because he *could* leave—more than likely would leave—and she just couldn't risk it?

She'd never had a relationship, much less fallen in love. And for fuck's sake, it was just a week. Nobody fell in love in a week. That was Lifetime Christmas movie shit. It made you feel good, but it was a sugar rush.

It always left a crash.

"I'm not a fucking groupie," Hailey muttered to herself. At this rate, she might pull out their ancient vacuum. Or clean windows. Her skin felt like it was crawling.

Her mother had chased relationships, left Hailey alone to fend for herself. She'd left Rachel behind completely, for fuck's sake. Worse, her mother had blamed her groupie behavior and her man-junkie tendencies on the fact that Rachel's father was her one true love, the one she'd never gotten over. Why that meant she went out and found a bunch of men to take care of her after, Hailey had no idea.

Of course, that might be why she felt so strongly about being "taken care of" by a man. Any man.

Hailey sighed, closing her eyes, leaning her forehead against the wall.

I'm not doing this. She'd made her decision. All the armchair quarterbacking in the world wasn't going to bring Jake back from Brazil, and until she got her shit together, it was probably just as well.

"Hello? Anybody here?"

Hailey sighed, then turned, facing the questioner who'd just stepped in. "Yes, hi, we're open. Welcome to Frost Fandoms. Can I help you?"

The woman was very thin. Her skin was sallow. She weighed maybe a buck twenty, soaking wet, but was tall and thin, like a sapling. Her hair was white-blond, like corn silk, and her eyes were a faded denim blue-gray.

"You're Hailey, aren't you?" The words were just over a whisper, and slightly singsong. She didn't look straight at Hailey.

A few more people wandered in, wearing *Mystics* sweatshirts and laughing raucously. Hailey waved at them, then looked back at the woman. "Yes, I'm Hailey Frost. My sisters and I own this store. Looking for anything specifically?"

"Just you," the woman said. "I'm—"

'Hey, is there anything signed left?" one of the newcomers interrupted.

Her companion, a sunny-faced guy with a flamboyant bouffant and a rainbow scarf, winked. "Girl, tell me you've got autographed pictures."

"They all sold out," Hailey said. "We should be getting more in, though, and we've got lots of other fandom stuff."

Just like that, the visitors started snapping up tchotchkes and trinkets, and going through the books. Hailey felt a burst of relief, and gratitude, as she turned back to the thin woman. "Sorry. What can I do for you?"

The woman sighed. "Well," she said, and pulled out a knife. "I guess you could die. For starters."

· ♥ · ♥ · ♥ · ♥ · ♥ ·

Jake managed to track down the producers, Phil and Veronica, on the main drag of North Bend. It was brisk, but the sun was shining—they were scouting the location, pointing to various restaurants and shops and buildings. He'd rarely talked to them in the past, only during a wrap party or the season intro stuff. They were more hands-off than other producers. He walked up to them, trying to keep his anxiety and impatience in check.

Ask them why, he told himself. *Make your case. Get this done.*

Don't be a dick, he reminded himself, grinning as he thought of Simon. *But don't back down.*

CATHY YARDLEY

"Hi, Veronica, Phil," he said. "Your, um, admin said you'd be here."

They looked at him, their expressions puzzled. Phil held out his hand.

"It's great to see you, Jake," he said. "I have to say, we're sorry to see you go, but we understand that that's how things sometimes work out."

For a second, Jake was too shocked to respond. The hell? Was that Hollywood speak . . . like corporate speak? "We're going in a different direction" or "you're being downsized."

They fired *him*, and now they're sorry to see him go?

"I wanted to talk to you about that, actually," Jake said. "Why am I going? Precisely."

If they looked puzzled before, now they looked downright confused. Veronica started looking pissed. "We had this runaround with your agent already, Jake. We did everything we could."

"You did everything *you* could?" He couldn't help it: the bitterness came out. "I went out and boosted my Q Score. I did everything I could to fulfill my contractual obligations. I did everything I could. But apparently, that wasn't enough!"

He ran his fingers through his hair, fighting to keep it together.

"I don't know if you understand this, but I loved your show. I'm a huge sci-fi and fantasy fan," he admitted, feeling irritated when Phil grinned. "I was a geek in high school. I frickin' loved this shit. When I read the script, I had to push my agent to put me up for it. I work really hard, even when I know you guys just had me on there as eye candy and I didn't have as many lines . . ."

"You never said anything," Veronica protested. "We were trying to figure out how else to use you, but you never agreed to any discussions on your character!"

That stopped Jake up short. "Wait, what?"

"We would've talked to you directly, but your agent made it quite clear that you don't deal with producers, or writers. Everything went through her." Phil's look was one of dawning awareness. "What did she tell you about those meetings?"

"She didn't tell me anything," Jake said, feeling an icy pit in his stomach.

"We hired you because you did a good job with Rick, and we thought you could do more," Veronica said, more gently. "We offered as much money as the budget allowed, but your agent made it clear that you had other offers. She turned us down."

Susie.

Now that icy ball in his stomach was the size of a grapefruit. She'd lied to him. Tricked him.

Betrayed him.

"I told her I wanted to do the show, no matter what," Jake said, finally. "I'm just now hearing about all of this."

They looked at each other. Phil's grin widened.

"I thought you were going off to film some movie in South America," Veronica said carefully.

"My agent—my *ex-agent*," Jake corrected, "wants me to do that film, yeah. I haven't even signed the contract yet, though." He paused dramatically. "And I won't . . . if I can do the project I really want to do."

Phil gestured down the street, toward a nearby coffee shop. "Well now, let's go sit down, have a cup of coffee, and talk about that."

Jake felt a bubble of hope. "Yeah, let's talk about that."

· ♥ · ♥ · ♥ · ♥ · ♥ ·

"Excuse me?" Hailey said, straightening and taking a step back. Now that she was really paying attention, the woman had crazy coming off her like mall perfume.

Shit, shit, *shit*.

Rainbow Scarf guy and his Midwest friend were staring. She saw the guy take out his phone, and prayed for a quick second that he was calling 911 and not, say, taking a . . .

The flash on his phone went off. "Crap," he muttered to his friend. "I meant video. This should be good."

Because of course getting this on TikTok is more important than calling the cops. It'd be funny if she wasn't right in the middle of it.

She got a good look at the knife. It was a big, *Crocodile Dundee* survivalist thing. That said, the woman didn't look like she was that heavy—she probably couldn't drive that thing very far into a person's body. She could get some lucky slashes in, but it'd be just that—luck.

Of course, she's crazy, Hailey reminded herself, looking around quickly for a weapon of her own. That meant she was probably stronger than she looked.

Shit, shit, SHIT.

"Listen, if this is about me and Jake—we broke up," Hailey said quickly.

"He's Rick. And he's mine," Ghost Blonde said, moving forward slowly, the knife staying surprisingly steady considering it looked heavy and the woman's whole arm was as thin as Hailey's wrist.

"Well, he ain't mine, so go nuts," Hailey said, then winced. Probably a bad choice of words.

Ghost Blonde picked up on it immediately. "You think I'm crazy, don't you?"

"I'm not judging you. The guy's wicked hot," Hailey said, looking over at the tourists. *Call the police, you idiots!*

The guy finally seemed to get the picture—both literally and figuratively. The woman he was with whipped out her phone. "Hello, police? I've got a situation," she said, then squealed when Ghost Blonde swung her knife around. They both fled out the front door.

Hailey saw the chance, and went to tackle her, but the psycho was quick—too frickin' quick. She sliced Hailey's arm and chest. It wasn't that deep—at least, Hailey didn't think it was, but she had enough adrenaline in her system to bench-press a bus—but it still had her moving back, heading for the kitchen if she could . . .

Ghost Blonde cut off that avenue, no pun intended. Hailey picked up a nearby book.

"I'm going to kill you," Ghost Blonde hummed, weaving slightly.

"But *why*?" Hailey said. "We're not together! We only knew each other for like a week. It's not like we were in love!"

"That's a lie!" the woman screamed. "I saw you two. He's never looked like that, at anyone. NOT ANYONE!"

Hailey blinked.

"You think you can understand him, but you don't. You don't know him like I do! I understand his secret soul! I know his pain! I know everything about him!"

Bleeding, hurt, scared, and pissed, Hailey felt frustration bubble through her. She was *not* going out this way. Not at the hands of some twiggy obsessive bitch.

"Oh, yeah?" she said, hoping to press her into making a mistake—and anger her more. "You don't even know his real name, for Christ's sake! He's not 'Rick,' he's Jake Reese! He's an actor, get it?"

"He's a Mystic Knight!" The knife slashed out, and Hailey dodged. Ghost Blonde's blue eyes were foggy but furious. "He and his brothers are trying to SAVE THE WORLD! They need women who understand the sacred mission

284

they've been given. Women who will support them. I have powers . . ."

"Yeah, I'll bet you do," Hailey muttered.

"I can take care of him. He was just dallying with you," Ghost Blonde said. "When you're dead, he'll need me more than ever."

"Fuck's sake, lady, when will you get it through your thick skull?" Hailey let her fury loose. "He's not even going to be on the *show*! He's going to South America or wherever, he's going to be ogling those A-lister women with no waists and huge tits and he's going to forget all about this crappy show, do you get it? It's *over*! He's *gone*!"

Ghost Blonde now paused. Then she smiled wickedly.

"You're lying. And jealous. He left you." Her tone was triumphant. "You were just a receptacle for his seed, and then he moved on. Just like he always would have. Did you really think a slut like you could keep him?"

That hit Hailey so hard, it was like getting the wind knocked out of her. Knife or not, she felt rage, like a bonfire. She grabbed nearby books blindly, throwing them at the blonde. They bounced off her shoulder, causing her to screech.

"FUCK. YOU." Hailey threw another.

"How dare you?" Ghost Blonde demanded.

"Are you kidding me with this?" Hailey dodged another stab, then wrestled with her. She got another lucky slash in, this time against Hailey's collarbone. She gasped. That had *hurt*—and was a little too close to her throat.

The fury, the fear, all dropped away as she clicked into a ready state: just this side of numb, hyper-alert.

Survive. Protect Cressida. Look for your opportunity.

"You'll never love him like I do," Ghost Blonde shouted. "I will NEVER let him go! I would give up EVERYTHING for him!"

"That's not love, that's fucking unhealthy," Hailey said quietly. Goading her. Heading toward the door—away from Cressida. *Get her out of the house*. "So, who'd you fixate on before *Mystics* started? No way you just started this with Jake, if you're already at the stalking and stabbing stage. Who got you started?"

"There's only ever been Rick," Ghost Blonde countered.

"If you really care about . . . Rick," Hailey echoed, "why trash his room? Why send him hate messages? Why try and kill me?"

"If you love someone, you sacrifice for him," Ghost Blonde said.

"If you love someone, you protect them." Hailey said, her voice sharp. *Just a few more steps.*

She was almost to the door . . . and then tripped. Fucking tripped on a pile of paperbacks that tumbled beneath her feet, making her heels slip out from under her. She screeched.

Ghost Blonde hovered over her, knife in both hands.

"He's *mine*."

Hailey tensed, putting her arms up defensively.

Then, suddenly, Ghost Blonde got clocked as a big tome hit her right upside the head. She grunted, her eyes rolled back, and she fell to the ground.

Hailey grabbed the knife away from her and stood up, looking Cressida right in the eyes. Cressida was panting, and held the heavy book in two hands.

"It's the *Hamiltome*," she said, her breathing uneven. "Thank you, Lin-Manuel Miranda."

"I always knew that damned show would save my life," Hailey said, then touched her slashes and wounds. "Ouch."

"The police are going to be here soon," Cressida said. She grabbed a nearby extension cord and tied the woman up. "You need to get to the hospital, get that . . . fixed. That looks like a lot of blood." She sounded weak.

"You okay?"

"I'm fine," Cressida said. "I'll probably break down a little later, when I've got my bearings. But yeah."

"I'll say," Hailey laughed, sinking down, hoping she wasn't going into shock. "You saved my life."

Cressida stood straighter, her eyes staying trained on the knocked-out blonde on the ground. "Guess I did. Told you I can take care of myself . . . even if I can't leave here."

"You can," Hailey said. Her body went cold, clammy. "You totally will."

"But even if I have to stay here—I swear, Hailey, if you stay, and think we're going to be two spinsters with a bunch of cats or something when we're eighty, you're out

287

of your mind," she said. "Yeah, I love the house. And you love me. But I want you to be happy, sweetie. You can't just stay safe. That's like saying jail is safe. You're meant for more than this."

Hailey started shivering. "I just want you to be taken care of."

"And I want to take care of myself," Cressida said. "I'm not thirteen anymore, Hales. I've got this. So do you."

The police came in. They took Ghost Blonde away, and Hailey was taken to the hospital in the ambulance. As they rode off, Hailey realized that Cressida was right.

She was through playing it safe. For somebody who talked a big game, she'd been running scared—hiding behind the very people she swore she'd protect and love.

She wasn't doing them any favors. She wasn't doing herself any favors. It was time to stop hiding.

That meant dealing with Jake.

CHAPTER 12

Jake stopped off at his room at the lodge. He'd had a really productive talk with Phil and Veronica, and now had a contract. He was having an entertainment lawyer look it over, but he knew that unless there was something really hinky, he was going to be signing it . . . for another three seasons. He was also excited about *Mystics* relocating from Vancouver, and the direction they wanted to take his character.

It was just what he wanted: the show, the role. Settling down in the Pacific Northwest. He knew that he'd love it here. There was hiking. He could kayak in the sound; he could fish, something he'd enjoyed with the guys. He'd get to hang out with Simon and Miles even more now, solidifying their friendship.

Most of all, though, it gave him the chance to do what he knew he really, really wanted to do: win Hailey. Convince her that he wasn't going to leave—that he was a guy that stayed. And that she was precisely what he wanted.

Don't be a dick, but don't back down.

His phone rang, and he glanced at it. Susie.

He'd emailed and messengered over a termination notice to his agent/manager. Jake wasn't surprised at all that she was calling. He just wasn't sure what he was going to say. He picked up the phone.

"Susie. The notice was clear. You are no longer my representation."

"What happened, Jake?" Susie said, sounding unnerved. "You're supposed to be in South America! I emailed you the plane reservations, along with PDFs of the contracts—you can DocuSign them. Was there some other problem? They're filming this week. This is just what your career needs. You'll be perfect for it, show them what you're really made of."

"I'm not going."

"What the hell? What *is* all this?" Susie said, her voice shaking, sounding pissed and confused . . . and maybe, just maybe, a little bit guilty. "I gave Bernardo my word you'd be on a plane . . ."

"Your word?" Jake snapped. "What about your word to *me*? I told you what I wanted. I wanted to be on *Mystics*. It was *all* I wanted. And you told me that the producers refused to pick up my contract. That they didn't like my character, and wanted to replace me!"

Susie sighed impatiently. "Sweetie, I say this with love: that show was all wrong for you. They didn't appreciate you, and never would. They just wanted you to be a beefcake, a pretty face. They never quite knew what to do with your character, anyway," she said, and her voice was so soothing, and supportive—God, she was a better actress than he'd realized. "I'm sorry, Jake, but you've just got to move on. You're going to be a huge star, and you're going to laugh off your days on a little network paranormal series."

He remembered Hailey's words. *I'm a lousy actress, but I'm a hell of a liar.*

"I talked to Phil and Veronica today," Jake said, pulling Susie up short. "They told me that they'd offered more money . . . and you turned them down."

"Hon, you know you're supposed to let me do the talking," she said, inanely, sounding defensive and angry and obviously regrouping. "It's like good cop, bad cop. If the stars talk to producers too much, they come off as pushy. I asked for more money. I'm an agent, that's what I do. You just let me do the talking."

"Apparently I let you do the thinking, too," Jake said. "That's on me. But I'm not making that kind of stupid choice anymore." He shut his eyes. "Damn it, Susie. I trusted you."

She was quiet for a minute. "I only had your best interests in mind."

CATHY YARDLEY

"You're fired," he said, feeling more tired than angry. "You've got it in writing and electronically. We're done."

"Your father is going to be furious," Susie said. Then, softly, "He put me up to it."

Jake was about to end the call, but he caught her last statement. "Wait. What did you say?"

"Kurt never wanted you on that show," Susie said, sounding miserable. "He didn't want his son on some . . . some teeny-bopper crappy sci-fi show. His words, not mine. It was bad for your reputation, for your career."

And by proxy, his, Jake thought. "Do you work for him, or for me?"

There was silence.

"For him," Jake said, feeling stupid as he answered his own question. He rubbed at his temple. "Always. All the guidance, all your helpful advice . . . you were always doing what he told you to."

"He wants what's best for you," Susie tried to argue weakly.

"No, he wants what's best for his image. He wants to live through me," Jake said. "And that's over."

"Jake, for whatever it's worth . . . I'm really sorry."

"Good-bye, Susie." He clicked off, then dialed his father.

His father picked up the phone immediately. "Congratulations!"

"What are you congratulating me for?"

"The film, of course. I heard about the director—they're saying he's the next Scorsese. Wouldn't mind working

292

with him myself, down the line. The studio threw a lot of money at him, and they're expecting big things." His father sounded unbearably smug. "This is the sort of work that'll break you out, kid. Not that little TV show."

"Dad . . ."

"I mean, I know television is where it's at, but they mean HBO, Showtime . . . that kind of thing. But basic cable? Really?" His father scoffed. "Trust me. You'll get much better offers. And you can always do a sci-fi film. Look at Chris Pratt, right?"

Not a great comparison. Jake sighed heavily. "Kurt."

His father finally stopped, mid-monologue. "What did you call me?"

"I called you by your name," Jake said. "Because I want you to listen to me. I appreciate that you're trying to help me. But you don't do that by pulling strings to get me on a film I don't even want. You don't do that by having my agent run my jobs past you, and then go against my advice and turn down stuff I tell her to negotiate."

"Jesus." His father growled. "Tell me. Tell me you are not fucking this deal up."

"There *is* no deal."

"You think I pulled strings? I pulled fucking *cables*, Jake," his father said, in his trademark growl. "You are going to make me look really bad."

"Do you honestly think I care?" Jake said, his own voice cutting. "Do you think that because you're Kurt Windlass, movie star, I need to bow down and do whatever the hell you tell me to? Jump when you say dance? You're my father, and barely that. You don't own me."

"Oh, really?" his father said. "I fucking made you! You really think you made it this far on your own? You think you'll be able to go any further without me pushing you—I swear to God, shoving you—every inch of the way? And this is the thanks I get?"

"I fired Susie," Jake said. "And I'm renewing my contract with *Mystics*. I'm staying here."

His father started cursing viciously. "This is a god-damned mistake."

"Yeah, well, it's my mistake."

"And when you realize what a big fucking mistake you're making . . ." Kurt said menacingly, his voice sounding like a gravel truck.

"Don't come crying to you?" Jake finished. "Is this the way I *repay* you? Dad, you're just using your old lines. And they sound tired. I promise, I'll never come to you for help. I'm never going to trust you with my career again. And yeah, that might mean I may never act again. And I'm actually okay with that."

"You don't have what it takes," his father spat out.

"You didn't have what it took to be a husband or father," Jake said quietly. "I may not have the hustle to survive Hollywood and claw my way to the top, the way you have. But I have what I want here. And I'm going to hold on to what I value."

His father was still spluttering when he hung up. Then
he grabbed the keys to Simon's car, and headed out the
door. It only took ten minutes to get from the lodge to
the bookstore normally, but he made it in closer to six.

He stepped in . . . and stopped immediately. Cressida
was there, cleaning up a pile of knocked-over books.

"Hey . . . are you okay?" he said, and stopped. He pointed to her shirt, the floor. "Is that blood? Are you all right?
What the hell happened?"

Her eyes were huge. "Um . . . I'm fine. There was kind
of an incident, though."

Suddenly, his chest clenched. "Hailey," he said, the
word like a bullet.

"She's at the hospital," she said. "On the plus side, your
stalker is in jail—the right one, this time, not some other
stalker. So there's that."

"Which hospital?" He was having trouble breathing.

"Evergreen. It's just up the hill, on the ridge," Cressida
said. "By Echo Glen . . . drive carefully, would you? She'll
be okay. She's tough."

He didn't care. He bolted for the car like he was on fire.

·♥ · ♥ · ♥ · ♥ · ♥ ·

If there was anything Hailey hated, it was hospitals. She
hadn't been in many, but they creeped her out. And the
expense—she had health insurance, but the ambulance

CATHY YARDLEY

ride and God knows what tests they might try to insist on or how long they'd want her to stay for "observation," had anxiety starting to bubble through her. She wondered if this was going to eat away all the profits from their sale, and felt tears burning at her eyes.

Nope. She wasn't going to start spiraling down that way. She was tougher than that. Maybe she'd sue Ghost Blonde the stalker. This was her fault, after all.

She rubbed the nascent tears away from her eyes, frowning. She needed to get some clothes. They'd given her stitches. She was going to look like Frankenstein, but there wasn't any serious damage. She needed to get home. As soon as the damned paperwork . . .

Her phone buzzed, and she grabbed it. Rachel. "I'm fine, Rache," Hailey said, without preamble, knowing it was the first thing Rachel would want—*need*—to hear.

"Stabbed?"

"Sliced, technically," Hailey said quickly, "and stitched up. I'm fine, seriously. No permanent damage. Just some wicked-looking cuts."

"Scarring?"

"Wouldn't surprise me." She let out a little broken laugh. "Hey, chicks dig scars. Isn't that what those memes say?"

Rachel sighed. "I'll get off work early, and skip out of class tonight. I'll be there as soon as I can."

"Stop that," Hailey said. "There's nothing you can do here, so why take the time? I'll spring for a cab home, and

296

hang out with Cressida." Ugh, which reminded her . . . she had to tell the casino she might need to miss tomorrow's morning shift. Although maybe it wouldn't be that bad . . . she could probably still deal cards, as long as she took it easy and the pain meds didn't make her loopy.

"Knock it off, would you? Stop being so *noble* for fifteen fucking minutes!"

Hailey's eyes widened. When Rachel swore, you knew things were serious.

"Do *not* worry about this. You've been trying too hard, working too hard. And I'm tired of seeing my sisters hurting because we've had financial issues. I've got this."

"You've got this?" Hailey laughed weakly. "How?"

"I've got enough money for us to last six months."

Hailey goggled. "How the hell did you manage that? Did you start making meth in a trailer or something?"

"I sold Ren's ring."

"Your engagement ring?" Now Hailey's jaw dropped. "But . . . no. Come on. That's . . ."

"That was ancient history," Rachel said firmly. "I should've done it years ago."

"You loved Ren. Like, *really* loved him." And, Hailey suspected, still loved him, even though she never talked about it.

"Yes, well . . . he didn't love me," Rachel said, and her voice was so monotone Hailey knew she was keeping it together only by sheer force of will, because there was a well of pain behind those words. "If he had, his parents wouldn't have bought him off and had him abandon me."

"C'mon. He was the love of your life," Hailey said, and now that she had more of a sense of what that felt like, she could only imagine the pain her sister was going through. "I know how much that thing means to you."

"It doesn't mean anything," Rachel said calmly, even though Hailey knew she was lying right down to her painted toenails. "I'd always held onto it for emergencies. And let's face it, it's way past time to admit: we're in an emergency. So I sold it."

"Already?" Hailey winced. "Can you get it back?"

"Even if I could, I'm not going to," Rachel said. "Damn it. I'm just sorry I was too involved in night school and doing the event planning job at the casino and the stuff with the bookstore . . ."

"Only those three things?" Hailey teased, trying to get her to lighten up.

Rachel plowed on, ignoring her interjection. ". . . to notice just how much you were struggling. You don't have to carry the family on your shoulders, Hailey. I'm more capable than you give me credit for." She was quiet for a long moment. "I want you to trust that I'll take care of you and Cressida, too, just like you take care of me. That I'm your sister."

"Of course you're my sister," Hailey said, but swallowed. Maybe that had been an issue, a resentment, a long time ago. But now, it wasn't. She loved Rachel.

Now, she needed to trust her.

"So take time off from the casino." Rachel's voice was stern. "For God's sake, Hales, you got attacked by a knife-wielding maniac. You need some down time."

"All right, all right. I'll . . . take time off," Hailey said.

"I love you."

Hailey's eyes welled up. "Love you, too, Rache."

She hung up. God. The world's turned upside down, she thought. She was used to being the rock, the one that everyone could count on. She was used to counting on herself. Now, she was relying on Rachel. Cressida saved her life. It should have made her feel frightened. Instead, she felt . . . loved. Cared for. She'd been vulnerable. They'd had her back.

It was mind-blowing.

What else was she missing out there?

There was a knock on her door, and she looked up. "Jake," she breathed. For a second, her pain was forgotten, and all the warmth that she'd been feeling magnified. She loved this man. She knew that, in every fiber of her being.

She just had to be brave enough to admit it.

He rushed to her side. "Oh, my God," he breathed, and she shifted a little, trying to pull the hospital gown up to cover the gash on her chest better.

"It looks worse than it is."

"This is my fault," he said, and the recrimination in his voice tore at her. "I should've insisted Vic stay with you guys. I should've known that she would . . ."

"Okay, stop," she said, taking his hand and squeezing firmly. "First, how could you know she'd attack me? We thought she was taken care of. Second, it's not your fault. It's her fault. Third—I'm fine, I really am fine. Just a few cuts. Not a big deal."

He stroked her cheek with his free hand, leaning against the bed. "I don't want you hurt. Ever."

"Well, I don't want to be hurt, so we're even." She blinked. "Wait. Aren't you supposed to be on a plane? You're supposed to be in South America!"

"Things changed."

She stared at him, looking deeply into his eyes. They hadn't known each other that long, but the seriousness, the caring, shocked her. She simply couldn't process the idea of anybody caring about her that way —not even her sisters. Not until now.

It was terrifying.

She was tired of being scared.

She patted the side of the bed. "Sit down."

He did, still staring at her, swallowing hard. "Hailey . . ."

"No, let me talk," she said. "I . . . listen. I didn't even know who you were a week ago. I mean, not other than general fangirl stuff. But the more I've gotten to know you . . . well, the more I . . . like you. Care about you."

Come on. Say it!

She swallowed like there was peanut butter stuck to the roof of her mouth. They'd left her some water. She hastily gulped some down.

"I like you, too," he said, pushing a curl away from her face. "I care about you. You know that, right?"

"I didn't understand what that could mean," she said softly. "But . . . I think I do. Now."

His smile was like a sunrise.

"I have some time off, apparently." She took a deep breath, like she was going to leap off a cliff. "So . . . I mean, I couldn't take three months off, or anything, and I'll be honest, I can't afford a ticket. But if you still want me to come to Brazil with you . . . I could. I mean, I will." She paused. "If you want."

His eyes were shining, and his hand gripped hers hard. She squeezed back, just as hard.

"And after that," she said, fighting off shivers, "I, um . . . well. I've never done the long-distance relationship thing. I mean, I've honestly never done anything relationship-ish. But if you want . . . maybe we could, um, see how it goes."

"You're willing to have a relationship with me?" he said carefully.

She nodded.

A nurse came in. "Are you all right?" she asked. "Your heart rate just went way up . . . oh!"

She'd finally gotten a load of Jake. Her eyes widened, and she smiled.

CATHY YARDLEY

"Well. I can see why that happened! My goodness!"

Hailey burst into surprised laughter. "Um, I just need a minute?"

"Of course, of course," the nurse said, winking at Jake. "The discharge paperwork will be ready in a few. I'll just . . . yes, of course." And she bustled out.

Jake was laughing, too. Then he leaned over and kissed her. It was gentle, but still full of promise.

"I am crazy about you, Hailey Frost," he said against her lips, before pulling back. "I do have one question, though."

She tensed. "Yes?"

"What if we didn't do long distance?"

She felt her heart fall. "I care about you. I could fall in love with you," she said, going for it, and was gratified when his eyes went wide. "I . . . think I already have."

He smiled at her, and the emotion in his eyes made her chest warm like a fireplace.

"But I can't leave my sisters," she continued. "I won't. I love them. And I know they can take care of themselves, but they're family. I want to be near them, too. I still want to help, if I can."

He nodded. "I wouldn't ask you to do anything less. It's part of what I love about you."

What he loved about her? Now it was her turn for her eyes to widen.

"I talked to the producers myself," he said. "I'm on the show."

She let out a whoop. "Holy shit! That's just what you wanted!" She grinned. "I'll make sure Charlotte can handle the four-hour drive to Vancouver, buddy. Take lots of vitamins during the week. Your weekends are all mine."

"There's more news, although you'll have to keep it a secret," he said, leaning forward and whispering to her. "They're moving production. They're going to be filming in North Bend."

"North Bend? As in, the next town over, just five minutes away North Bend?" she goggled.

"So you'd better get used to seeing me constantly."

She hugged him, hard, then yelped, wincing. "God-damn stitches."

He kissed her, gently. "I'm not letting you get away that easily," he said. "And I'm not letting go."

She smiled. "I'm not letting you get away, either." And sealed the promise with a kiss.

EPILOGUE

One month later...

"Are you sure you know how to put together a book-shelf?" Hailey called, then grinned when she heard Jake's derisive snort.

"I am useful," he called back from the kitchen. "I can. Ow, goddamn it!"

"Do not hurt yourself," she said, with a low chuckle. "I can always get Kyla's brother to help us out. Hell, I can get Kyla."

"You think you're insulting me with your traditional masculine roles jibes, but you're not," he said. "Besides, this is from Ikea. You don't need to be male to build this, you just need to be able to follow instructions." He paused. "In Danish. Jeez, how many pieces does this thing have?"

"Stay strong." She burst into laughter, and she saw him bend backward through the doorway, giving her the finger before getting back to work.

"This is so awesome," Cressida said, caressing the pieces as she put them away. There was a lot of stuff from shows, books, and movies they loved. Arrow, Firefly, Doctor Who, The Sandman, Attack on Titan . . . you name it. Cressida was lining up Marvel bobbleheads next to a Supernatural-themed Monopoly game and a Mystics version of Risk. Jake had been instrumental in getting a lot of signed stuff for them, too—from Mystics, obviously, but also from industry friends and people he knew. He had a new agent now, and she knew that he was still hurt over Susie's betrayal and his father's duplicity, but mostly he was happy. The show was on hiatus while they moved production from Vancouver to North Bend, so he'd spent every moment he could with Hailey. And since Hailey had gotten attacked, she'd had two weeks off, and had taken time off from the casino. Now, with the influx of money from Rachel's ring, they were putting what they could into revamping the store.

"Frost Fandoms," she said, nodding at the sign Kyla had painted for them. "I like it."

Fans across the internet knew that production was moving, which meant more fans coming in. And news of Hailey's attack had spread, thanks to Rainbow Scarf's video and photos. Hailey was becoming a celebrity in her own right. This was not something she was necessarily comfortable with, but she loved being with Jake, so it was worth the inconvenience and weirdness. Besides, she loved fans. It wasn't so hard, especially when they could geek out and talk about stuff they loved.

Ghost Blonde—whose real name was Samantha Deiter—had a history of stalking and mental issues. She was in a criminal psych ward, which helped Hailey feel better.

"I love this," a woman enthused. "It's kind of out of the way, but I love everything you've got here. I can see myself spending plenty of money."

"That's what we love to hear," Rachel said. It was a weekend, so she didn't have to work at the casino or go to school, and she was putting all she could into boosting the store. They'd repainted, and were putting in new shelves, new displays. The whole crowd was there, it seemed.

Miles came in. "I got those shirts you wanted." He was friendly, kind, and obviously a good friend to Jake, which made her like Miles even more. Simon was funny, and also cared about Jake. He seemed to have his own issues with Snoqualmie, and wasn't thrilled when they moved to North Bend, but she'd get him to hang out in the store eventually, she thought.

It was working out. She was almost scared to trust how well it was working out.

"Done," Jake said, bringing out the new, plain bookshelf. "There we go. What do you think?"

"I want a Doctor Who display," Cressida said.

"We said that it'd be a Mystics display," Rachel said.

"We already have that, there," Cressida said.

"Yes, but . . ."

They started debating. Hailey felt Jake sidle up behind her, wrapping his arms around her waist, just below her breasts. He pressed a kiss to her neck, and she sighed.

"They're going to be at that for a while," he murmured. "Think we can sneak upstairs for a bit?"

Hailey shivered. She couldn't get enough of him, it seemed. And she didn't have to worry about it.

"I'm taking a break," she said, as the sisters absently nodded and continued their arguing. Then she and Jake crept upstairs.

His mouth was on her before her bedroom door closed.

"And you said you never bring sex home," he teased, taking off his shirt as she took off hers, as well as her bra.

"I don't bring sex home," she said, shimmying out of her pants and underwear. Then she stared at him, her heart feeling so full, she thought she'd explode with it.

She took a deep breath.

"I brought love home," she said, softly.

He paused in the act of stripping off his own pants. "Hailey."

CATHY YARDLEY

"Come here and love me," she said, trying to brush past it. To not focus on the fact that she'd never said that word—love—to any man before. That she'd never felt it before—and certainly not like this.

"I love you, too, Hailey Frost," he breathed, his heart in his eyes.

It was like falling, she thought. No. It was like flying.

She grinned. "Hurry up," she said, laughing with pure joy. "We've got work to do."

"All right," he said, grinning back at her like a fool, stripping the rest of the way and diving at her. "But to make up for it, we do slow tonight."

"We'll do everything tonight," she said, and held him like she was never going to let him go.

· ♥ · ♥ · ♥ · ♥ · ♥ ·

Thanks so much for reading Hailey and Jake's story. Next up is Game of Hearts! *When Kyla needs help in her family's auto shop so she can meet a cosplay competition deadline, she reaches out to her brother's best friend Jericho... but they've both changed a lot since they hung out as kids. Can she resist the hot, hunky mechanic? And does he want her to?*

A NOTE FROM CATHY

Hi!

Thank you so much for reading *One True Pairing*, the second book in the Fandom Hearts series. This series is all about finding the things you're passionate about — the things you're *geeky*
about — and going all in. I loved writing this series, and I hope you enjoy reading it just as much. The series is complete (I think? For now? Although some of those secondary characters *have* been nudging at me!) and
each book can be read as a stand-alone, although they can be enjoyed in chronological series order for the full experience. And there are other series to enjoy if you're looking for more fun, geeky love stories!

If you do enjoy the book, please take a minute to write a review of this on Amazon and Goodreads. Reviews make a huge difference in an author being discovered in book searches and shared with other readers!

And if you'd like to connect with me, I love hearing from readers! You can stop by www.CathyYardley.com to email me, or visit me on social media. Or join my Facebook readers group, *Can't Yardley Wait,* to see early reveals, read exclusive content, and share a lot of shenanigans with a very fun group.

Enjoy!

Cathy

ABOUT THE AUTHOR

Cathy Yardley writes fun, geeky, and diverse characters who believe that underdogs can make good and sometimes being a little wrong is just right.

She likes writing about quirky, crazy adventures, because she's had plenty of her own: she had her own army in the Society of Creative Anachronism; she's spent a New Year's on a
3-day solitary vision quest in the Mojave Desert; she had VIP access to the Viper Room in Los Angeles.

Now, she spends her time writing in the wilds of Eastern Washington, trying to prevent her son from learning the truth of any of said adventures, and riding herd on her two dogs (and one
husband.)

Want to make sure you never miss a release? For news about future titles, sneak peeks, and other fun stuff,

CATHY YARDLEY

please sign up for Cathy's newsletter *here*.

LeT'S GeT SOCIaL!

Hang out in Cathy's Facebook group, Can't Yardley Wait

Talk to Cathy on Twitter

See silly stuff from Cathy's life on Instagram

Never miss a release! Follow on Amazon

Don't miss a sale — follow on BookBub

ALSO BY

THE PONTO BEACH REUNION SERIES

Love, Comment Subscribe

Gouda Friends

Ex Appeal

THE FANDOM HEART SERIES

Level Up

Hooked

One True Pairing

Game of Hearts

What Happens at Con

Ms. Behave

Playing Doctor

Ship of Fools

SMARTYPANTS ROMANCE

Prose Before Bros

STAND ALONE TITLES

The Surfer Solution

Guilty Pleasures

Jack & Jilted

Baby, It's Cold Outside